To Susan –
I hope you enjoy
Sara and her search!
Jan

Sara's Search

Jan Christensen

Sara's Search

Jan Christensen

Quiet Storm Publishing • Martinsburg, WV

Published by Quiet Storm Publishing
PO BOX 1666
Martinsburg, WV 25402

www.quietstormpublishing.com

Cover by : Clint Gaige

ISBN: 0-9749608-3-7

Library of Congress Control Number: 2004105432

Printed in the United States of America

DEDICATION

This novel is dedicated to my daughter, Debbie, whose motto is, "It could be worse."

She is usually my first reader and has been an enthusiastic cheerleader during my writing phase of life. More importantly, she battles two fatal illnesses daily without complaint: Wegener's Granulomatosis and end-stage kidney disease. She is an inspiration to all who meet her and a bright, shining light in my life.

However, none of the characters in this book is Debbie. She is simply too unique to be able to capture on the page.

Debbie, this one's for you!

THANK YOU

Thanks to these writers who helped me with this particular novel. Most just saw a chapter or two, but a few went through the whole thing with me. I can't tell you how much it helped and how much your support has meant to me.

Nancy Baer, Bunnie Bessel, Terry Calvin, Jan Clark, Carole Cummings, Elizabeth, Chuck Gatlin, Dorothy Greninger, , Mark Noe, and Jonathan Shipley.

You are all terrific!

CHAPTER 1

The door was ajar, so Sara pushed it the rest of the way inward and entered the apartment. The stereo blasted, and clusters of people--drinks and food in hand--stood about, talking, gesturing, laughing. Across the room, the New York City skyline twinkled through the huge picture window.

Sara edged inside and began eavesdropping--her favorite party occupation.

"I never watch TV myself," a tall, thin, thirtyish woman told her companion. He was fat, forty and funny-looking.

"Not Johnny? Letterman? How about CNN? The Discovery Channel?" She shook her head after each question. "Well," he told her, turning away, "I need to find someone who saw Donahue yesterday. I have some serious questions about that show." The anorexic was left standing alone with Sara. The woman looked around, then headed quickly toward another group.

Sara followed her deeper into the living room, found the bar, and asked for a Vodka Collins. While waiting for her drink, she heard a man say, "Hey, pretty lady." The guy looked to be at least fifty, old enough to be her father. And drunk. He weaved as he stood there. Always polite, Sara smiled at him and tried to edge away. She didn't want him to touch her. She'd always had an aversion to drunks.

"Where did you come from?" the man asked, breathing heavily into her face. At this rate, she wouldn't need a drink herself. She could get high on this guy's fumes. And she didn't know how to answer his question. She came from outside, from her office, from New Jersey, from her mother's womb.

"Where'd you come from?" he repeated, slurring his words even more, and swayed. But, surrounded as they were, he couldn't fall down. She could imagine him, out cold, propped up by the crowd, going from one group to the next, no one noticing unless someone asked him a question.

"I'm from New Jersey," she told him.

"Ah, I could have guessed. That sleek look--lovely brunette hair, soulful brown eyes, pretty face and good figure." He winked and she blushed.

"Thank you. Where are you from?"

"Brooklyn. Brooklyn, can you believe? Lived there all my life."

"How fascinating."

"Here's your Collins," the bartender told Sara. She thanked him and sipped it gratefully. "Oops," she told the drunk, "I see someone." She raised her hand in a wave and made her way quickly through an opening.

Behind her she only heard, "--your name," but she hurried on, like the rabbit in *Alice in Wonderland*. She needed to find her friend, Belinda, hostess and therefore the cause of all this chaos.

"It was awful," Sara heard a woman say. Sara paused to listen. "It's like they say. You feel as if you've been violated. The burglar broke all the locks, and he took everything. The stereo, the TV, the silver, all my jewelry." Sara moved away, the woman still inventorying every item as if her listeners were insurance adjusters.

Sara couldn't get around a large group, and she noticed the drunk staring at her. He made her uncomfortable. A man speaking gestured wildly. As he waved his hands, Sara kept waiting for some of his drink to come sloshing out onto his listeners, but it miraculously stayed inside the glass.

"Quit cold turkey eight weeks, three days and," he looked at his watch, "twenty-seven minutes ago. Only way to stop smoking. Quit, never look back. And boy, do I feel like a new man. All you who still smoke need to quit, you know. I breathe better, sleep better." He winked at a couple of the women. "Make love longer."

"Good going, George," another man said. "You also talk longer." As the rest of the group laughed, Sara saw an opening and slid through it, bumping up against a knot of people standing in the dining room archway.

She broke free and glimpsed the food-laden table across the room. Her stomach rumbled, and she headed in the direction of dinner. Glancing at her watch, she realized she hadn't eaten since a breakfast of cereal early this morning.

"I dreamt I switched the couch and loveseat. When I got up the next morning, they were moved and my arms and back hurt."

"Come on, Maureen. You expect us to believe that?"

"But it's true." Maureen frowned and took a sip of her drink.

Sara paused to listen, her hunger forgotten for the moment.

"Hey, I believe her," another woman said. "My husband got up one night and started digging in the garden. I heard this noise outside, scared me to death, and I turned on the light. There he knelt, in his pajamas, digging up the potatoes. He was tired the next morning, too. I didn't stop him, you know. Figured that was the only way I'd ever get him to do it. Now I whisper suggestions in his ear, like vacuum the rug, or clean the toilets, but he never does--" the speaker's voice trailed off and she stared into space.

Sara felt her stomach rumble, reminding her where she was headed. Once again, she noticed the drunk standing there, watching her. She began to feel decidedly uncomfortable. The more she saw him, the more he looked a little familiar. He had nice even features and intelligent-looking eyes. Thinning hair didn't cover the squarish head very well. He was of medium height and build, and there was nothing outstanding about him. But, she thought, there's something . . .

She saw an opening, squeezed through and came to another bunch of people who were discussing mixed drinks.

Sara moved away.

"They've been big since seventh grade," a woman whispered in her ear. Sara drew back and realized that she had stumbled into a group of women in a corner who were trying to have a quiet conversation in the general hubbub.

"Well, at least yours don't look like two mosquito bites. I waited and waited, and nothing ever happened. Flat as a pancake. That's when I decided to have surgery. Now I'm tired and achy all the time but can't convince my doctor it's just since the operation."

"Oh, doctors never listen to women. What do we know?"

Sara found herself looking at all the women's breasts. Some were large, some were small, but generally they seemed to go with the rest of their figures.

"Yeah, that's right, doctors don't listen," a large, bony woman said.

"But you should never have unnecessary surgery anyway. We need to worry about a society that puts so much importance on physical attributes. Now, the way I see it--"

Sara had heard it all before, and she smelled food. She ducked between two of the women--one with small breasts, one with large--and headed toward the aroma. Still no sign of Belinda, her newly rich best friend, or Blinky, her husband. Belinda really had done well, marrying the uptown doctor who was fourteen years older, but still handsome. Belinda wanted to introduce Sara to some new man, and although Sara knew such introductions were generally disastrous, she had come to the party with some hope in her heart.

"Oh, excuse me," she said when she bumped into someone. "Why, JoAnne! How nice to see you." Sara could feel a fake social smile split her face. JoAnne's grin looked equally forced.

"Sara. Of course, I should have expected you to be here." She looked to the right and left of Sara. Only the drunk stood very close. "Are you alone?"

"I'm meeting someone," she said, stretching the truth.

"Oh, well, this is Arthur Benson. Arthur, Sara Putnam."

The three of them--or four, if you counted the drunk--stood there awkwardly for a minute before Sara thought to ask, "Well, JoAnne, how do you like your new job?" JoAnne had been transferred to the legal department two weeks before.

"It has its good points and bad. Lawyers can be difficult."

"I'll bet. And is Arthur a lawyer?"

"Goodness, no. He works at G.S. in New Jersey."

"Oh, I know where that plant is. I live in Montclair."

"What a coincidence," Arthur said. "I live there now."

"Really? What street?"

"Grove."

"Honestly? I lived on Columbus right off of Grove." Sara noticed JoAnne was getting a bored look on her face. Good, she thought, and smiled wider. "What intersection are you near?"

He told her the name of the nearest cross street, but she didn't know it. Then he said, "This reminds me of a story." JoAnne rolled her eyes.

"Later, Arthur," she said. "I see someone over there I want you to meet." She turned to Sara. "We must keep in touch."

"Of course," Sara said, and when they were gone, did her own eye

5

rolling.

As she turned to go to the table, she found herself stuck at the edge of a group of five women, all complaining about their bosses.

"Did you ever have one who told you to call someone for him, and he stands there while you do it and will not get on the phone until the person answers?" asked the thin woman Sara had noticed when she first came in.

"Oh, yes, my boss gives me lists of people to call every day, and I have to keep a log of who he talked to and when, who called him back, and who didn't. I can hardly get anything else done as long as he's in the office. He regularly phones me from airplanes and tells me to call so and so and give him a message. It's all a power trip." The speaker was a very tall blond.

"Don't you know it," a petite redhead with lots of freckles chimed in. "Mine leaves his files and computer disks at the office and calls me in a tizzy to send them to him Federal Express. Then he downgrades me on my evaluation for being forgetful." She took an angry puff on a cigarette.

"Anyone here still have to get coffee? No? Well, I do, and my boss is female."

Groans greeted this announcement. Another woman said, "Well, I have a real nice female boss, but another one, a guy, always brings me something at five to five to type and needs it to go to the post office that night."

"Don't you hate it?" the blond said. "I had a boss do that once, and I told him the typewriter was switched on, and I hoped he knew how to type because I had a five-fifteen appointment. I didn't tell him it was an appointment to be in rush hour traffic and on my way home to my family."

"Yeah," the thin one said. "If you're late to work, all hell breaks loose, but they don't care if you're late getting home to your family."

"Ain't it the truth," the redhead said.

"What a depressing subject," the thin one said. "Where did everyone go on vacation? I flew to Myrtle Beach and played golf. It was wonderful."

"Oh," the blond replied. "I went to Florida to visit my folks, and it rained the whole time, and I didn't meet any cute guys or anything."

"Have you ever thought of vacation insurance? They pay you back if it rains."

"Never heard of it. Where do you get it?"

"Through a travel agent, I think."

"How weird. Wonder if they give you your money back if you don't meet guys?"

Everyone laughed, and Sara remembered she still hadn't eaten. She saw an opening, took it, and found herself at the wrong end of the table--the plates, napkins and silverware were at the other end--at least twenty feet away. Well, obviously she was going to starve to death among all these people with all this food right in front of her. As if not appreciating her little joke, her stomach gave a large enough rumble for the man next to her to hear it during the sudden lull that always seems to occur at such moments. He stared at her.

"Sorry," she mumbled.

He laughed, his face crinkling up pleasantly. "That's all right. Sort of involuntary. Have some finger food until you can get to the other end. I'll hold up everything while you nosh."

"Thanks," Sara said as she grabbed a shrimp, dipped it in sauce and tossed it into her mouth.

"That won't help much. Have some cheese and crackers."

She followed his suggestion, but quickly realized she couldn't stand here long and do this when the woman behind them said, "What's the holdup, Chester? People waiting, you know."

"My wife," Chester said quietly to Sara. "Always in a hurry."

"I'll just go to the other end. Thanks for your help."

"Why don't you take some crackers with you."

"Good idea." Sara took as many as she could hold, leaving her empty drink glass sitting on the table. She also needed to find the bar again.

And she wanted to put some distance between herself and the drunk who lurked close by, staring at her.

She moved around Chester and was halted by a group whose present speaker was at least fifty pounds overweight. "I started on this new diet last month and already lost fifteen pounds."

"What is it?" another large woman asked as she picked peanuts out of her left hand and put them into her mouth with her right. Where had she found them? Sara's mouth watered.

"Well, mainly grapefruit, hard-boiled eggs and tuna fish."

"Ugh," a third woman said. She was eating a piece of cake. "Is that the one where you eat the tuna without mayo or anything--just dry?"

"Well, yes," the first woman said. She held a celery stick, but gestured with it instead of eating it. "But it's worth it." Sara eyed the celery stick hungrily and moved on.

She was almost there when she heard her name called.

7

"Sara!" Belinda stood right behind her. "You came. We thought you chickened out." Belinda took her arm. "Come on, I want to introduce you to Henry. Now where did he go?" She led Sara away from the table, easily snaking between groups, and suddenly Sara found herself back in the living room in front of the picture window.

"Belinda," she said when they finally stopped moving, "I'm starving. I was headed toward the buffet. It took me over an hour to get there, and now you've taken me away. This is a great party, by the way. Happy Anniversary! Lots of interesting people. I now have some hope for Henry."

"What did I tell you?" Belinda said, hugging her. Gold bracelets jangled on Belinda's wrists. She wore a slinky gold dress with a slit up to there, gold high heels, gold hoop earrings and a stunning necklace. Sara thought, she can get away with it with her figure.

"You hired a clown?" Sara exclaimed when she caught sight of the funny figure in a corner talking to the drunk. Sara couldn't tell if the clown was a man or a woman.

"What?" Belinda asked as she turned to look where Sara pointed. "Blinky must have hired him. I didn't. He is funny, isn't he?" she asked as the clown made a dog out of a balloon and placed it on the drunk's head.

"I guess so," Sara said dubiously. "Where is this paragon you're going to introduce me to?" Sara asked.

"Shh. There he is. Oh, Henry!" Belinda waved at a movie-star handsome man standing in a group that hotly debated the right to strike for teachers. "Henry!"

Henry finally noticed Belinda and came over. Belinda quickly introduced them, then left. Sara didn't know what to say, and Henry seemed equally ill at ease. Her stomach rumbled during another lull. She grimaced and said, "Sorry about that. I've been trying to get to the buffet for hours, it seems."

He nodded, but did not make a reassuring remark as Chester had.

"So, tell me," she finally said, desperate. "Have you been robbed lately?"

Henry shook his head, staring at her.

"No? Just give up smoking? No? On a new diet?" He'll think I'm nuts, she thought. Maybe I am. Why do I always do stupid things when I meet attractive, eligible men?

Henry continued to gaze at her as if hypnotized.

8

"Have any interesting dreams? Watch much television? Hate your boss? Have a terrible vacation?" She gave up, breathless, aware that she'd made a fool of herself. He shook his head no to everything. "Well, what do you do?" she finally asked. That should be a safe question.

"I'm a lawyer."

Why couldn't he elaborate? He wasn't helping her at all. Maybe he wasn't worth knowing after all. "Know any good stories, then?"

"No, it's all privileged information."

"I see. Could we go to the bar and get a drink?"

"I don't drink."

"I see." What a stuck-up snob, she thought. "Well, I drink at parties a little," she told him, thinking, and I need one after this nonconversation with you. "It was nice talking to you, Henry," she lied and walked away. When she got to the bar she turned and saw Henry back with the group he had been with before.

"Vodka Collins, please." When the bartender put it in front of her, she took a long sip, then saw the peanuts in a bowl in front of her. Before she could take one, a hand reached in and grabbed them all. Startled, she gasped. She thought the drunk stood behind her, and she turned quickly to see.

Arthur, JoAnne's friend, smiled at her as he chewed the last of the peanuts.

"Well, hello, Arthur," Sara greeted him, happy to see him instead of the other man. "Tell me a story." She realized Arthur didn't feel threatening to her, as Henry had.

"Really?"

She nodded.

"You really mean it? No one wants to hear my stories."

"Well, I do. I want to find out why no one wants to hear them."

He grinned at her, and putting his elbow on the bar began. "Okay." He proceeded to tell the most boring story Sara had ever heard about something that had happened to him at work. When he finished, Arthur popped a peanut into his mouth. Sara watched him chew for a minute.

"That was amazing. I don't know what to say."

Arthur looked pleased.

Out of the corner of her eye she saw JoAnne approaching. She took another long swallow of her drink, said a quick, "Goodbye," to Arthur and headed toward the buffet, not stopping to listen to anyone, even the group discussing Reganomics and Gorbachev's coming visit. She was tired, her feet hurt, and she wanted to leave, but she was too hungry to go all the way home without food.

When she got to the dining room, they were dismantling the table, and the only thing left was a plate of olives. Sara finished her drink and put as many olives as she could into her glass and headed for the front door, eating olives as she went.

Next time she'd eat before going to a party given by Belinda. Her stomach rumbled as she reached the elevator. She decided to walk down even though it was twelve floors. She hated elevators, and she'd probably get in there with lots of people who weren't talking, and her stomach would growl. She hit the exit door and practically tripped over the man lying on the landing. The man who had been following her during the whole party. The man who wanted to know her name. He must have passed out. She touched him lightly with the toe of her shoe. He didn't move. She bent down to get a closer look.

That's when she saw the blood seeping out under his collar. She screamed and dropped her glass of olives. They bounced down the stairs in a wild dance. Sara screamed again and went rushing back to the party for help.

CHAPTER 2

When Belinda woke the morning of her anniversary party, she felt terrible. She ached all over as if coming down with the flu, tired because she'd tossed and turned all night. Blinky tugged on her arm.

"Come on, sleepyhead, time to rise and shine."

She moaned. "Just a little while longer, please, Blinky."

His tone of voice hardened. "Lots to do, Babe. Have to get ready for the blowout, remember."

She groaned again. "Call it off! Tell everyone I died."

"That's not even funny."

"Oh, Blinky," she said, contrite, "I'm sorry. Happy Anniversary."

"To you, too, Babe," he said.

Carefully, because she felt a little dizzy, she swung her legs around to put her feet on the floor. She looked at her husband through sleepy eyes. God, he was handsome. She still felt like the luckiest girl alive every time she looked at him. If only she didn't feel so tired and run-down all the time. He'd sent her to the best specialists in New York. No one could find anything wrong. They asked her about her stress level, feelings of anxiety, depression. She denied it all, truthfully. Mentally, she felt great. Why shouldn't she? She loved her husband, he loved her, they had more money than they'd ever be able to spend in their lifetimes. All she needed to feel totally complete was a baby or two. But the way she felt right now, she didn't think she'd have the energy to handle even one.

Blinky held out his hand to her, and as she grasped it, a slight thrill coursed through her. She wondered at the fact that this still happened when he touched her. After all, they'd known each other for three years and were celebrating their first wedding anniversary today although tomorrow marked the real date. June 30, 1984, she thought dreamily. Suddenly, a feeling of almost unbearable happiness swept through her. She let Blinky pull her up and slipped into his arms and hugged him with all her strength. She raised her face towards his, and they kissed. Blinky broke the embrace and gave her bottom a slight pat.

"Lots to do, Babe," Blinky said again. "Time to get dressed and get to it."

Belinda sighed as the tired feeling swept over her once again. She bit back a bitter reply and went to her dressing room. As she removed her nightgown, she caught sight of herself in the full length mirrors which lined the walls and closet doors. She still couldn't believe it was her body in those mirrors. Sure, she kept it toned and in shape, but Blinky had done the best part--her breasts. Looking at them now, she knew why he was considered one of the top plastic surgeons in the country. They were absolutely perfect.

Sweeping her long, black hair out of the way, she put on a bra and panties, then slipped into jeans, a T-shirt and tennis shoes. Quickly, she applied mascara to already long lashes, some rose blush and lipstick. Then she brushed her hair vigorously and fastened it into a ponytail.

Ready now to do battle with caterers, florists, and bartenders, she went to the kitchen for a cup of coffee. Hilda, the housekeeper, handed her a mug as she entered the sunny room. Blinky already sat at the table, reading the paper and eating eggs and toast. He looked up and nodded at her approvingly. She smiled and asked Hilda for a bowl of cereal and some orange juice.

"Listen to this!" Blinky said, rattling the newspaper. "This fellow has invented a robotic vacuum cleaner. You just set it on the floor, and it goes around the house, vacuuming."

"Huh," Belinda said. "Does it put itself away when it's finished?"

Blinky ignored the question. "They're going to put you out of business, Hilda, if they keep inventing these machines."

Hilda sniffed. "Not likely. Someone still has to set up the silly things. Does it do windows?"

"Come on, ladies, it just moves around by itself and vacuums. It doesn't do windows, dust, clean the toilets or put itself away."

"If men had to do housework, it would have been invented years ago," Belinda said, grinning at her husband. "And it would have vacuumed the house from top to bottom and done the windows, too."

Blinky sighed. "You're probably right. I thought you'd be interested."

12

"We are!" Belinda and Hilda said together.

"We're amazed," Belinda said. "How does it work, really?"

"The article didn't go into many details. The first models will cost over two thousand dollars, though."

"That's a bit more than a broom," Hilda said, turning away to put the dishes in the dishwasher.

"We'll get you one as soon as they come out, Hilda," Blinky assured her.

Hilda sniffed and continued putting the dishes away. "In the meantime, I'll have to vacuum the place the old-fashioned way before the caterers arrive."

The rest of the day flew by in a flurry of activity. While Blinky rushed to the hospital to check on his patients, Belinda had her hair done, directed the placement of flower arrangements, showed the caterers where to set everything up, sent Charles, the chauffeur, to get her dress at the dressmaker's, picked out the jewelry she planned to wear, and checked to see that finally, everything was the way she wanted it. By four in the afternoon, she was exhausted.

"I'm going to lie down for an hour," she told Blinky and Hilda. "Call me at five."

She fell asleep before her head hit the pillow.

She woke to Blinky kissing her neck so lightly that at first she thought a bug was crawling on her. She almost swatted him away.

"Let the festivities begin!" Blinky said and kissed her on the mouth.

She didn't feel much better than she had when she'd lain down, and she had to quell her impulse to push him away. Instead, she fiercely kissed him back. It isn't fair, she thought. I should feel wonderful. She felt tears welling and had to swallow painfully. Blinky broke the kiss, and she looked away from him, breathing hard and fast so she wouldn't cry.

He got up and went to his bureau. He brought back a small package wrapped in shiny gold paper. "Happy Anniversary, darling," he said, placing the gift in her hand and sitting back down on the bed.

She'd been dying to know what he'd gotten her for days. Fingers trembling slightly, she unwrapped the present, opened the box and exclaimed at the beautiful gold locket with a huge emerald cut diamond at its center. "It's gorgeous!" she exclaimed. "But it's only our paper anniversary. What will you do for gold and diamond?"

He smiled at her. "Open it up."

Inside was a tiny piece of paper. In Blinky's fine, spidery handwriting, she read, "To Belinda. I'll love you forever. Love Blinky."

She let the tears come now as she kissed him long and hard. When they broke apart, she got up and brought him her gift--a planner with a leather cover, his name embossed in gold on the front.

"Paper," he said. He sounded a bit disappointed.

"Look under the S's," she commanded.

When he did, he found a notation: "Smithfield, Dr. Bancroft A., II. I'll love you forever, Blinky." She'd signed it, "Babe."

"Great minds . . ." he murmured as he pulled her down onto the bed.

Her eyes noticed the readout on the clock, and this time she did push him away. "It's almost six o'clock, and it'll take me at least an hour to get ready. Let me up, Blinky."

He groaned. "Infernal party. Whose stupid idea was it, anyway?"

"Yours," she said, laughing. "You know you'll love every minute of it."

"Um," he said, nuzzling her neck. "But now I have a better idea."

She pushed on his chest, and he moved away with a sigh. "Pushy woman," he said and got up.

Belinda laughed again and headed for the shower.

She'd managed to be dressed and ready to meet the first guests, the locket against her skin feeling warm. It constantly reminded her of Blinky, even after they got separated in the crush.

Her exhaustion disappeared as she greeted and talked to her guests. A warm glow came over her as people complimented her on the party. She was particularly glad to see so many of her old co-workers from Nort International. They didn't mingle much, though--just stood around in a group and talked about work. Belinda hung with them awhile to catch up on everything.

JoAnne introduced her to a new boyfriend, Arthur. Belinda thought cattily that he was better looking than most of the men JoAnne latched onto.

"Do you know what your old boss has been up to?" Ginny Haymaker asked Belinda.

"I can imagine," Belinda said.

"No, you can't! He got so mad one day that he threw the telephone against the wall. A piece broke off and cut his face. He's suing for Workman's Comp."

"Sounds like him," Belinda said. "He threw a pen at me once. I told him if he ever did anything like that again, I'd be sure it hit me, and I'd sue his pants off.

14

He said, go ahead, it would be his pleasure. I had to leave his office before I could accuse him of sexual harassment. He always knew where to draw the line though, the bastard. I thought of going to his boss, but she wouldn't have believed me. They were tight as two ropes on a hammock. She still there?"

"Ms. Jefferson?" Sandy Jarvis, Jefferson's assistant, asked. "You bet. As daffy as ever. Misses more planes than I'll ever get on. Works until two in the morning, comes in at eight. The higher-ups love her."

"Sure, with no family, she's made work her whole life. I almost feel sorry for her," Belinda said.

"Don't waste your pity. She's eaten up and spit out more subordinates than anyone I've ever met. We keep waiting for her to screw up so bad they'll have to fire her. Doesn't look as if that'll happen soon," Sandy said. "I don't know how much longer I'll be able to last."

"Well," Belinda said, "I can't say I'm sorry to be gone from there, although I do miss you guys."

"It was nice of you to invite us to your party," Ginny said.

Belinda smiled at them and excused herself to mingle, wondering where Sara was. Later, she noticed that all her old colleagues had left, except JoAnne.

Belinda got stuck with a group discussing the launch of Discovery with the first Arab in space which she had not followed. Actually, she realized, she didn't read the paper or listen to the news much since she'd stopped working and married Blinky. She'd been too busy setting up the apartment and adjusting to being married. All she knew was that Reagan was president.

Her attention was drawn to the group next to the one she was in. They seemed to be talking about breast implants. She heard one woman say something about being tired and achy since she got them. Belinda caught sight of Sara, but decided to stay and listen to more of the conversation as Sara moved away.

"We need to worry about a society that puts so much importance on physical attributes," a woman with the strident voice of a true militant was saying. "Now, the way I see it, women should only worry about their health, not how they look."

"Oh, come on, Andrea, women have always been concerned about how they look. You'll never convince the majority to stop doing things to their bodies to attract men. Too much competition."

Belinda felt confused. She didn't see what was wrong with improving your looks just about any way you could. That's why she'd had the implants. A good thing, too, or she never would have met Blinky. Dreamily, she remembered the first time she'd seen him in his office when she'd gone to inquire about them.

She abruptly came back to the present when one of the women in the group began to list her symptoms since getting implants.

"They're all so vague," she said. "Mainly, I'm so tired! I get these little rashes that come and go, and my eyes and mouth are dry sometimes. One day my knee will ache, the next my ankle, another my shoulder. Why did this all start about a month afterwards? I'd never had any problems before."

"I've talked to other women at the Woman's Collective that have the same problems, Mary," another woman said. She looked grandmotherly, and Belinda wondered fleetingly how Blinky knew her well enough to invite her to their party. "There must be something to it."

"It's hard getting the doctors to listen," Mary said. Belinda knew that feeling. Suddenly the grandmotherly woman looked towards Belinda and must have recognized her. She shushed the others and motioned them away.

Belinda's group had finished discussing the space mission and was talking about Reaganomics.

Belinda left them and went looking for Sara. After a few minutes, she found her. Although happy to see her, she felt her hostess duties pressing, so she took Sara to the living room to meet Henry. Before she could get them properly introduced and started on a conversation, she saw the caterer motioning to her. Hurriedly, she excused herself and went to see what he wanted.

"I'm sorry, Mrs. Smithfield," he said after they were in the kitchen. "I have to wrap it up. I got an emergency call that my father is in the hospital." The man looked distraught.

Belinda patted his arm and said, "That's all right. You do what you have to do. Tell me what I can help you with."

"Just tell the others, would you? They'll pack up when the party's over."

Belinda nodded and went to speak to the second-in-command. She mingled some more in the living room. When she walked into the dining room later, she was dismayed to see that the caterers had dismantled the table, and the guests were beginning to leave.

"What are you doing?" she asked the caterer's assistant when she found him the kitchen, packing everything up.

He looked at her, surprised. "I thought we were supposed to go."

"Oh, no." She explained, then said, "But it's too late now. You might as well leave."

She returned to the living room, disgusted. She saw Sara approaching through the thinning crowd and was surprised by her friend's expression. Shock? Fear? Both, she decided as she went to meet her in the middle of the living room. Sara's eyes looked enormous. Her hair was in slight disarray.

"What's wrong?" Belinda asked.

Sara took her arm and steered her towards the study. "Can't talk here."

"Sara, what is it?" Belinda demanded, alarmed by Sara's obvious distress.

Sara didn't say a word until she'd firmly closed the study door behind them. Then she collapsed onto the couch and said, "Did you see that man who was so drunk?"

Belinda shook her head. "I saw several. Why?"

"This one seemed to be following me around. You didn't notice him?"

"I'm sorry," Belinda said, perplexed. "I really didn't."

Sara clasped her trembling hands together. "He's . . . he's out on the landing. Dead, I think. I saw blood on his neck. He . . . he might have been murdered."

Belinda gasped. "Ohmygod." She ran to the phone on the desk, dialed 911, and told them to come quickly, explaining exactly where. "We'd better go out there and wait, don't you think? Let's find Blinky, first."

Sara shook her head. "I don't think I can."

"Oh," Belinda said.

"You didn't see him, Lin. I just can't do it. There was something about him. He kept following me around, watching me. He seemed somehow familiar, but I'm sure I didn't know him."

Belinda walked over to the bookcase and pushed on the spine of *The Great Gatsby*. Part of the case swung around, revealing a bar with a small refrigerator. She plunked some ice cubes in a glass and filled it with vodka.

"Here," she said, handing the drink to Sara. "You stay put. I'll be back as soon as I can."

"Thanks," Sara whispered.

Belinda rushed out of the study and began searching for Blinky. She found him in the kitchen looking for a lemon, muttering about the caterers

17

leaving so early.

"Blinky," she said, more loudly than she intended.

He turned around, looking startled.

"Come quick," Belinda urged. "Someone's hurt in the hallway."

"What? Where?" Blinky asked, following her towards the front door.

"On the landing," she said impatiently, making her way easily through the thinned crowd in their living room.

At the hallway exit door, she hesitated uneasily. She decided it would be better if Blinky went first.

He pushed open the door, then bent down quickly towards the man lying there looking almost as if he were asleep.

Belinda put her hand over her mouth to stop herself from crying out. "Is he . . ." she asked.

Blinky had his fingers at the man's throat, and when he took them away, she saw the blood. "He's dead," Blinky said. "Go call 911."

"I already did. Sara found him and came to tell me."

Blinky stood up. "Who is he, do you know?"

Belinda shook her head. "Sara said he seemed to be following her around at the party. Don't you know who he is?"

"Never seen him before in my life."

"Then he crashed the party."

"Huh," Blinky grunted, looking at the man more closely. He shrugged and said, "Let's wait in the hallway, shall we?"

"Okay," Belinda said, shuddering. She couldn't help taking one last look at the man. There was something about him . . .

After what seemed like forever, the police arrived. While Blinky explained to them what he knew, the paramedics also showed up. The police asked Belinda and Blinky to go back to their apartment and posted an officer at the door so no one would leave.

Inside the penthouse, one of the officers told a shocked group what had happened while they were partying.

JoAnne approached Belinda and whispered, "Who was it?"

Belinda frowned at her and said, "I don't know. Never seen him before."

"Really?" JoAnne asked.

Belinda stepped away. "Excuse me, I need to find Sara."

Annoyingly, JoAnne stayed right behind her as she walked to the study. Sara had finished the vodka, Belinda noticed as they entered, and a little bit

18

of color had come back to her pale cheeks.

Sara stood up. "Is he really dead?" she asked.

Belinda nodded.

"Did you find him, Sara?" JoAnne asked.

"Yes," Sara said.

"Oh, tell me what happened. Do you know him?"

Sara shook her head. "I was leaving the party and decided to walk down the stairs when I found him. I don't know who he is." Her voice sounded strained.

"Look," Belinda said. "I think we should go out and stay with the others until the police decide what they're going to do with us."

"What did you do after you first saw him?" JoAnne asked. "Did you scream? I didn't hear you. How was he killed, do you know?"

"JoAnne," Belinda said, letting the exasperation sound in her voice. "I don't think Sara feels like talking about it right now. I'm sure she needs to save her energy for answering any questions the police might have."

Sara flashed Belinda a grateful smile and led them back to the living room where they found about a dozen people waiting, most of them looking rather tense. Blinky kept them all supplied with fresh drinks and dishes of peanuts and pretzels.

Finally a police office came in and announced, "We have a tentative identification of the deceased from his driver's license. Does anyone know a Howard Lyndquist?"

Sara gasped. The officer looked at her. "You know him, miss?"

"No. That is, yes. I mean, he's my father."

"Then you can help us identify him."

"No," Sara said, tears streaming down her cheeks. "I've never met him. He's my birth father. I've been looking for him for the last two years."

CHAPTER 3

Dazed, Sara watched the officer turn to Blinky and ask for a private room where they could set up to interview the guests. Blinky showed him to the study while everyone else sat or stood quietly. Sara continued to snuffle into the tissues Belinda had handed her, embarrassed by her outburst. It was all too much. First she found the body, then that policeman told them who it was. She had no warning, no idea that it could be her father, although now she realized why he looked at bit familiar. He looked like her, or rather, she looked like him. Same dark hair, blue eyes, squarish face.

Belinda sat next to her on a couch, occasionally patting Sara's arm. JoAnne stood nearby, staring at her as if hungry for her innermost thoughts. Most of the others avoided looking at her. She felt slightly relieved when the police officer asked her to come with him to the study. Legs shaking, she followed him into the now-familiar room.

A man in plain clothes sat behind the desk. He rose to greet her, holding out his hand. She took it as he said, "I'm Detective Beecham. You're Sara Putnam?"

"Yes," she said, studying him. Of medium height and build, he appeared to be around forty with thinning sandy hair, sharp green eyes and pale freckled skin. His handshake was firm without being crushing.

"Have a seat," he said in a neutral tone.

Sara sat, carefully adjusting herself so she felt comfortable, thinking the interview might be awkward. She noticed that the other policeman sat off to the side. He was drop-dead handsome, and in other circumstances, she

20

might have tried to get to know him better. "How did you know my name?" she asked the detective.

"With extensive work, we can find out anything," he said and smiled.

She realized he'd tried to make a joke, and she smiled weakly back at him.

"We asked your host."

"Oh."

She glanced up and saw a black spider about the size of a quarter making a web on the eight-by-ten picture of Blinky's father behind Detective Beecham's head. She wondered if she should say anything, and decided against it.

"Please state your address, phone number, and place of employment," he said.

"Sara Putnam, 363 Linden Avenue, Montclair, New Jersey. I work at Nort International Wholesalers." She gave him her phone numbers.

Looking down at a yellow pad, he said, "I understand you found the deceased?"

"Yes."

"Would you tell me about that?"

"There isn't much to tell. I left the party, decided to walk downstairs until I got tired, or all the way, if I could. When I pushed open the door, I saw him." She paused and swallowed hard, then watched the spider for a minute. It swung back and forth on a strand of web.

"Want some water?" he asked.

"Please," she said. The web had become quite intricate, and it glistened slightly in the lamplight.

He poured her a glassful from a pitcher on a tray near the edge of the large desk.

"Your first reaction?"

"I thought he'd passed out. From drinking, you know."

"So you knew he'd had a few?"

"Yes." Somewhere, in a mystery story perhaps, she'd read it was best not to volunteer too much information to the police. Her brain seemed to be working on two levels--one extremely conscious of everything that was being said. On a deeper level, her mind jumped around like a skittish horse, dancing here and there, scared of lights and people and everything, but especially the unknown.

"How did you know this, Miss Putnam?"

21

"What?"

"That this particular person had had too much to drink. You saw him at the party?"

"Yes. He spoke to me, and I caught glimpses of him several times afterwards." The spider seemed to be taking a rest. She hung from a fine strand, motionless. Sara wondered if she waited for prey, if she was hungry.

"He spoke to you?"

She nodded.

"What did he say?"

"He wanted to know where I came from and my name."

"What did you tell him?"

"That I was from New Jersey. I didn't tell him my name."

"Why not?"

"Because he was drunk."

"How did you know that?"

Sara took a sip of water. "How do you know anyone is drunk? He slurred his words. He swayed as he stood. He reeked of liquor. His eyes were bloodshot." Her hand shook as she took another drink of water. She watched the spider some more as she began again to spin her web.

"Why did his being drunk have such a negative effect on you, Miss Putnam?"

"I . . . I don't know," Sara said, really not knowing. "He looked sort of familiar, but I couldn't figure out how. I've never liked to be around people who are drunk."

"Okay," Detective Beecham said, apparently deciding to let that ride for the moment. "So, you thought when you saw him on the landing that he had just passed out. What made you change your mind?"

Sara lowered her eyes. "I saw the blood," she said softly.

"Where?"

"On his neck."

"Then what did you do?"

"I . . . I think I screamed. I ran back here and got Belinda and told her. She called you."

"That's all?"

She nodded again.

"Why did you decide to walk downstairs instead of taking the elevator, Miss Putnam? It's a long walk. Twelve stories, I believe."

"I hate elevators. I got stuck in one once when I was visiting my

22

father--my adoptive father--in the hospital. For hours. I've never trusted them since."

"Then you're claustrophobic?"

"No. I just hate elevators." The spider worked steadily now. Sara suddenly realized how lucky she was. She wasn't afraid of much. Spiders didn't bother her at all, nor any other creepy crawly things. Don't be so smug, Sara, she told herself.

Detective Beecham made a note or two on his pad, then looked up. "Now, you claim Howard Lyndquist is your father."

"Yes."

"But you'd never met him? Would you explain a little about that, please."

Sara nodded and cleared her throat. "I'm adopted. A couple of years ago, after my adoptive father died, I decided to try to find out who my birth parents are. I figured time might be running out, that they could die at any moment, too."

Sara paused and stared at the spider. She had worked fast and the web now almost covered the entire picture.

"Go on," Detective Beecham said.

"You probably know that adoptees are allowed access to their records now. I got a copy of my birth certificate. It named my mother and father. I found out later that my mother had died when I was four years old. I never could find my father. Until now," she whispered and buried her face in her hands. She wanted to scream, to yell out about the unfairness she felt. She had no relatives now except her adoptive mother. She felt so alone. Vulnerable.

The young officer came over and handed her some tissues. She blotted her eyes and blew her nose loudly. She was at the point where she didn't care what these men thought of her. She wanted to go home, crawl into bed and stay there for days and days until she felt better.

"Do you have anything to add, Miss Putnam?"

"No."

"Then you may go," he said, surprising her. "Turn on the overhead fan, will you, Pete?"

When the other officer turned it on, Sara realized how warm the room felt. The sudden gust of air made the spider swing out over the detective's head and hang suspended in front of his face. He gave a short shout and jumped out of his chair, overturning it. He fumble-bumbled around, grabbing at the desk for support, sending papers flying as he did so.

Sara started to laugh as she watched him. The spider climbed up her strand and went back to the picture as if affronted by the detective's reaction. The other officer came over to the desk.

"Want me to kill it, sir?"

Detective Beecham had managed to get his bearings and turn around to face his adversary. "I think I can handle it," he said, approaching the spider with a rolled-up bunch of papers. As he swung, the spider maneuvered herself out of the way, the rush of air from the paper helping her along. Detective Beecham aimed again, and again missed. He swore softly under his breath, and hit out once more. This time he smashed the spider against the picture glass. When he brought his paper away, they could see the spider's remains on the cheek of Blinky's father. It looked like some strange mole.

He didn't have to do that, Sara thought. The spider wasn't hurting him.

Detective Beecham's face had become red from his exertion. He turned to Pete and said, "Clean that up, would you? Miss Putnam, as I said before I was so rudely interrupted, you may go."

"Home? Or just to the other room?"

"Home. We know where to find you." That sounded ominous.

Sara got up, looked one last time at the two policeman, and left the study.

When she got to the living room, Belinda and Blinky came over to her. "How'd it go?" Belinda asked.

"All right. He said I could leave."

"Good," Belinda said. "You look beat. Blinky, call her a cab, would you?"

"Sure," Blinky said. He went to the corner of the room to the phone while Sara told Belinda about her interview. JoAnne came up to them while Sara talked, so she finished her story quickly, as usual feeling annoyed with JoAnne's nosiness.

Blinky came back. "A cab's on the way. I asked that officer over there if I could see you downstairs. He said he would. He thinks the detective might be calling me soon."

"Thanks," Sara said, tiredness suddenly overwhelming her. She gave Belinda a quick hug and said a general goodbye, wanting to get away as fast as possible.

She didn't even protest to the officer about the elevator. She felt too weary to walk down now. If it got stuck, she'd just curl up in the corner and go to sleep. They rode in silence, and the officer waited until he'd seen Sara safely into the cab before going back inside.

Sara relaxed as much as possible on the short trip to the Port Authority Building. There she caught the next-to-last bus home to Montclair.

When she entered her apartment and saw her roommate watching TV in the living room, she closed her eyes briefly, thinking, oh, no, I just can't explain everything all over again. She opened her eyes. Eileen barely looked up from the horror movie.

"Hi," Eileen said. "You ought to watch this. It's a good one. How was the party?"

"I'll tell you tomorrow, okay? I'm beat."

"Sure," Eileen said, waving her thin hand in dismissal, eyes glued to the TV. A creature, with an orangutan's face and an alligator's tail, spit some horrible-looking stuff at a beautiful girl, who screamed and screamed. Sara shook her head and went to her bedroom.

After she got into bed, she thought she'd fall right to sleep. But her mind went over and over what had happened that evening. She'd been so close to meeting her father, without even knowing it. Now she never would. What had he done that someone wanted to kill him? And why had he been drunk? Why was he watching her? Did the thought of meeting her make him feel a need to get drunk? If he knew who she was, how did he find her? Or maybe he really didn't know who she was. Maybe he was hitting on her, without realizing she was his daughter! She decided she'd have to learn all she could about him by meeting the people he had known. With that thought going through her mind, she finally fell asleep.

* * * * *

The next day when Sara got up, Eileen had already left the apartment. After coffee and toast, Sara decided to go for a walk. She walked down the two flights of back stairs in the old Queen Anne Victorian, hoping to avoid the landlady and her young son. Stepping outside into the summer air, she breathed in the scent of trees and flowers and grass. Setting off briskly, Sara walked for several blocks, admiring the other old houses along the way, as she always did, before turning around and heading back.

As she turned, she noticed the hedge in front of the house about two doors away moving as if someone had gone through it. Probably a kid, she thought, shrugging. She looked through the leaves as she walked by, but nothing stirred.

How could she find out more about her father? Dummy, she thought, look in the paper. There was probably a whole write-up about the murder.

Moving quickly now, she rounded the corner. Something made her look over her shoulder. A man behind her stopped walking abruptly when he saw her staring at him and bent down to tie his shoe lace. Sara scowled at him for a moment, then rushed up the side walkway and into the house.

The *New York Times* was on the table at the bottom of the stairs where Mrs. Abbot left their mail and newspapers. Sara grabbed it and dashed up the stairs, two at a time.

The story made page three.

> Inventor Murdered in Hallway. Howard Lyndquist was found with his throat slashed in the apartment hallway of famous plastic surgeon, Bancroft Smithfield, II. Mr. Lyndquist had attended a party given by Dr. Smithfield last evening. Police say they are working on several leads.
>
> Mr. Lyndquist was the inventor the robotic vacuum cleaner and numerous other innovative household products. He is survived by his son, Kevin.

And daughter, thought Sara, a sudden lump forming in her throat. Unwanted daughter. Until yesterday? What had happened to make him want to see her, meet her? She was sure, now, that he had wanted to. He'd followed her around, watching. He'd wanted something from her. But what? Had he got drunk for courage?

She threw the paper down in disgust. Call Belinda, she thought suddenly. Maybe she knows something.

Belinda picked up on the third ring, sounding sleepy.

"Did you see the paper?" Sara asked. "Great party last night, by the way. You do have unusual entertainment."

"Sara? Are you being sarcastic and mean, or just trying to be funny?"

Sara sighed. Why did she always get flip when stressed out? "Doing a horrible imitation of a comic," she told Belinda

"Well, save it for some other time," Belinda said, sounding irritated. "I haven't seen the paper. I'm hardly out of bed yet. The police were here until four a.m.! What did the paper say?"

"Said you did it," Sara couldn't resist saying.

"Cut that out! Really, read it to me."

Sara did.

"Your father invented the robotic vacuum cleaner?" Belinda exclaimed. "We read about that in yesterday's paper. We were talking about it before the party."

"Really?" Sara said, excitement in her voice. "Hold on while I see if the paper's still here." She found it under several of Eileen's diet and recipe books. "Got it," she told Belinda. "Hold on while I read it.

"I can't believe it, Belinda," Sara finally said. "My father was practically famous."

"You keep referring to him as your father," Belinda said. "Don't you think that's a bit unfair to Marshall?"

"I know Marsh raised me," Sara said. "And I loved him dearly. But I wasn't a bit like him or Mom. I always felt as if I were the cuckoo in the strange birds' nest."

"I know your adoptive parents were different from you," Belinda protested, "But a lot of kids are unlike their real parents."

Sara sighed. "I can't explain it, Lin. As hard as they tried, I didn't feel like part of the family."

"Was that their fault, or yours?" Belinda asked softly.

Sara thought for a moment. "I don't know," she said slowly. "As small as I was when my real mother died, maybe I still remembered her and couldn't love Mom and Marsh as I should."

"Do you remember *anything* about your real mother?"

"Just a few bits here and there because I was only four when she died. I think I remember going shopping with her once for groceries. And I remember her lying on the couch one day, and I couldn't wake her up. I was so scared! She finally got up, though. She took a drink from a bottle, not a glass. A long drink. I can see her throat moving as she tilted the bottle." Sara felt a shock of insight go through her. "She was an alcoholic! That's one of the pieces that's been missing all these years. I knew Mom and Marsh were holding something back. Something shameful. Wonderful," she said bitterly. "The last memories I have of both my

27

parents is of them drunk."

"Don't be so hard on them," Belinda said. "You don't know the whole story yet."

"No. No, I don't," Sara said. "But I'm going to find out."

"How?"

"From my mother. She knows more than she ever told me."

"Sounds like a plan to me. Tell me if you need any help."

"Thanks, Lin. I will."

They hung up, and Sara immediately dialed her mother's number.

CHAPTER 4

Belinda hung up the phone. She rubbed her eyes, looked at the clock and sighed. Ten-thirty already. She wondered how long Blinky had been up. Good thing Sara called, or she'd still be asleep. It was so strange, no spooky, that Sara had searched for her father for so long, and then found him here murdered, in her apartment building. Belinda shivered and rubbed her arms. She got up, did a few stretches, then took a shower.

She found Blinky in the sitting room reading the *Times*. He liked this room best because of the way the natural light streamed in.

"Hi, Babe," he greeted her. "We made page three."

"Aren't we lucky," she said, making a face and sitting down on the sofa. "Poor Sara."

"Yeah. It sure was rough on her," Blinky acknowledged, handing her a section of the paper. "You look a bit tired. Can I get you some coffee?"

"Please."

When he brought it back, Belinda put the paper down and took her mug gratefully.

Blinky joined her on the couch, patting her leg.

"Sara just called," Belinda told him. "She's all set to find out all she can about her father now."

"Don't you think that's a bit dangerous? There is a murderer loose out there, you know. She should let the police handle it."

Belinda nodded. "She wants to find out more about her father, not just who murdered him." That chill went through her again. She remembered Howard Lyndquist's body on the landing, so gray, so dead. But she knew, too, how much Sara longed to know about her parents.

Blinky put his arm around her, and she set down her coffee mug. "Want to talk about something else?" he asked.

"Uh huh."

"Well, did you enjoy the party last night? I mean up until the last part, of course."

"Yes. Yes, I did." Her hands had begun to shake, and she didn't want Blinky to see. She held them in her lap and looked at them as she spoke. She had to be careful how she approached the subject she needed so badly to talk to him about. "I heard one group talking about breast implants," she said timidly.

"Oh?"

"Yes." She looked at him. His face showed no discernable expression. She let her eyes fall back down to her lap. "They were discussing a few symptoms some women have after getting implants."

"I've heard about that. Not proven medically and scientifically." His face took on the set look she'd come to expect when they discussed the subject.

"But Blinky, they were describing the symptoms I've been having. Tiredness, achiness, that rash that comes and goes."

"It's all coincidence, Belinda. And those symptoms are so vague."

"Vague to you, maybe," she said with some heat. "Being tired all the time may not kill me, but it sure gets in the way of enjoying life sometimes." She looked up at him, then, and saw the anger, quickly masked with a false smile.

He patted her arm. She pulled away.

"You think I'm imagining it." She felt the tears in back of her eyes. I refuse to cry, she thought. If I do, I'll just be an emotional female to be patronized by the all-knowing doctor. Surprised by the bitterness she felt, she stood up quickly and went to the window. Sometimes she forgot how the view of New York always took her breath away. So much left to do, just in this city alone, she thought. And now not always the energy to do it.

"I don't think you imagine it, Belinda," Blinky said from behind her. "It's real to you, I know that. But we can find no cause--"

"No known cause." She turned to face him, feeling her face hardening with anger.

He shrugged. "I'll see what I can find in the literature. Again."

She felt herself soften inside. She knew he'd searched already, and talked to every doctor he knew. He'd just made a big concession for her. She turned to him and slipped into his arms. "You're wonderful. Thanks."

"Don't thank me yet," he said gruffly, holding her tight, stroking her back with his amazing hands. "What do you want to do today?" he murmured into her hair.

"I want to go to the Cloisters. I've only been once, and I want to go again."

"All right. Let's do it. Lunch first?"

"Yes," she said, happy once more.

* * * * *

Monday morning Belinda woke late, as usual. It was five to eleven, and Blinky had already left for his office on Park Avenue, so she decided to laze around. Most people had to rest up on the weekends because they worked hard all week, she thought ruefully. I have to rest up during the week from being so busy on the weekends.

Throwing on a robe and slippers, she padded to the kitchen where Hilda was cleaning the stove. The newspaper lay neatly folded next to Belinda's place setting. She glanced at it and noticed the date. July 1, 1985.

"Oh, no," she said, "I'm late getting my driver's license renewed. I was supposed to do that last month."

"You'd better wait until Charles gets back on Friday from his vacation so he can chauffeur you," Hilda advised, pouring orange juice and coffee. "What do you want to eat?"

"Just toast and corn flakes, Hilda. I'm going to get it done today. I may need to drive around the rest of the week."

Hilda shrugged as she put a piece of bread in the toaster.

After breakfast, Belinda got dressed, made phone calls for the cancer drive, ate a late lunch at two, then drove to the Department of Motor Vehicles. She had to stand in line for fifty minutes, staring at the public service posters, smelling the dank musty air. By the time she reached the chest-high counter, her feet hurt and she had a headache.

"May I help you?" The woman behind the counter was small with a round face. Each of her large silver earrings dangled a cat, the tail waving. They pulled the woman's lobes down obscenely, making the pierced holes gape. Belinda made herself stop staring.

"Yes. I need to renew my driver's license." She handed the clerk her

31

expired one and waited while she typed some information into her computer.

"Oh, but you're deceased. I can't renew this." The clerk took some large scissors and cut Belinda's license in half.

"What do you mean, I'm deceased? Of course I'm not dead. I'm standing right here in front of you, aren't I?"

"Well, yes, but the computer shows you died last month on the eleventh. Nothing I can do about it."

"Of course there is. That's my birth date. Just change the information in the computer. You can see I'm still alive."

"How do I know you're who you say you are?"

"Well, if you hadn't cut up the license, you could have seen from the picture, although I admit I don't look much like it."

"See there? Next." She gestured to the woman behind Belinda.

"Wait a minute," Belinda exclaimed. "What am I to do? I need a driver's license."

"Go over to that line," the clerk pointed. "Maybe they can help." The sign above it said, "New Licenses," but Belinda went over and got behind a large woman in a floral dress and waited.

At five to four a man shouted, "Everyone not already at the counter will have to leave and come back another day."

People began straggling out, defeated-looking. "Wait," Belinda said. "Oh, wait. That woman cut up my license. How am I supposed to drive home?"

"Did the computer declare you dead? When it does that, we're required to cut up the license," the man said.

"Well, yes. Does this happen a lot?"

"Not too often, but sometimes. Come back tomorrow with your birth certificate, and we'll take care of it. Oh, and please drive carefully." He gave her a big smile and turned away.

Dejected, Belinda left and drove off cautiously in her new, 1985, silver Jaguar, looking in the rear view mirror more often than usual, checking for police cars.

Then she saw one. The cop had on his flashers and was waving her over. She pulled up next to a fire hydrant. Slowly, the policeman got out of his car. Her hands began to tremble. She told herself to get a grip, she hadn't broken any laws.

Finally, he was at her window, looking down at her. She pushed the button to lower the window, letting in a blast of hot air. "What's wrong?"

"Your inspection sticker has expired."

She couldn't see his eyes behind his dark glasses, but she could feel him looking her over. Belinda did not feel flattered.

She looked at the corner of the windshield. The sticker had the number five on it. She'd forgotten that, too. Blinky would be upset with her.

"I need to see your license and registration."

She opened the glove compartment and got the registration and handed it to him. He checked it over and gave it back.

"Your driver's license?"

"I don't have one. I went to DMV just a while ago to renew it, and the lady said the computer showed me as deceased, so she wouldn't renew it. Then she cut up my old one."

"Wow," the cop said. "That's the best excuse I've heard yet."

"But it's true!"

"Yeah, lady, and I'm Santa Claus. Okay, show me some form of identification, then get out of your vehicle and come with me to mine."

She fumbled in her purse for her American Express (don't leave home without it) card and showed it to him.

"Don't you have something with your address on it?" he asked.

She looked some more, but couldn't find anything. "Just the registration," she said finally.

"All right," he said, "let's go."

Belinda got out of her car and stumbled a bit. The officer gave her a sharp look and followed her to his car, opening the passenger door for her. She got in, and he slowly went around to his side.

"All right," he said, putting his sunglasses in his pocket. He radioed dispatch and gave them her name and address. A voice came back and said something Belinda could not understand.

"Huh," he finally exclaimed. "It does show you as deceased. If you are who you say you are." He gave her a sharp look again, and she tried to make her face seem sincere. "Too weird to be a lie, I guess. These new computers are more of a pain than they're worth sometimes. Well, I won't give you a ticket for driving without a license, but I have to give you one for the inspection being overdue."

"But you can't give a dead person a ticket at all, can you?"

He rubbed his chin, then threw up his hands, finally smiling. "All right. You can go." He stared at her chest and licked his lips. His eyes fell to her left hand where her diamond ring sparkled at him. He cleared his throat. "Make sure you get that sticker and get the mess with your license straightened out."

"I will, Officer, I promise." She couldn't believe she'd talked herself out of it. Maybe it hadn't been what she said, but how she looked.

When Belinda got home, it was after five. She flopped down on the living room couch, kicking off her shoes, and closed her eyes.

A few minutes later, Blinky arrived.

"How are you, Babe?" he asked and gave her a kiss. He pushed her legs off the couch so he could sit down with her.

"Dead," she said.

"Me, too," he told her, moving his hand along her leg.

"No. I'm really dead. Deceased, kaput, gone, passed away. According to the Department of Motor Vehicles, anyway."

"What do you mean?" Blinky asked, his hand stopping on her knee.

She explained what had happened.

He smiled. "Yeah, you are a little pale." She glared at him. "Really. Belinda, I've said it before. You shouldn't leave things until the last minute."

"So, it's my fault?" She frowned.

"I didn't say that. It's just that if you were a little more organized--"

She scowled harder. "I happen to be super-organized."

"No, you're not. What's for dinner, by the way? You did remember that it's Hilda's night off, didn't you?"

"Dead women don't cook," she told him, jumping up from the couch.

She headed for the bedroom, furious. She'd expected sympathy and gotten hassled instead. Blinky didn't follow her, and her anger quickly turned to depression. She felt so damned tired! Maybe what was wrong with her would prove to be fatal. Then the Department of Motor Vehicles would be right. Up until now, she'd thought that whatever the problem was, Blinky and his doctor friends would find out how to cure it. Now she didn't feel so sure. What if what she had couldn't be fixed? What if she just got worse and worse?

Don't be silly, she told herself. Stop feeling sorry for yourself. Resolutely, she got up off the bed and went to the kitchen. Blinky must have heard her rattling around. He poked his head in. "Is it safe to come in?" he asked.

34

"Yes," Belinda said. "I've been reincarnated as a cook, super-organized, of course. Because of my supernatural powers, dinner will be ready in less than five minutes." She put the leftover lasagna in the new microwave oven and set it for four minutes.

"I'm impressed," Blinky said, getting out napkins and silverware to set the table.

They had a companionable dinner. Afterwards, Blinky went to his study to catch up on some paperwork. Belinda dragged herself to the bedroom and fell asleep with her clothes on.

She woke the next day feeling ratty, took a long, hot shower, and ate a leisurely breakfast.

Then she drove to the Department of Motor Vehicles. Again. The lines were a little shorter, she noticed, thankfully. When it was finally her turn, she didn't know quite how to explain her situation. "I'm Belinda Smithfield. I was here yesterday."

"Yeah?" The clerk, a woman of about thirty and chewing gum loudly, barely looked at Belinda.

"I tried to renew my license. Belinda Smithfield."

"Yeah?"

"Well, the computer said I was deceased. A man said to come in with my birth certificate." Belinda opened her purse and handed the certificate to the clerk.

"This says you're Belinda Anderson."

"Yes, I know. I'm married now."

"Did you bring your marriage certificate?"

"No. No one told me I would need it."

The clerk handed her the birth certificate. "You do."

"No," Belinda said, quietly, so furious she could barely speak. "You people made a mistake. You fix it. NOW."

The woman snapped her gum. "You don't understand. We have to have the proper paperwork--"

"You do," she shouted now. "I did all this before. You screwed up. You fix it!"

The crowd applauded, startling Belinda. She'd forgotten they were there. The clerk glared at them and at Belinda, then motioned for the man behind Belinda to step forward. "Bring in your marriage certificate," she told Belinda.

Belinda frowned at the woman. "I want to talk to your supervisor."

35

"He can't help you."

"I'll talk to him anyway." Belinda did not move from her spot.

"Oh, all right. Hal. Oh, Hal!" the clerk shouted over her shoulder.

The same man who had told her the day before to bring her birth certificate stepped up to the counter.

"What's the problem, Esther?"

"This woman doesn't have the proper paperwork."

"You told me yesterday to bring my birth certificate. You didn't say anything about a marriage license."

"Ah, you're the deceased licensee." He smiled at her.

Belinda frowned at him.

His smile faded.

"All right. Please step over here." They went down to the next open counter space, and he started up the computer.

"Name?"

She told him.

"Date of birth?" She told him and handed him her birth certificate for good measure.

"Oh, here we are." He typed a few characters, had her take the eye test and took her picture. The computer spit out some heavy stock perforated paper, and the man pasted her picture to it, tore the license out and laminated it. He then gave her her new license.

She wrote a check. "Thank you, Hal," she said as she handed it to him. "Thanks, Esther," she shouted. Esther looked up, startled, and Belinda waved her license at her triumphantly, then went out to her car where she checked it over carefully. The middle initial was wrong, but she shrugged, and put it in her wallet.

Next she drove to the 10-minute inspection station where it took her an hour to get her car checked out.

Tiredness overwhelmed her when she finally entered the apartment again. She went to the bedroom, kicked off her shoes and flopped down on the bed. The clock said five-thirty. Sara should be home by now, she decided, as she dialed the number.

Her friend answered on the second ring.

"Hi," Belinda said. "What're you doing?"

"Belinda. I was just thinking about you! How are you?"

"Well, I was dead this morning, but I feel better tonight."

"What do you mean?"

Belinda told her, and the whole episode became funny. Belinda laughed so hard, tears came to her eyes. She began to choke. She just hoped it wasn't some kind of cosmic joke foretelling her immediate future. She sputtered and couldn't stop coughing.

"Belinda, what's wrong?" Sara asked, all laughter gone from her voice.

"Nothing. I just swallowed the wrong way."

"Are you sure you're all right? You sound strange."

"I'm okay," Belinda protested. Except for battling bureaucracy, the police, my husband and having a murder take place outside my door, she thought.

"Belinda. This is Sara. Tell me."

Belinda swallowed hard. "I can't tell you over the phone. We need to get together and talk." She wanted to talk to Sara, but in person, so she could see her face.

"It's serious then."

"Oh, you . . . No, I'm all right. Lunch Saturday? Do you want to come to Manhattan?"

"Sure."

"We'll go to Four Seasons. You always like that."

"Okay," Sara said. "But now I'm worried."

"Don't be," Belinda whispered. Then, forcing her voice to be stronger, she said, "Any news about, you know, the murder?"

"I talked to Mom, but it's a long story. I don't know anything more about the actual, um, murder, though."

"When we see each other on Saturday you can tell me what your mom said, and maybe we'll know something more by then."

"That sounds good to me," Sara said.

They hung up. A sudden ache made Belinda put her hands to her breasts. They no longer made her feel good about herself. She decided that perhaps she should see another doctor. A doctor who didn't know who she was or who her husband was. She'd thought of it fleetingly before but hated the idea. Aching all over, Belinda got the phone book from the nightstand and opened the Yellow Pages to Physicians.

CHAPTER 5

After Sara spoke to Belinda on Sunday morning, and before she had a chance to think about what she was going to say, she called home.

"Mom," she said over her mother's greeting. "Have you read the paper? Did you see what happened last night?"

"I'm just finishing the ads, Sara. Calm down, now, and tell me. Slowly."

Why does she always have this effect on me, Sara wondered. I don't usually rattle off like that. I handled the police well last night. This is my mom. It should be much easier to talk to her than to them.

She took a large breath of air. "Page three. Howard Lyndquist. He was murdered last night outside Belinda's apartment." Her breaths started coming in short gasps. She could feel the blood racing to her temples. "I found him. I found him! It's just too incredible."

"Really?" Lucille's voice hardly changed inflection. Sara tried to imagine her expression. Probably the face remained smooth, unmarred by any expression. Perhaps the eyebrows raised slightly. A look of distaste might have passed fleetingly across the patrician vestige. God, she was getting fanciful. "Is that all you can say? Really?" Sara knew her tone bordered on the disrespectful, but no one could make her more frustrated than her mother.

"What did you want me to say, Sara?"

"Oh, I don't know. That you were perhaps surprised, shocked, sorry I had to find him. Any number of things."

"Well, I am all of those things, of course. That should go without saying."

"It did," Sara said, grinding her teeth.

"Really, Sara, I think maybe we should start this conversation over again."

"I agree. I'll come over there so we can sit down and talk. Okay?"

"All right. What time can I expect you?"

"Do I have to give you an exact time?"

Silence answered her.

"Okay. Let's see. I'll be there in an hour. How's that?"

"That will be fine, Sara. I look forward to seeing you then."

Sara clenched her fist as if ready to throw a punch and said goodbye.

As she hung up the phone, Eileen strode in, long legs taking her across the living room and to the kitchen in just a few strides. Her waist-length red hair streamed behind her, and her green eyes shone brightly with excitement.

"Isn't it a beautiful day?" she asked, putting a grocery bag down on the kitchen counter. She began to unload doughnuts and yogurt.

"Wonderful," Sara said. "What kind of diet are you on now?"

"The doughnuts were an impulse. A treat. After we eat them, I'm going on a yogurt, fruit and grain diet." She pulled out a loaf of dark wheat bread, two bananas and three apples.

"Eileen, you know you don't have one ounce of fat on you. Why do you do this to yourself?"

"You're kidding. Look at these thighs. These hips."

"Eileen, pinch some fat somewhere."

Eileen pulled up her T-shirt and pinched a smidgen of flesh near her waist between finger and thumb. "See?" she asked.

Sara shook her head and opened the doughnut box. "I've decided to just consider this a strange hobby. Like quilting or throwing pots. Or your mania for decorating." She waved her hand around and took a large bite out of the doughnut, feeling the powered sugar coat her lips and tongue.

Cows had invaded the apartment in the last month. A big wooden Holstein sat on a long side table, and other, smaller ones were placed on end tables. A large papier-mâché bovine lay on the floor next to the couch. Cow magnets, cow canisters, a spoon rest, and a calendar with cows on it graced the kitchen. It was a black and white world.

Eileen took a doughnut herself and sat down on the cowhide-covered bar stool next to Sara. "How was the party last night?" she asked between nibbles.

"Interesting," Sara answered. "I found my father, murdered on a stairwell landing." She got up to get some orange juice.

"What?" Eileen squawked, almost choking on her doughnut. "You're kidding."

"No. Really." She came back and tossed the newspaper to Eileen. "Read all about it."

Eileen bent her head over the paper, her bright hair covering her face. When she looked up, brushing it away impatiently, she said, "The *Times* doesn't waste any time, does it? This is so short, it hardly tells me anything."

After pouring two glasses of juice, Sara sat down again and explained everything.

"You poor kid," Eileen said when Sara finished. "What are you going to do now?"

Sara looked at her watch. "Go see Mom. Damn, now I'll be late." She stood up, grabbed her purse and headed for the door.

"You're not going like that, are you?" Eileen asked.

Sara stopped and looked down at what she wore--T-shirt and shorts. "Damn," she said again and headed for her bedroom. Tearing off the shirt and shorts, she put on a slip, and a skirt and blouse, pantyhose and pumps. Quickly, she applied a bit of blush and some lipstick and caught her shoulder-length brunette hair into a ponytail.

Dashing down the back stairs, she almost ran over Eugene, the landlady's son, entering his part of the house. She apologized.

"Where are you going?" he asked.

"Out," she said.

"But where?"

"To see my mom." She figured out long ago that the best policy was to answer his questions quickly and try to escape. About a month after she and Eileen moved in, she noticed that sixteen-year old Eugene had a huge crush on twenty-three year old her. They'd lived here a year, and he hadn't gotten over it. She wished he'd get a girlfriend. At first it had been flattering. Now she felt mildly annoyed whenever she met him on the stairs or in the driveway.

"How's your mom doing?" Eugene asked, standing in the middle of the stair so that she couldn't get around him.

"She's fine, Eugene. I'm really in a hurry, if you don't mind."

He blushed slightly and stood aside. She avoided touching him as she went by. Unfortunately, his mother stood at the bottom of the stairs, the *Times* in her hand.

"Sara, are these the Smithfields you know?" She held up the newspaper where she'd folded it so that the article about the murder faced outward.

"Yes," Sara said wearily.

"My goodness." Mrs. Abbot's chins quivered. "Did you see the man who was murdered?"

Sara sensed rather than saw Eugene coming down the stairs behind her. She felt surrounded, weary of explaining.

"Yes. I found him. He's my long lost father. I don't know who did it or why. I'm going to see my mother now and try to find out some things. And I'm late. Would you excuse me?"

Mrs. Abbot's eyes widened, and her mouth opened to say something, but nothing came out. A momentary feeling of satisfaction came over Sara. For the first time ever, she'd made her landlady speechless.

She rushed past her, out the door, Eugene following her.

"Is it really true?" he asked. "Did you find him? What was it like? Did you know he was your father?"

Sara stopped short and spun around. What had made his mother tongue-tied had opened the floodgates of Eugene's mouth. He looked like a gangly puppy dog standing there, his nose practically twitching, his tail almost wagging. Lank dark blond hair hung down a bit over his eyes and halfway down to his collar. His light blue eyes looked guileless and innocent.

She reached out and put a hand on his arm. "Listen, I promise to tell you all about it when I get back. Okay?"

He nodded at her, smiling.

"I really have to hurry now."

"That's all right," he mumbled, back to his shyer self. "You won't forget, though, will you?"

"No. I promise." Sara unlocked her car door and slipped inside.

She made it to Caldwell in fifteen minutes. The house hadn't changed since she was a little girl--same white exterior with black shingled roof and black trim. The shutters had Scottie dog cutouts. A huge pine tree took up almost half of the small front yard. Sara pulled into the long side driveway and parked in front of the detached garage near the rear of the deep property.

Lucille stood at the back door, her face neutral. Not happy, not sad. Not calm or angry. Just there. Of medium height, she held her slender body stiffly upright, stomach and buttocks tucked in. Every bleached blond hair on her head had been sprayed into submission. Makeup was perfect. She wore a flowery shirtwaist dress, hose and pumps. The only time Sara had seen her in just robe and slippers had been in the middle of the night when Sara was ill.

Pushing the screen door open for Sara, Lucille held it, then let it ease shut so it wouldn't bang. They entered the kitchen together. This room never changed either. A new refrigerator had replaced a worn-out one, but that was it. Even the breadbox and canisters were the same tin ones from long ago. An old *Better Homes and Gardens* cookbook lay open on the counter.

"Let's sit in the sunroom, shall we?" Lucille suggested.

"All right," Sara said.

"You go ahead. I'll bring the iced coffee."

Sara nodded and went through the dining room into the sunroom. A long, narrow room the length of the driveway side of the house, sun streamed in the bank of windows along the wall. Plants crowded the space, all healthy and lush. Sara liked this room best in the house, except for her old bedroom upstairs, now a sewing room.

Her mother came in with coffee on a tray. She set it down on the coffee table and handed Sara a glass. Its coldness felt good in Sara's hand. She felt slightly flushed, as if she had a fever. She took a long refreshing swallow and held onto the glass in order to enjoy the feel of it longer.

Settling herself on a chair opposite, Lucille said, "Now, tell me about everything that happened."

Sara told her, watching her face. Her mother's expression hardly changed at all, except when Sara told her about finding her father. A slight frown marred her forehead, but it quickly became smooth again as she took a sip of coffee.

Sara finished telling her about the night before, and then said, "This morning I talked to Belinda, and she told me about the article in yesterday's paper about Howard Lyndquist being an inventor. He invented the robotic vacuum cleaner. Did you know that?"

"I knew he was an inventor. I didn't know about the article in the *Times*. I must have missed it. I often don't read Saturday's paper."

"You never told me," Sara said, taking a sip of coffee to see if it would rinse away some of the bitterness she felt.

"Sara, we've been over this. I just don't understand why you need to know about this man who abandoned you. Your father and I did our very best by you, and it hurts me that you feel the need to dredge all this up." Sara couldn't hear a trace of hurt in her mother's voice.

Sara set her glass down sharply on the table. She felt like getting up and pacing around, but made herself sit still. "This has nothing to do with you or Dad. It's so hard to explain. It shouldn't hurt you. It's like some part of me is missing. There's an empty spot inside that can only be filled with information about my relatives. I'm a blank, different, apart. Wouldn't you want to know?"

Her mother looked startled by the question for a moment. "No," she said firmly. "No, I'd be grateful for what I had and let sleeping dogs lie."

"Okay," Sara said. "That's another way we're different. Don't you see? I won't be happy until I know all there is to know."

A look of resignation passed over her mother's face. She wiped her lips with a napkin, then put it aside. Clasping her hands together, she began to speak. "I'm going to tell you all I know. Then we will not talk about it again. Is that understood?"

Sara held her breath for a moment, then let it out in one long sigh. "Yes," she whispered and leaned forward.

"Well. Your mother was married to your father, Howard Lyndquist, for only about two years. He left her soon after you were born, and they divorced. When you were four, your mother took an overdose of sleeping pills with some liquor. It must have killed her rather quickly." Lucille paused.

Sara arranged her face into a mask. She felt as if a body blow had connected with her stomach. Her mother a suicide. Maybe Lucille was right. Maybe she should have left it alone. She took a shaky breath. "Go on," she said.

Lucille looked at her sharply, then continued. "You were at a neighbor's. When the neighbor brought you home, she found your mother. No one could locate your father, so a social worker took you into custody. Marsh and I wanted a child, and since I couldn't have any, we decided to adopt. I'm not overly fond of babies, and we wished to give a home to an older child, perhaps one who wouldn't otherwise be adopted."

She paused and took a sip of coffee. Sara stared at her steadily, waiting for more. She could believe that Lucille wouldn't want a baby. Too messy.

"You'd only been in custody a week when we brought you home. They warned us that they would continue looking for your father for a year. He never turned up, so we were able to adopt you. I didn't want to tell you that you weren't our child, but Marsh insisted that we do so. He said you might remember things about your other family and might get confused. We waited until you were about twelve, I think."

Sara remembered. It had been Marsh who told her, not Lucille. He'd come to her room one night while she studied for a history quiz. He'd asked politely if she had a minute to talk. Sitting at her desk, she put a pencil in the book to keep her place and closed it. Marsh sat on her bed, awkward-looking in Sara's pink, lacy bedroom. He cleared his throat a couple of times before beginning.

"I don't know any other way to say this," he began. He gave her a pleading look. "You're adopted. Your mom and I adopted you when you were four years old."

Somehow the news hadn't shocked her, nor surprised her much. She'd always felt different. When she found out that some of her friends thought they were adopted, she knew that lots of kids went through a time when they believed that. But there were other, little things that let her know that something was different about her family. Her parents never talked about when she was a baby or about anything before she began kindergarten. The photo albums held no baby pictures. She had her adopted mother's coloring, but otherwise didn't look like either parent. Marsh watched her closely, probably expecting some big dramatic scene. She didn't know what to say to him.

Finally, she said, "That's all right."

"Aren't you surprised?" he asked.

"Not really. I've always wondered . . ."

"You never said anything."

"I didn't want to hurt you and Mom if it wasn't true."

"Oh," he said. "Do you have any questions?"

"Not right now," she'd answered, and kicked herself ever after. Because she couldn't bring it up again for years, and they never did. So when she finally told them that she wanted more information, they thought it a closed subject and were reluctant to give her any. Lucille flatly refused, and then Marsh died, and she became really frantic to know.

Finally her mother gave her names and dates, but that was all. Sara wrote letters, searched newspaper files at the library, looked in every telephone book she came across for Howard Lyndquist. She had no clues about his whereabouts, didn't even know if he was alive. Now it was too late. Sudden anger coursed through her. Sara looked away from her mother so she wouldn't see. She took a deep breath, then another, trying to calm down.

Lucille's serene voice continued. "I knew your birth father's name, and I read an article several years ago in *Newsweek* about inventors. His name was mentioned. Since I wasn't positive it referred to your father, I never told you. That's all I know."

Sara stood up abruptly. "Why didn't you tell me about the article when I was searching the libraries? I probably could have found it, maybe learned where he was."

"I really didn't want you to find him, Sara," her mother said, a faint exasperation seeping through her outward calm. "I thought you knew that. I have the article. You may have it, now."

Now when it wouldn't help, Sara thought resentfully, staring out the window at the driveway. She swung around. "You have it? Where? Let me see it!"

Her expression never changing, Lucille got up from her chair and left the room. Sara followed her upstairs to Lucille's bedroom where her mother pulled a shoebox off the top shelf in her closet.

She took it to the bed and opened it. "Here," she said, thrusting a packet at Sara. "There're some letters he wrote to you, too. You might as well have them now."

"What?" Sara gasped, automatically holding out her hand. "How long have you had these?"

"Only a few months."

Sara stared at her mother a moment, speechless, then turned around and ran down the stairs, almost stumbling in her pumps. She let the screen door slam behind her as she dashed out of the house. She jerked open the car door and jumped in. Her first impulse was to read everything right now. Her heart pounding, her breath coming in short gasps, her hand trembled as she placed the packet on the passenger's seat. It would be better to be in her bedroom at her apartment, the door closed, to look at it all, she decided. Gunning the motor, she took off for her apartment. She'd never been so angry at Lucille before in her whole life. She needed to get out of there before she did or said something she'd regret later.

45

CHAPTER 6

Sara rounded the corner to her apartment, driving faster than she should have. A man crossed the street in front of her. She slammed on the brakes, missing him by inches. She sat a moment, stunned, staring at him with her mouth open. He glared at her, then took off running around the corner, and was gone. He looked odd running in a suit and tie. She listened through her open window until she couldn't hear his leather soles slapping on the sidewalk any longer. He'd looked a bit familiar, but she was sure she didn't know him. Must be a neighbor, she thought, out for a Sunday walk, still in his church clothes.

Her hands shaking, she drove carefully into the driveway and got out of her car, taking the packet with her. She made it to her floor without meeting the landlady or her son. Thankfully she found that Eileen had gone out again. She just wanted to go to her bedroom, lie down and read the letters in peace.

Stretching out on the bed, she took the elastic band off the envelopes. There were three, plus the clipping from *Newsweek*. With shaking hands, she organized the letters by postmarked date. One in March, one in April, the last one in May. Each had Howard Lyndquist's name and return address in Brooklyn in the corner, and her name and old address in the middle. None of the letters looked as if it had been opened, but Sara wondered if perhaps her mother had steamed and resealed them. At this point, she could believe anything possible.

Carefully, she opened the oldest envelope. Crisp, heavy paper crackled in her hand. The letter began, "Dear Sara." She read quickly through it, then again, slowly.

> *I hope I have the right Sara. Sara Lyndquist, daughter of Howard and Gloria, adopted around age four soon after Gloria died. If this is you, please write me at the address on the envelope. I need to see and talk with you.*

It was signed, "Hopefully, Your Father."

She threw the letter down and began beating her fists on her thighs. Damn her mother for not giving this to her. She could have met him, talked to him. Now it was too late. She would never forgive Lucille. Never.

Taking a deep breath to calm herself, Sara opened the letter from April and read it through blurred eyes.

> *I am writing again thinking that perhaps you did not receive my first letter, and therefore, could not answer. Please write to me soon if you are the daughter of Howard and Gloria Lyndquist. I must talk to you. If I have the wrong Sara, could you please drop me a note and let me know. That way, I won't bother you again.*

It was signed the same way as the first.
And the third.

> *I feel like I am dropping these letters into a great void. I've enclosed a self-addressed stamped envelope. Please get in touch with me soon to let me know either that you are my daughter, or not. I understand that you may not want to talk with me, feeling that I abandoned you. It will be in your best interests to write. Believe me.*

It was signed, "Waiting Anxiously, Howard."

She noticed that he didn't put, "Hopefully, Your Father," this time. It almost broke her heart, and tears slid down her cheeks as she imagined him writing to her, thinking she hated him and didn't want to get in touch with him.

Sara put the third letter down and leaned back against the covers. She didn't remember ever being this upset and angry in her whole life. The clipping caught her eye. She scanned through it quickly. Howard's name was mentioned only once with several other inventors. It probably wouldn't have helped her if she'd seen it earlier. But it might have.

The unfairness of it overwhelmed her. What had he wanted to see her about? Could it have anything to do with his murder? Heart pounding, Sara got up and paced around the bed with its animal print cover. She passed the bureau with the carved wooden animals--an elephant, zebra, giraffe and rhinoceros. Feeling like the caged lion in the picture she'd painted over the chest of drawers, her mind veered from idea to idea. She wanted to strangle Lucille. She wanted to call Belinda but was too agitated to talk coherently. She could go see her. No, she thought, as she looked at the clock. Four-thirty. Too late. She could call the cops, see if they had found out anything. But she didn't want to bring attention to herself. She stopped and looked at the return address on one of the envelopes. Brooklyn. An overpowering urge to go there, to see where he had lived, overwhelmed her. But she didn't know anything about Brooklyn. Didn't have a map. She wished Eileen were here. They could go together.

She didn't know where Eileen had gone or when she'd be back. She was probably out with her new boyfriend whom Sara hadn't met yet. Who did she know that could find their way around Brooklyn? JoAnne. JoAnne grew up there. She would love to help. With her inquisitiveness she might even be useful.

She called JoAnne who quickly agreed to go. After they hung up, she changed into jeans, a T-shirt and her running shoes. Then she went downstairs and outside to wait for JoAnne, pacing back and forth in front of the house. Suddenly she stopped. A feeling of being watched had overcome her, and she looked around for some sign. Although she didn't see anyone, her unease remained. She looked toward the house. Maybe Eugene watched her from his bedroom window, but she couldn't see him there.

Relieved to see JoAnne drive up, Sara rushed over to the car and said, "Hi. Thanks for coming. Should I drive, or do you want to?"

"Let me," JoAnne said. "Since I know the way, it will be easier. What's the address?"

Sara got in and gave her one of the envelopes. JoAnne looked at it a moment and said, "I think I can find it."

As they took off, Sara unobtrusively moved an old food wrapper from White Castle away from her foot. JoAnne lit a cigarette. Sara was glad the

48

windows were open and that they were in JoAnne's car. She didn't want hers all stunk up with stale cigarette smoke.

"You don't mind, do you?" JoAnne asked after she'd taken a few puffs.

Sara shook her head, suppressing a cough. "How long do you think it will take to get there?" she asked.

"Close to an hour. I'm not exactly sure where that street is, but I think I can find it all right."

Sara nodded, clutching the door handle as JoAnne took a corner rather fast.

"That was some party Belinda gave last night, wasn't it?" JoAnne said.

Sara didn't know if she meant it or if she was being sarcastic. "I thought it was very nice. Lots of people. How did you meet Arthur, by the way?"

JoAnne laughed. "At the pet store, would you believe? We both have fish."

"Have you been seeing him long?"

"Just a month or so. Isn't he cute?"

Adorable, Sara thought. "Yes, he's cute. Does he have a brother?"

JoAnne laughed again, entering the highway, and immediately pushing the speed up to seventy. "No brothers or sisters. An over-protective mother is all."

"Uh, JoAnne, I'm not in that much of a hurry. You're going to get a ticket."

"What? Oh, no, I won't. I never do." She pointed to the radar detector, pushed her speed up to seventy-five, and lit another cigarette.

The wind tugged so hard at Sara's ponytail she felt like her head might come off. She wanted to close her window, but wouldn't be able to stand the smoke. The car bounced over the rough road like an old stagecoach, and Sara was glad she had buckled herself in or she'd be thrown into JoAnne's lap. "How's it going in the Legal Department?" Sara asked, raising her voice to be heard over the wind.

"Pretty good," JoAnne replied. "I'm still learning the ropes. Some of those lawyers can be pretty demanding, too."

"So I've heard. I think I'll just stay in Training and Development."

"Probably wise." JoAnne swung out into the middle lane to pass a car. Sara glanced at her. JoAnne's short brown hair didn't get in her face at all. A slight frown marred her narrow forehead as she concentrated. She had a long, thin face with a pointed, sharp nose, and small lips. Large gray eyes saved her from being homely. Her slender fingers were easy on the wheel which made Sara realize that JoAnne had good control of her car. After they passed the slow car, JoAnne got back in the third lane, and Sara relaxed a bit.

"I'm not absolutely sure, Sara, but I think someone may be following us."

"Really?" Sara asked and twisted around in her seat to look.

"Don't look!" JoAnne said. "You don't want him to know we know."

"Why not?"

"Um, I don't know. I just think that that's how it's done."

"Done where?"

"You know. In detective novels. On TV."

Sara looked in the side-view mirror. "What color is the car? How long have you noticed it?"

"It's blue. A Chevy, I think. He's been there since we got on the parkway," JoAnne told her.

"Could be just coincidence. Why would anyone follow us?" Sara asked.

"I don't know. Why would anyone murder your father?"

Sara winced at JoAnne's bluntness.

"So tell me about your father. Howard, wasn't it? I'll keep an eye on the Chevy."

Sara thought JoAnne had missed her calling. She should have been a private detective, or at least a journalist. "I've been looking for him for a couple of years. My mom had these letters and just gave them to me with the address this afternoon."

"You have any idea who might have murdered him?"

Ah, Sara thought, payment for the ride is that she gets to pump me for information.

"No idea at all," Sara told her.

JoAnne frowned and lit another cigarette. "You going to try and find out?"

"Yeah," Sara said. "I think I am."

JoAnne nodded, then remained silent for several miles, and Sara put her head back gratefully.

Around six, they exited the Brooklyn Battery Tunnel and entered Brooklyn.

"That Chevy's still behind us," JoAnne said.

Sara forced herself not to turn around and stare.

JoAnne slowed down and began looking for the street. She rounded a corner and said, "Darn. I thought it was right here, but I guess I was wrong. I'll just go down here a ways, then start crisscrossing streets and see if we can find it."

"Why don't we just ask someone?"

"Who'd you have in mind?" JoAnne asked.

Sara looked around. A drunk leaned against a brick storefront. Several youths were grouped on a corner near a small grocery store. Another drunk crossed in front of them, and JoAnne waited impatiently, tapping her fingers on the steering wheel, as he zigzagged by. When he got safely onto the curb, he turned and gave them the finger. JoAnne flashed him a peace sign.

"I see what you mean," Sara said, grinning at JoAnne's elegant response to rudeness. "This isn't the best of neighborhoods."

JoAnne drove on down the street, and they looked at every sign.

After half and hour, they found themselves in a slightly better part of town, but still hadn't found it. "Let's ask her," Sara said, pointing to a middle-aged woman carrying a grocery bag.

"Okay," JoAnne said, pulling over. "Do you know where Michigan Avenue is?"

The woman looked at them a moment, then shook her head and hurried away.

"Better ask a man," Sara said.

"Right, although sexist," JoAnne muttered. They saw a man in a suit up ahead, and JoAnne pulled over again.

He gave them directions, waving his arms and pointing, involving six or seven turns and landmarks.

"Did you get all that?" JoAnne asked as she pulled away from the curb.

"I'm not sure," Sara answered, getting anxious. It wouldn't get dark for another hour or so, but they still had to drive back to Jersey.

They headed in the direction the man had pointed and made several turns before admitting they didn't know where to go next.

"Let's try a gas station. Maybe they'll have a map," Sara suggested. Why was this so hard? Why was everything so hard? Then she remembered the Chevy. "Is that guy still following us?"

"Naw, I think we lost him. Probably all the turning I did."

"Good," Sara said. At least that was one less worry.

At the gas station Sara hopped out and got both a map and directions.

"It's quite a ways," Sara told JoAnne as she got back in the car. "That man gave us the wrong directions, I think."

"You navigate." JoAnne lit a cigarette. "Find us on the map?"

"Yes, and where we're going, too. Make a left ahead."

Finally they came to the street. When they turned onto it, JoAnne said, "Uh-oh. Someone else is following us."

Sara automatically turned to look and saw a black hearse. She gasped. "How long has he been behind us?"

"Just a couple of blocks. Eerie, isn't it?"

Sara shuddered. "Yes. Look. I think that's the building up ahead. But it's a warehouse." She looked around. The street was filled with warehouses. "Can this be right?" She looked at the map, then at the address on the envelope, then at the long, low building as JoAnne pulled up in front of it.

"The hearse is behind us," she whispered. "Lock the door and close your window!"

Quickly, Sara did as JoAnne suggested. They sat, waiting to see what would happen. After a few moments, the driver's door on the hearse opened, and a tall, thin man got out. He wore black slacks that were too short, allowing his white socks to show above his hightops. He had on a T-shirt with a black suit jacket over it. Long, straggly gray hair bushed out around his thin face and flowed below his collar. He looked at their car curiously but didn't slow down in his dash to the front of the warehouse. He produced a key, unlocked the door, and entered.

"He doesn't look much like a funeral director," JoAnne commented.

"No, he doesn't," Sara said, unlocking her door. "I'm just going to go look at that hearse."

"Don't do that!" JoAnne said. "He might come back out."

"He looked pretty harmless. I don't think he followed us. Just coincidence that he was behind us and we were both going to the same address. I won't be a minute."

"Sara, don't."

"Quit worrying. Be just a sec."

She went over to the vehicle, checking it out. She couldn't see anything except through the windshield. As she peered at the dash, she felt a hand on her shoulder. She jumped back and bumped into someone. She gave out a little yell.

"What are you looking at?" the driver asked, scowling at her with his bushy gray eyebrows.

"You scared me!"

"I'm sorry. I just wondered why your car was in front of my building, and then you came to look at my hearse."

"Your building? Not Howard Lyndquist's?

The man's face turned sorrowful. "Mine and Howard's. Until his unlucky demise." He looked at her more closely. "You are the daughter," he said. It was not a question.

"How'd you know?"

"You look like him. Come, have some coffee. Get your friend. We need to talk."

Sara hesitated. The man looked loony-tunes. Only someone crazy would drive a hearse, wouldn't he? But was he harmless crazy or dangerous crazy? Guileless blue eyes returned her gaze. Sara shrugged. "I'll go get JoAnne."

He nodded and went to the warehouse entrance to wait. Sara walked over to the driver's side of JoAnne's car.

"I saw him come out, but he was so fast he got there before I could do anything," JoAnne said as she rolled down the window.

Sara realized if he'd limped over carrying a couch under one arm and a chair under the other, JoAnne wouldn't have done anything. But what would I have wanted her to do? If he owned the building with my father, he must have trusted him. Then she remembered that her father had been murdered. She looked at the strange man standing in the doorway. Maybe he did it! Maybe he was luring her inside to murder her, too. Don't be ridiculous, she told herself. Why would he want to murder her? There was no logical reason he should. So, he looked strange. She'd just get JoAnne to go in with her, and with two of them there, he wouldn't dare try anything.

"The man knew my father--they owned the building together. He wants us to come in and talk to him."

"I'm not going in there with him!" JoAnne said, starting to roll up her window.

"JoAnne. Please. We came all this way. He's harmless, believe me."

JoAnne left the window half rolled up and looked over at him, and he smiled and waved at them.

"He drives a hearse, for God's sake."

"Don't you want to find out why?" Sara asked. "And what's in the warehouse? My father was an inventor. Might be lots of neat stuff in there."

JoAnne hesitated again. Sara knew she almost had her. "Come on. He might even help us find out who murdered my father."

That did it. JoAnne retrieved her keys from the ignition and got out of the car after rolling up the window the rest of the way. She carefully locked the doors, checking both before going up the sidewalk with Sara.

The man turned and went inside ahead of them.

Sara followed, JoAnne behind her. They stopped just inside, and Sara and JoAnne gasped at the immense space filled with machines. Machines that looked like robots, machines that looked like boxes. Computers were everywhere. Sara saw a model train in a corner. A dollhouse sat next to it, lights on in the windows. Model cars, boats and planes filled another corner, remote controls beside them. Dolls, stuffed animals and clowns were arranged on shelves. In the center of the room stood a strange-looking vacuum cleaner. Sara wondered if it was the robotic one.

Sara and JoAnne began walking around, looking at everything. The man stayed by the door. Here was a lounge chair with an electrical cord behind it and a remote control. There was a stereo system, partly disassembled. In another corner was a hammock with electrical wires on its frame.

"Why do you have the toys?" Sara asked as she turned around to look at the man. Her voice echoed in the large space.

He came towards them. "Come in the office, and I'll explain while we have some coffee."

He led the way towards the back. They entered a room with two huge open rolltop desks covered with papers, a counter with coffee pot and mugs, and a drafting table. In a corner were an old battered couch and chair of indeterminable colors.

"Have a seat. I'm Ira Levine, by the way. You must be Sara. And you are?" he asked JoAnne.

"JoAnne Justin, Mr. Levine. Nice to meet you."

He bowed, then turned away to make coffee. Sara and JoAnne exchanged looks, then gingerly sat on the couch together.

When he'd finished fiddling with the coffee pot, he came and sat down in the chair while the coffee perked. "Your father was most anxious to meet you." He crossed his legs which made his white socks much more noticeable. Sara tried not to stare.

"My mother just gave me his letters today."

Ira nodded. "You know he's dead?" His eyebrows seemed to droop at the edges, making him look like a sorrowful puppy.

"Yes. I found him."

"What?"

Sara nodded. "I think maybe he wanted to talk to me that night, but he never said who he was. He was drunk, following me around. When I left the party, I found him."

"That's terrible. Terrible," Ira said. "What a situation. Howard never drank, you know."

"Really?" Sara asked.

Ira nodded. "Hated liquor. Said it should be illegal. He believed that the brain was sacred, inviolate. He didn't believe it should absorb anything harmful. No smoking, drinking or drugs of any kind, except in life-threatening situations. Like penicillin, you know." He got up to get them coffee.

"But he really was drunk. I could smell it on him, and he could barely walk or talk."

Ira brought the mugs over and set them down on the scarred coffee table. "He was distraught. Against all he believed in, he finally hired an investigator to find you."

"But why?"

Ira sighed. "It's a long story. The bottom line is, he wanted to disinherit his son and make you his sole heir."

Sara put her mug down quickly on the table, afraid she'd drop it. "Why?"

"They were having some difficulties. As I said, it will take a long time to tell you."

"Do you know if he disinherited his son?" Sara asked, her mind churning.

"I'm not sure." Ira looked at her sadly and took a sip of coffee. "I guess we'll find out when they read the will after the funeral."

55

CHAPTER 7

The funeral! Sara stared at Ira Levine, a tingle running down her back. She hadn't even thought about it. And her half brother. A brother her father had been angry enough with to disinherit?

"My brother," Sara said, the word sounding strange and feeling forced on her lips. "He had an excellent reason to murder my father."

Ira nodded. JoAnne watched him, mouth slightly open.

"Do you know if the police questioned him?" Sara asked.

"Yes, they did," Ira replied. "Right before they talked to me. He has an alibi. A very good alibi. He was with me, here at the warehouse." ·

"Oh," Sara said. She looked closely at Ira, a thrill of fear making her shiver slightly. Suddenly, she wanted to leave this strange place inhabited by this strange man who drove a hearse and could alibi the strongest suspect in her father's death. Her brain felt like it was in information overload. She needed to go home and think about everything she'd learned.

Then she thought of something else. "What about his mother? I mean, my half brother's mother?"

Ira nodded. "She lives here in Brooklyn. She and Howard are, were, legally separated. About two years ago."

"If they weren't divorced, wouldn't she inherit his estate?" JoAnne asked.

"Normally," Ira acknowledged. "However, they had a separation agreement. He paid her a large settlement, and she signed a paper waiving rights to his estate." His mouth pressed itself into a straight line. "She thought it better to have the money two years ago than perhaps not have any later."

"Why would she think it would be gone?" JoAnne asked.

"In our business, it can go quickly. We put most of our money back in, and if the newest idea is a bust, we go bust, too. We'd just sold a patent for a pretty large sum. Howard decided to see if he could buy Miriam off."

"What was the patent for?" JoAnne asked.

Ira shook his head. "The company that bought it is still in the development phase. I'm not at liberty to discuss it."

Sara and JoAnne looked at each other, JoAnne raising an eyebrow. Sara looked at her watch. "I didn't realize it was so late. We need to get back to Jersey. Work tomorrow, you know." Standing up, she smiled a smile that felt false. She felt so strange--light-headed, almost dizzy. She knew she should ask him more questions, but she couldn't think of any more. She felt claustrophobic all of a sudden, as if she were in a stuck elevator. "It was very nice meeting you, Mr. Levine," she managed to say.

"Call me Ira." He stood up. "I'm glad we finally met, Sara. I'm sorry it was too late for your father. He was a good partner. It will be difficult to continue without him. He had most of the ideas. I just tried to implement them."

They began walking towards the front of the building. "You never did tell us about the toys," JoAnne said.

"Ah, yes. They serve as inspiration, and we use, used, them to try out things on a small scale."

Sara nodded. "Makes sense. Can I ask you a personal question?"

He stopped walking and looked at her warily. "I suppose," he said finally.

"Why do you drive a hearse?"

He laughed. A laugh that sounded like a donkey braying. Sara took a step backward, bumping into JoAnne.

"Nothing sinister about it," Ira said when he caught his breath. "We got it cheap, and we could use it to haul all our stuff around. It's been a dependable vehicle."

"Doesn't it make you feel creepy to drive it, though?" JoAnne asked.

Sara thought it a rude question, but she had wondered about that, too.

"Maybe a little at first," Ira said, giving JoAnne a piercing look, as if he'd just noticed her. "Now I don't even think about it anymore."

They continued to the front door. Sara felt really anxious to leave. They shook hands. Ira said, "Come back to visit anytime. Will you come to the funeral?"

Sara nodded. "I guess so. I'll try. When is it?"

"Thursday at two. You come by here at one-thirty, and I'll take you there."

"In the hearse?"

He smiled ruefully at her. "I guess that wouldn't be appropriate, would it? Perhaps we could take your car."

"I'll have to get time off from work."

"That shouldn't be a problem," JoAnne said. "He was your father."

"Right. Okay. Let me have your phone number, Mr. Levine, in case I can't make it."

"Ira. Call me Ira." He took a small notepad from his pocket, and a pen, and wrote down the number for her. He asked for her number, and she gave it to him.

The sun was setting as they drove towards New Jersey. Neither of them said anything for awhile, each thinking her own thoughts.

"A strange man," Sara finally said.

"Very," JoAnne acknowledged. "Maybe you have to be in order to be an inventor."

"That would mean my father was strange, too."

JoAnne shrugged. "Seems likely," she said bluntly.

Sara winced. She realized that when she'd gone searching for her birth parents, she hadn't thought much about what they might be like. And how she would feel if they were not normal, average, middle-class American type people. Maybe Lucille was right. Why borrow trouble? But no, she was glad she knew something about them. She could be proud of her father. He'd had high personal standards, and he'd had a worthwhile life. Suddenly, she wanted to meet his wife, Miriam. She could tell Sara a lot of things that Ira wouldn't know. Personal things.

JoAnne dropped her off at home. Sara climbed the three flights of stairs to her apartment and found Eileen still out. When Sara went to get a glass of milk, she saw they only had about half a cup left. They'd need some for morning coffee, too. "Damn," she muttered as she grabbed her purse. She drove to the nearest convenience store.

Upon entering, she greeted Mike who had been working there for over two years. Sara thought it was a bad sign that she knew the clerk by name. It meant she used the high-priced store too often because she didn't plan her purchases better. She should be buying this stuff at the grocery store

58

for much less. Also, it was disquieting that Mike had kept the job for two years because he couldn't find anything better. He'd told her he was looking for something else, but had had no luck.

He seemed like a personable, reasonably bright individual. Average looking, he was neat and clean. He asked how she was doing, and she told him a little about the last day and a half. She was the only customer, so they chatted awhile. The door opened, letting in some fresh evening air along with an antsy-looking young man in torn jeans, a plain white tee and a black leather jacket. Sara glanced outside, but didn't see any cars in the lot, except hers. She thought the boy might not be seventeen--too young to drive. She walked to the back of the store to get her milk.

When she came back to the counter with a gallon container, the young man had a gun pointed at Mike. "Empty the register into a paper bag," he said as he waved the gun. "And give me two packs of Camels. Hurry up." His voice cracked, and his hands trembled.

Sara almost dropped the milk, but she grasped the bottom of the jug and set it down on a shelf.

The young man said, "Stay right there, lady. This will only take a minute. Just do what I say, and no one will get hurt."

He sounded like a television character, Sara thought. Her eyes were mesmerized by the gun.

"Young man," she said, her voice much higher than normal, "does your mother know what you're doing right now? What would she say?" She sounded like Lucille. Her mind was going ninety miles an hour trying to think of a way to defuse the situation. She tried to concentrate on the boy instead of herself, but it was hard to do.

"Shut up," he squeaked at her. "Just shut up." He waved the gun at Mike again. "You hurry up."

Mike was putting the money in a bag, but Sara thought he moved rather slowly.

"Really," Sara said. "Have you thought about the consequences of what you're doing? What will you do with the money?"

"Probably drugs," Mike said.

"I don't do drugs," the boy said indignantly, shifting from one foot to another.

"So, what's the money for?" Sara asked again.

"Just stuff," he told her.

"Like the gun?" Sara looked at it more closely. She'd been to the toy store last weekend, looking at games for Eileen and herself. She'd gone by a display of toy guns. They looked so real. She squinted at the weapon. There was something about it, and the way his hand held it as if it didn't weigh anything at all. If it were real, shouldn't he be holding it with his two small hands?

Suddenly, Mike had a gun, too, and he was pointing it straight at the young man. "Drop it, now," he said. Neither his hands nor his voice shook.

The boy looked panicked, but kept his gun up. He started backing out of the store.

"Drop it, I said," Mike told him again.

"Mike," Sara's voice sounded funny in her own ears. "I don't think he has a real gun--"

"Dammit, I said to drop it, or I'll shoot."

"No, Mike," Sara screamed as the boy dropped his weapon, turned around and fled out the door. "Let him go!"

She watched while Mike slowly lowered his arm and took a shaky breath, then she walked over to where the boy had dropped his weapon. Carefully, she stooped down and looked at it. When she picked it up, Mike said, "Don't touch it. I'll call the police."

"Mike, it's plastic. Look." She brought it over to him. He examined it closely.

"Still," he said.

She went and got her gallon of milk. "He was just a kid. Maybe he learned a lesson. No good education in jail."

"Yeah." Mike's shoulders slumped, and he put his gun away underneath the counter and rang up the price of the milk. "Yeah. God. I could have killed him!" He wiped his brow with the back of his hand. "I really need to look harder for another job."

"You were so calm. Have you been robbed before?"

"Five times."

"Five!"

"Yeah. I always just gave them the money before. But I got tired of it, so I bought the gun.

"I never knew," Sara said. "Gee, Mike, what will you do next time?"

"I don't know." He shook his head. "I just don't know." He took the plastic gun off the counter and hurled it in the trash with great force, making crumpled paper cups, straw wrappers and napkins come flying out.

Sara looked at it lying there on top of all the trash for a moment, then on a whim, she went and retrieved it and stuck it in her purse.

"Souvenir," she said. "Well, I've got to get home." She stood a moment looking at Mike. "Will you be okay?"

He nodded and started to put the money from the paper bag back in the register.

"Bye, Mike."

"Come again," he answered automatically.

When Sara got into her car, she began to shake all over. Thoughts flew through her head. What if it had been a real gun? What if Mike had shot the kid? What if she had somehow been shot?

She couldn't quit shaking. She hugged herself tightly to make herself stop.

After awhile, she started up the car and drove slowly and carefully home.

In the empty apartment, Sara put the gun in her nightstand--where else would it go, she wondered sardonically. She checked all the windows and double-checked the door. After she poured herself a glass of milk, she sipped it while making a sandwich for supper. She sat thinking for a while, then took a long, hot shower and got into bed, wondering where Eileen was.

Sara didn't think she'd ever fall asleep, but she finally drifted off. A few hours later, a noise woke her. She sat up straight in bed, straining to hear. There it was again. Someone was in the living room, picking up things and putting them down again. She heard something fall on the floor. Eyes wide, Sara got up and crept to the doorway. She tried to open the door a crack without making a sound. She peeked through the space. Holding her breath, she strained to see into the darkness. A figure, back to Sara, picked up one of the cows on an end table and took it to the bar, placing it there. As the form turned, faint moonlight coming through the window illuminated her face, and Sara sagged against the doorjamb with relief. Eileen. What on earth was she doing?

Sara turned to look at her clock on the nightstand. Three a.m. She opened the door and entered the living room.

"Eileen, what are you doing?"

Eileen didn't answer. Instead, she walked over to the large papier-mâché cow on the floor and pulled it toward her bedroom.

"Eileen," Sara said sharply. She followed her into the bedroom where Eileen placed the cow on top of the bed. She walked past Sara without acknowledging her presence.

Sara suddenly realized that Eileen was sleepwalking. She hadn't seen her do it since they first moved in. Helplessly, she watched as Eileen moved each cow to a different location, then moved them all back again. Sara perched on the couch, watching, afraid to wake her roommate, afraid to go to bed in case Eileen left the apartment or somehow hurt herself. Eileen's auburn hair fell like a curtain over her blank face. Her bare feet moved soundlessly back and forth, back and forth. After the cows were all in their original places, she began to remove the dishes from the cupboards. Then she put them all back.

Sara felt her eyes start to close. She was so tired. She snapped them open and watched Eileen begin to put clean dishes in the dishwasher. She wanted to go wake her up and get her to bed. Sara went into the kitchen and took Eileen by the arm. "Come on, you're tired. Let's go lie down."

Eileen ignored her, and pulling her arm away, she put another glass in the dishwasher.

"Eileen," Sara said in her ear. "Time for bed. Come on."

Eileen began to take all the dishes out of the dishwasher and throw them away in the trash can under the sink.

Appalled, Sara tugged on Eileen's arm again. Eileen ignored her, continuing to throw away the dishes.

Sara felt tempted to just go to bed. She had to go to work in the morning. Later this morning. She looked at the clock. Four-thirty. She tried one more time, taking Eileen's arm, whispering in her ear to come to bed. This time it worked, and Eileen let Sara steer her toward the bedroom and help lay her down. Sara covered her carefully and tiptoed out of the room with one last glance at her roommate. A slight snore escaped Eileen's lips, and Sara smiled a tired smile and went back to bed herself.

She had drifted off when she heard a sound in the living room. I'm not getting up this time, she thought. She won't hurt herself. She'll be all right, and I have to get some sleep. Another sound, as if someone had bumped into a piece of furniture. "Damn," she muttered, throwing the covers off herself, swinging her legs angrily over the side of the bed.

This time she didn't linger in the doorway but strode into the moonlit living room.

She gasped when she saw the strange man standing in the middle of the room with a gun in his hand.

62

Jan Christensen

CHAPTER 8

"What do you want?" Sara asked, her voice hoarse with fear.

He didn't answer--just motioned her with the gun into her bedroom. Slowly, Sara backed into the room, her eyes never leaving the stranger. He was dressed in black, like a caricature of a cat burglar, even to the black ski mask. The gun was black, too, of course. Sara had no doubt that it was real. But a feeling of unreality settled over her as she faced the second gun within twenty-four hours.

This can't be happening to me, her mind screamed. What is he going to do? She wanted to yell out loud, but no sound would pass her lips. She was afraid that if she did anything to make him mad, he'd shoot her. This was a well-built man dressed all in black--turtleneck, jeans, shoes and socks. Not a young, scared skinny boy. She could see sharp blue eyes and a tuft of black hair peeking out of his cap.

He kept motioning with the gun, one black-gloved finger to his lips. She backed farther into the room until her legs pressed against the edge of the mattress. He pointed, indicating that she should sit. When she did, she had to look up at him, her neck at an uncomfortable angle.

He grabbed a pillow. She thought for a moment that he planned to smother her with it, and her insides turned to jelly. Never taking his eyes off her, he shook it out of its case with his left hand. Rather gently, he pushed her facedown onto the bed. She tried to scream, but only a muffled sob escaped her. Putting his knee on her back, the stranger tied her hands behind her with the case. He got the other pillowcase and tied her feet together. He's not going to rape me, she thought, since he tied my legs

63

together. But he still might kill me. She should have struggled with him, not let him do this to her. He found a scarf in a bureau and fixed it around her mouth. She was too shocked and scared to resist.

Sara's breathed in short gasps, and she thought she would choke when he put the scarf over her mouth.

Paralyzed with fright, she lay motionless, only turning her head to watch him methodically search her room.

He opened every drawer in her bureau, moving everything aside, then back again. He removed each drawer and looked carefully underneath the wood drawer separators. He did the same with the chest of drawers, then searched her closet. Next he looked under her bed, and he even lifted up the corners of the rug. He moved each acrylic painting of different jungle cats she'd done, looked behind the curtains, and shook out every book in the room. She wanted to scream at him to hurry and get it over with.

In her nightstand, he found the letters from her father, and he read each one, then stuffed them into his jeans' pocket. Sara felt her eyes widen with surprise. Is that why he's here? she wondered. Is he looking for a will? He moved her address book and saw the toy gun. His eyes shifted to her, then back to the gun which he picked up carefully. When he discovered what it really was, he shook his head and tossed it back into the drawer. Deliberately, silently, he inspected every inch of her bedroom, but when he had finished, he'd taken nothing except the letters. He looked at her. She held her breath, imagining what he might do next. Thoughts of torture and death whipped through her mind. Tears she could not contain began falling down her cheeks. He seemed unmoved, and without looking back, the burglar left the room, closing the door behind him.

Sara didn't know what to do. He could still be in the apartment, and if she made a sound, he might come back into her bedroom. Being as quiet as she could, Sara rolled over onto her side and shrugged her shoulder up towards her mouth, trying to work the scarf off her face. Finally, it came loose and fell around her neck. Sara pulled her feet up to her hands, and tried to untie the pillowcase. She broke a fingernail working at the knot. Sweat joined the tears on her cheeks, and she was sobbing by the time she finally undid the knot. Her wrists ached and her throat felt parched.

Swinging her legs off the edge of the bed, she stood up. Her legs wobbled as she made her way to the door. She pressed her ear onto the wood, listening. She couldn't hear anything, but he had been silent in the bedroom, so Sara didn't know if he still lurked in the apartment or not.

Finally, she couldn't stand it anymore, and she turned around to grab the doorknob with her bound hands. She pulled it open slowly, then turned and stared into the living room. Early dawn light gave the room a misty look. Sara realized she was holding her breath as she moved cautiously into the room. She glanced all around, then hurried to Eileen's room, and opened the door. Afraid of what she'd find, she was relieved to see Eileen asleep on her bed, unbound, snoring slightly.

Sara bent over her roommate and whispered her name.

Eileen came awake slowly. When she realized that Sara was in the room, her eyes popped open wide. "What's wrong?" she asked.

It took Sara a moment to speak. "A burglar broke in. He tied me up." She turned around so Eileen could see her hands.

"Holy cow! Is he gone?" Eileen asked as she jumped out of bed and ran to the doorway. "What did he look like?"

"He'd be the only one here with a mask," Sara said. "He's gone, Eileen. I wouldn't be here if he hadn't left, would I? Could you untie me, please?"

Eileen turned and looked at her, wide-eyed. "Holy cow," she said again. She went behind Sara and began undoing the knot. "Did he hurt you? He didn't rape you, did he?" she blurted out, her hands stopping their work on the knot.

"No. No, he just tied me up and searched my room. Please hurry and untie me." Sara felt as if she was going to start crying again, and she didn't want to. She needed to sit down.

Finally, free, she staggered away from Eileen, tottered to the living room and collapsed into the armchair. Eileen followed her and began searching the apartment.

"He's gone," Sara told her, rubbing her wrists.

Finally satisfied, Eileen stood in front of Sara and said, "I'll call the police." She went to the phone and had a quick excited conversation.

While she talked, Sara thought with dread about the police. More explaining. These would be different cops in a different state, even, so they wouldn't necessarily know anything about her father's murder. This whole incident must be related to that. Why else would anyone search her room and take only her father's letters? The letters! The only link she had with him. Gone.

Until now, she'd led a normal, uneventful life. Her thoughts flew around her head like deranged butterflies beating their wings fruitlessly against her skull. Get a grip, she told herself. At least he hadn't hurt her.

But she felt violated nonetheless. She could still feel the pillowcases around her limbs, the scarf over her mouth. She shivered.

Eileen hung up the phone and turned back to Sara. "Can I get you something? How about some coffee? Or tea? Or even a drink?"

For a moment, Sara couldn't say anything.

Eileen stood there, watching her. "Coffee or tea? I'd suggest brandy, but we don't have any."

"Tea, I think," Sara finally said. "Hot, though. I'm suddenly cold." She hugged herself.

Eileen brought her a blanket and helped Sara wrap herself up. Then she brought tea and toast. Sitting down opposite her with her own cup of tea, she asked, "What do you think he was looking for?"

"I don't know," Sara said, taking a grateful sip of the warm liquid. "It must be related to my father's murder." She sat up straighter. "Maybe he was looking for the weapon? Maybe he thinks I did it?" She took another long swallow of tea. "I don't even know what the weapon was. I can't believe someone killed my father only the night before last. It seems as if so much has happened since then."

"A lot has," Eileen said. "Do you think he might have been looking for a will? Do you have one, or any other papers that might cause someone to do what he did?"

"No, nothing. Just the letters. He took those."

Before Eileen could say anything, the doorbell rang, making them both jump.

Eileen got up to answer it. "Hello," she greeted someone.

Sara could tell by her voice that the someone was male and good-looking.

"You called and reported a robbery?" a deep voice asked.

"Yes," Eileen replied. "Please come in. I'm Eileen Rogers, and this is my roommate, Sara Putnam. She's the one you need to talk to."

Two officers entered the apartment and introduced themselves, but Sara couldn't concentrate and immediately forgot their names. She felt as if she should stand up, but didn't feel strong enough to do so. Instead, she stayed wrapped in her blanket while Eileen asked the men to sit and offered them tea. They declined, and the younger, blond one took a notebook out of his pocket. "We checked all around outside before coming up, but didn't see anyone suspicious," he said. Then he began questioning her.

Sara told them everything that had happened. When she finished, he

Jan Christensen

asked her, "He took only the letters? You're sure?"

Sara nodded. "Nothing else in the bedroom. I don't see anything missing in here, do you, Eileen? All the cows seems to be accounted for."

Eileen looked around, then shook her head.

"What do you think he was after?" the officer asked.

Sara sighed. She'd have to tell them about the murder now. A wave of weariness overcame her, and she looked helplessly at Eileen.

"Do you mind if I fill you in on that?" Eileen asked. "Sara's a bit tired."

More tired than you know, Sara thought. I hardly got any sleep at all between your sleepwalking and my burglar. She wanted it to be over. She wanted to crawl into her bed and sleep for a week. She'd call in sick. She wouldn't be able to work, anyway. She tried to remember what she needed to do at work today, but couldn't concentrate.

Eileen's soft voice, along with the hot tea and warm blanket lulled her, and she drowsed.

She woke with a start, hearing Eileen say, "Isn't that right, Sara?"

"What?" Sara blinked her eyes at them. What were the police doing in their apartment? Then she remembered, shivered, and rubbed her wrists.

Eileen had picked up the stuffed cow and petted it as she looked at Sara. The two police officers also looked at her expectantly, the blond one holding his pencil poised above his notepad. They were both so good-looking. If the circumstances were different . . .

"I said," Eileen told her, "that you haven't heard any more about your father's murder since what you read in the paper."

Sara nodded. "That's right."

"I remember reading about that," the one with brown hair said. "Something came in about it this morning. They found the weapon."

Sara sat up straighter in her chair. "What was it?" she asked.

"They're not sure. Never seen anything like it before. They think it's some new kind of kitchen tool. Probably something he invented."

"How awful," Sara said. She wrapped the blanket more tightly around herself and stared at the floor. She didn't want to think about it anymore. She wished *she* were sleepwalking instead of living this waking nightmare. She looked up and found the other three looking at her expectantly.

As if she knew something they didn't. But she didn't. She felt so helpless, so lost.

CHAPTER 9

Belinda sat in the strange waiting room, trying not to stare at the other women. She couldn't help wondering why they were there. Since most seemed to have small or almost non-existent breasts, she assumed they all wanted implants. One woman did have an enormous chest. Belinda guessed she had come to see about a reduction. Unless she was there as a follow-up to implant surgery. Surely not, Belinda thought, and looked away.

At last the nurse called her name. Her hands icy and trembling with fear, she entered the examining room. The nurse pointed at a pile of paper gowns with silly pink flowers and told her to remove everything from the waist up and put one on, opening in front. After the nurse left, Belinda took off her blouse and bra and donned the gown. A feeling of vulnerability washed over her as she sat there waiting. It seemed as if her body had betrayed her. She could no longer trust how she felt. If one more doctor told her he couldn't find anything wrong, she didn't know what she'd do. See a psychiatrist? She hated the thought. All her new friends in the City did that. Like doing lunch, going to the nail salon, having a bi-weekly massage, they fit in one, two or three weekly visits to their "shrinks." What would Blinky think? What would Sara think? More importantly, how would it make Belinda herself feel?

If the doctor said the implants needed to be removed, she didn't know what she'd do. How would she be able to tell Blinky? What would it do to their relationship for him to know she sneaked behind his back?

Finally, the doctor came bustling into the room, followed by the nurse.

68

Short and thin, the physician had black bushy eyebrows, a long straight nose and full sensuous lips. His almost black eyes looked her up and down before he greeted her.

"Mrs. Smithfield?"

Belinda nodded.

"I'm Dr. Alverado. What can I do for you today?"

Her hands clasped tightly in her lap, Belinda stared at them while speaking. "I'm having some problems since I got breast implants, and my doctor can't find anything wrong."

"What kind of implants are they?"

"What do you mean?" Belinda asked.

"Silicone or saline?" the doctor asked impatiently, pulling up a steel stool and sitting down in front of her. She had to look down at him as she sat on the treatment table.

"They're silicone."

He nodded. "We've been seeing some patients with apparent reactions to this type of implant. They can leak and then the silicone gets into the system causing all kinds of problems. If you'll lie back, I'll take a look."

The nurse helped her lie down and stood next to her head as the doctor parted one side of the paper gown and began massaging her breast. Belinda refrained from gritting her teeth. He started off gently enough, but soon began to push hard, and she let out an involuntary gasp.

"Just relax," he told her.

Easy for you to say, she thought. No one's pushing on *your* tender parts.

He covered the breast and uncovered the other one, doing the same exam. When he finished, he absently pulled the gown back over her and said, "You may sit up now."

She did so while the doctor washed his hands.

"Tell me about your symptoms," he said, turning away from the sink and facing her.

"Mostly tiredness, sometimes I ache all over, and I have a rash that comes and goes. It's not there now."

"Where?"

"On my legs."

"What does it usually look like?"

She thought for a minute. "Round, about the size of a dime. Pretty red."

He nodded. "Okay, you can get dressed now. Then come into my office and we'll chat awhile. Nurse Dunning will show you where."

After they left and closed the door, Belinda put on her bra and blouse. She took her brush from her purse and pulled it through her hair. She found Nurse Dunning waiting outside. She showed Belinda into a small office decorated in Queen Anne style--claw feet everywhere. She stared at pictures of the doctor's family and his desk for another twenty minutes, wondering what they were going to "chat" about.

At last the doctor entered the office, moved quickly to his desk and sat down behind it, rolling the chair up close. His black eyes looked at her appraisingly before he spoke.

"I believe you have had a reaction to your implants. We can replace them with saline implants, and no one, except possibly your husband, will ever know the difference. My nurse can set up the appointment for you." He looked at her, eyebrows raised.

"I don't know," Belinda said. Her stomach hurt all of a sudden, and her hands felt clammy. She wiped them across her skirt. "The surgeon who did the operation said that there's no scientific evidence that the implants are causing my problems."

"Ah," Dr. Alverado said, leaning back in his chair. "Of course this is what he said. He is afraid of a malpractice suit. I have never used silicone implants, by the way. I understand that some patients like them because they say they feel more natural. But the ingredient is not natural. Saline can do no damage if it leaks--it just leaves the body in the urine. These symptoms you have--they started when?"

"About four months after the surgery."

"You never had them before?"

Belinda shook her head. She could feel the tears starting behind her eyes. "You're sure that the symptoms are caused by the implants?"

"Well," Dr. Alverado hedged, "as sure as I can be. There are no tests as yet. We go by patient testimony. Your rash does sound a bit different from others, but that may be that the silicone reacts to your body differently. You have no leakage from the nipples, so I do not have that proof. Better that we take the implants out and be wrong than leave them in, and I be right. No?"

Belinda nodded, looking down at her lap.

"Who was your doctor?" he asked suddenly.

Belinda looked up, surprised. "I'd rather not say."

Dr. Alverado shrugged. "You need time to think about it," he said, his voice kind.

Belinda nodded.

He stood up, reached into a holder on his desk and handed her his business card. "For when you decide." He patted her on the shoulder. "Don't wait too long, now."

And he was gone. Belinda sat a moment, bracing herself to walk out of Dr. Alverado's office. Suddenly she remembered Sara's reaction when Belinda told her about the implant surgery.

"But why?" Sara had exclaimed. "Your breasts aren't big, but they're there. It's not nice to fool with Mother Nature," she paraphrased. Her eyes had widened. "What if something goes wrong?"

But Belinda had been walking on air. She'd just been to Blinky's office and met him for the first time, and she was highly attracted to him. From the way he'd acted, she thought he felt the same way. She cautioned herself that he might treat all his patients that way, but somehow she didn't think so.

He first saw patients in his office, not the treatment room. He'd told her he did that because he thought it made them more comfortable, and she agreed with him. After an initial conversation, he glanced over the questionnaire she'd filled out in the waiting room and asked her a few questions about her reasons for wanting the operation. Then he told her to go to the treatment room with his nurse to get ready for him to examine her.

She'd felt a tingle go through her when she thought of him touching her. But her breasts were so small--34A. He wouldn't like them. He must like large breasts, mustn't he? After the implants, she'd look so much better. He'd see her then, too.

He had been totally professional when he examined her. When finished, he again met with her in his office and explained everything thoroughly. She couldn't remember now what the list of complications included, but in the early eighties there hadn't been a whisper about the implants leaking.

Blinky had remained professional throughout. It wasn't until a month after he had discharged her as his patient that he'd called her and asked her out.

Belinda got up from the chair in Dr. Alverado's office and walked slowly towards the elevator. When the door opened, she was startled to see a clown and a woman glaring angrily at him. Belinda couldn't help staring at the clown who was dressed as a female with a mid-thigh length polka-dot skirt, black and white striped blouse, wildly patterned stockings, and huge red shoes. He--had to be a he, Belinda decided since he was over six feet tall and black whiskers were peeking through the whiteface--held a pink feather duster upright like a bouquet. He had red hair in wild disarray topped with a funny hat. He was a sad clown with downturned mouth and a tear on one cheek.

"Talk to me, dammit," the woman whispered loudly as they arrived at the ground floor.

Belinda jumped and looked at her. But she was speaking to the clown. He shook his head sadly and motioned Belinda and the woman out of the elevator. He followed them carefully, his big shoes flapping on the marble floor.

Belinda walked over to the newsstand to pick up an *Elle* and *Vogue* before leaving the building. The strange couple followed her, the clown getting a package of breath mints.

"You have to tell me what the doctor said," the woman demanded as they hustled towards the exit. "Did you talk to him, at least?"

The clown nodded.

"Why won't you talk to me?"

The clown shrugged.

They were outside the building now. The woman and the clown stopped and faced each other. Belinda lingered, wondering what would happen. Streams of people wove their way around the small group. No one even gave the clown a second look.

Belinda checked out the woman more closely. Of medium height, she wore a navy power suit, navy pumps and carried a navy designer-label handbag. Her medium-length blond hair had been fashioned into a pageboy. Altogether, she made a striking contrast to the clown.

"I'm your wife," pleaded the woman. "Why won't you talk to me anymore?" She looked at her diamond-encrusted watch. "I have to be back to work soon. You know. The job where I make the money so we can live decently?"

A bit better than decently, Belinda thought while the clown hung his head.

Suddenly, the feather duster began bobbing in the clown's hand. "You talk enough for all of us," it seemed to say. The clown's lips had not moved. The voice had been a high, sharp falsetto.

"Dammit," the woman screeched. "I'm tired of your silly games. Talk to me like an adult."

"No fun," replied the feather duster, bobbing.

"Life isn't always supposed to be fun," the woman replied through her clenched teeth.

Stitch that on a pillow and put it on your couch, Belinda thought.

"Why not?" asked the duster.

"Look, Dusty," the woman said, "I'm trying to talk to Monroe here. Why don't you stay out of it?"

The feather duster had a name! For some reason, this surprised Belinda more than anything else.

"Monroe doesn't want to talk right now. He's all talked out from being with the shrink."

"So, he did talk to the doctor. What about?"

"That's privileged information," the duster said primly.

"Did he talk about me?" the woman asked.

The clown and feather duster remained still.

The woman glared at them. "Well, did he?" she demanded.

The clown held out the hand not holding the duster, palm up, and shrugged. A passerby put a quarter in it. The clown looked at the money, grinned and stuck it in his pocket.

Angrily, the woman grabbed the feather duster and began hitting the clown with it. This action finally drew a crowd.

"Ow, ow, ow," the duster groaned. "That hurts. You're ruffling my feathers."

The crowd began to laugh. The woman began to cry, and then people became uneasy, looking at each other, mumbling and moving away. A few stuffed some change or bills in the clown's large pocket as the woman's blows became less severe. One person even managed to put a bill in the woman's suit pocket.

Finally, the clown grabbed the woman and took the feather duster away from her. He pulled her towards him, and she rested her head on his chest, crying softly.

Belinda turned away, suddenly sorry she'd stayed and watched the strange pair. She hesitated, and finally decided against giving them any money. It could have been an act, but she didn't think so.

She suddenly remembered the clown that had been at her anniversary

73

party. She'd meant to ask Blinky about that. She hadn't hired him, and she wondered why Blinky had. The clown at the party hadn't put on any kind of show. He'd come in late, mingled a bit, then left.

Belinda retrieved her car from the building's parking garage and drove to the New York City Public Library. After finding a parking spot in the lot and feeding the meter, she hurried past the stone lions and walked into the massive building with her usual sense of awe at being there. She asked for the microfiche department, and there, pulled up a chair at a carrel.

An hour later she only had a few articles to look at about reactions to silicone breast implants. She read them carefully, making notes. The doctor was right. Her rash didn't seem to be the same kind that other women were reporting, but all the other symptoms matched.

Disgusted, she got up and stretched. Her elbows hurt, and one ankle had a stabbing pain in it. She looked down and saw that it had swollen a bit. That had never happened before. Picking up her purse, she limped to her car and drove to her apartment.

At home, Belinda took a nap until just before Blinky was due to arrive from his evening hospital rounds. Still groggy when the alarm woke her, she stumbled into the bathroom to wash her face and brush her teeth. Looking for a lipstick, she fumbled with her handbag and knocked it onto the floor, spilling most of the contents.

Blinky came into the bedroom calling her name.

"In here," Belinda answered, stuffing her wallet back into her purse. She found the lipstick and put it on the counter. Blinky came in, saw what had happened and bent down to help her.

She saw him pick up the business card and closed her eyes for a moment.

"What's this?" he asked.

"Just a card," Belinda said.

"It's not just a card, Belinda," Blinky said, obviously trying to make his voice sound patient. Patronizing, Belinda thought. "Dr. Alverado is a plastic surgeon. See? It even says so right here." He pointed.

"Is he good?" Belinda asked.

"As a matter of fact, he is. What I want to know is why his card was in your purse."

She could feel the tears starting behind her eyes. Her nose tingled. Staring at Blinky, she couldn't help noticing with one part of her mind how attractive he looked. Her heart thudded in her chest at the thought of losing him. She loved him so much. She couldn't take the chance. So what if she was tired some of the time? Her ankle throbbed, but she chose to ignore it.

She turned away from him to compose herself.

Blinky took her shoulders and slowly turned her back towards him. Staring into her eyes, he said, "If you really believe that the implants are doing this to you, we'll get them removed. I couldn't do it myself now that you're my wife, but I don't want you to do it behind my back!"

"Oh, Blinky," Belinda sniffed. "No. No, I don't want them removed. I'm sure they're fine." She paused and took a deep breath. "Katie gave me the card today and asked me to ask you if Dr. Alverado is a good surgeon. She says since we're friends, she's too embarrassed to see you." She put her head on his shoulder so he couldn't look at her too closely while she lied to him. She'd never lied to him before.

Blinky hugged her tightly. "I see," he said, sounding relieved. "Yes, he's fine," he murmured into her hair. "Katie should be very pleased with him."

Then he kissed her until she almost swooned.

Later she was careful to cover her swollen ankle artfully with the sheet so he wouldn't see it.

CHAPTER 10

Sara rode with Eileen to work on Tuesday. When Sara arrived in her area, Maurice was at his desk, but Helen had not yet arrived.

"Feeling better?" Maurice asked. He had an expectant look. She wondered if he was hoping to catch her in a lie.

"I'm much better, thank you," Sara replied, and coughed. "Did I miss much yesterday?" she asked. The yesterday she'd spent dozing, emotionally recharging from all that had happened since Saturday night. She didn't want to think about it. Work was the best thing right now to keep her mind away from worry and sadness.

"Only the fire drill. People still can't get that right." Maurice shook his head, and a look of disgust crossed his face. "Ignorant, stupid--" he stopped abruptly and smiled at Sara, his large teeth gleaming. Maurice was large everywhere, with a big nose, wide mouth, large staring eyes. His sizeable hands and feet seemed to be constantly in motion.

She turned away without comment and went to her desk. Logs for yesterday's classes, returned training modules, the mail and two notes from Helen, her other supervisor, cluttered it. Sara thought about her first day in the department. Her desk then had been bare.

When she had arrived, late because first she'd stopped at Personnel to finish her paperwork, she had heard strange noises coming from the training room. Cautiously, she had peeked in and seen Maurice bending over a woman in a jogging suit. He was unzipping her top. Sara gasped, and Maurice looked up and smiled at her. "Hi, Sara. Meet Annie." While Sara held her hand over her mouth, Maurice continued to remove the

76

woman's top. "Just need to clean out her tubing," he explained. Sara could feel her eyes growing larger and larger. She heard a snap, and Maurice removed part of the woman's chest, and Sara saw that it was a plastic dummy.

Just then, Helen had come up behind Sara, said, "Hi," and put her arm around her shoulder. Sara jumped and Helen laughed. "Maurice up to his old tricks, huh? He likes to initiate new hires with a little strip tease of Resussiannie. Did he fool you?"

Sara managed a strangled, "Yes," while watching Maurice remove the tubes for cleaning.

"Spit builds up in here, so we need to flush it out every once in a while. Come here, and I'll show you how, since it will be your job. Put it on your calendar for every two or three weeks, depending on how often we use her. The baby over here needs to be cleaned, too." He had pointed at the small doll on the nearby table.

Eventually, Sara had learned CPR herself and even been certified to teach it. She did so occasionally when Maurice or Helen had other things to do. She also taught first aid which she liked better than CPR.

Sara sighed, shook her head to bring herself back to the present and looked at her cluttered desk. Helen's notes told Sara she would be late, and that they needed more alcohol wipes for Annie and the baby doll.

She took the two logs from yesterday's classes and began entering the information into employee staff development records in her new 8086 IBM computer--a tedious job.

When she was about halfway through, Maurice came out of his office and said, "I have a project for you." He showed her a picture in a booklet. The caption cited a publishing company, the book's title, edition, and date published. "I want to use this drawing and two others," he said as he flipped some pages and pointed to a second and third picture he'd marked. "We'll have to get permission from the publishers. Would you call them and see what we need to do in order to use these?"

"Sure," Sara said and took the booklet from him. Maurice went back to his own office. Sara studied the illustrations a few minutes, determining that all three came from books from different publishers. One was in Philadelphia, one in Los Angles, and the third in New York. No phone numbers, of course. She got out the Essex County phone book and looked up the area code for L.A. and Philly--she knew New York's. Then she called directory assistance in each city for the numbers. No problem there.

She decided to call the Philadelphia publisher first, for no other reason than it published the first picture Maurice had shown her.

"Hello," a mechanical sounding voice answered after two rings. "You have reached Westlake Publishers. If you know your party's extension, please dial it now." Pause. "If you need Customer Service, press 101." Pause. "If you wish to place an order, press 102." Pause. "If you wish to talk to someone in the Children's Books Division, press 103." Pause. "If you wish to talk to someone in the Adults' Book Division, Fiction, press 104." Pause. "If you wish to talk to someone in the Adult Book Division, Non-fiction, press 105." Pause. "If you need the Accounting Department, press 106." Pause. Sara yawned. "If you need Personnel, press 107." Pause. "All others, stay on the line and someone will be right with you."

"Thank goodness," Sara said out loud.

"Westlake Publishing. May I help you? Please hold."

Sara had opened her mouth to explain what she needed. She closed it again. Looking around her area, she decided the ivy needed watering, and she should dust the top of the file cabinets. It seemed the janitors didn't dust.

"I'm sorry to keep you. What can I do--Oh, please hold."

Sara sighed and pulled an order form out of her desk to requisition the wipes for Resussiannie.

"Sorry about that. May I help you?"

Sara explained what she needed.

"Let me put you through to that department." Another pause.

"Hello," a male voice greeted her.

"Hi," Sara said.

"You have reached Lenny Rumloff's office," the voice continued over hers. "I'm sorry I'm not at my desk right now."

"You're sorry? How do you think *I* feel?" Sara said.

"Please leave your name, your phone number and a brief message, and I'll get back to you as soon as possible." There was a loud beep.

Sara explained her mission, then hung up.

She sat stunned a moment, realizing she had just had a longer communication with a machine than with a real live person. She loved her new computer, but she wasn't sure she liked the way automation was handling the phone. After she made some notes on a pad about the time and who was supposed to call her back, Sara dialed the number in New York. It was too early to call L.A.

Jan Christensen

"Hello. You have reached Quillan Publishing Company. If you are calling from a touch tone phone, please press any button, now." Sara sighed and pressed the O. She listened to another long message until it got to the part where she should stay on the line and the next available operator would assist her. Long pause while Jim Croce sang, "Time in A Bottle." Sara hummed along.

Helen arrived, looking rushed, and smiled at Sara. "You on hold?" she asked. Sara nodded. "You okay?" Sara had to think for a moment, then she remembered she'd been out sick the day before. She nodded again. "Good," Helen told her and went to her office.

The music had switched to "Killing Me Softly with His Song." Sara was ready to kill someone, but she didn't have any names.

"Good morning. Quillan Publishing."

Click.

They were cut off. Sara looked at the receiver a moment, then placed it none-too-gently into its cradle.

Angrily picking it up again, she jabbed the redial button.

"Hello. You have reached Quillan Publishing Company . . ."

Sara pushed the O repeatedly while the message ran its course again, but it droned on to the bitter end. She was listening to "Memory" sung by Barbra Streisand when a real, live voice said, "Good morning. Quillan Publishing."

Sara knew she was asking a favor, so she sweetly said, "Good morning," and went on to explain what she needed. She was surprised when put through to another real, live voice. She again explained her mission, and she was transferred to another human being.

When told what Sara needed, the live being said, "That's easy, just fax us a request on your letterhead stating what you want to use, what type of publication you'll use it in, and the name of it, and about how many copies you'll be printing." The person gave Sara her fax number.

Sara got up from her desk and told Maurice what she had learned. He instructed her to draft a letter on her computer and bring it to him for signature. Later, she was both ticked off and amused when he made two minor changes in the letter she had composed. She knew it was just to show off his power. After he signed the final version, she headed for the fax machine which T&D shared with Personnel and Legal.

As she walked past the Accounting Department, Leslie, whom she used to work with, saw her and waved at her to come in. Reluctantly, Sara did

79

so, keeping a watch out for Bernie Puntz. Unfortunately, he came out of his office as Sara entered the outer reception area for the department. He greeted her by putting an arm around her waist, and she winced when he squeezed her side.

He was a rabbity-looking guy--short with bushy brown hair and sad brown eyes, slightly protruding teeth, large ears, and a tiny pursed mouth. Somehow he was connected to the company's owners. Sara could never remember how exactly, but she thought he was married to an owner's granddaughter. It was rumored that his family had lots of money, but he wouldn't get it all until he was thirty-five. For now he lived on interest and his salary from the Accounting Department. Bernie had started there just before Sara got transferred to T&D, and she had never liked him. She felt unclean when he was around. He practically smacked his meager little lips when he saw her, and he never missed an opportunity to touch her. She knew she could legally complain of sexual harassment, but didn't believe it would be worth it. She told JoAnne about every instance of his touching her, and also kept a log of dates, times, and incidents. Just in case. She wondered how many other women were doing the same thing at their jobs-- keeping logs and keeping quiet. She didn't know of anyone who had brought sexual harassment charges against someone, so she didn't know what the consequences might be.

She shuddered and pulled away. He let her go.

"Tell us about T&D," Leslie demanded, ignoring Bernie. Sara had always liked Leslie, but Bernie made her so uncomfortable that she gave an excuse about an urgent fax and left, promising to come by and chat another time.

Sara hadn't used the fax very much since the company had bought it about six months ago, and she approached it slowly, trying to remember exactly what to do. When she saw the machine, she remembered to put the paper with the writing against the glass that looked like a window. Then she dialed the number and pressed copy. The machine copied her papers, then sounded the error alarm. She quickly pressed "stop" and stood a minute studying the thing. She remembered she should have waited for the beep, then pressed "start," not "copy." This time she did it right, and when finished, the machine printed out a confirmation message. Sara took it and her papers back to her area.

Her phone was ringing when she got back to her desk. She grabbed it, put her papers on the desk, and sat down, getting notepad and pen ready to make notes, if necessary.

"It's me," Belinda said after Sara's greeting.

"Hi!" Sara said. "What's up?"

"Not much. I wanted to see how you were. I talked to Eileen last night, but she said you were resting after all the excitement. Have the cops found out anything?"

"The New York cops, or the New Jersey cops?"

Belinda laughed. "It is getting confusing, isn't it? Either. Both."

"Not that they've told me. I'd probably be the last to know, anyway."

"Right. You're doing okay? You're back at work."

"Yeah. I'll survive."

"Okay, I know you're probably busy, but I wanted to make sure everything was all right. I'll call you tonight, around eight?"

"Great," Sara said.

Maurice came out of his office and stood next to Sara's desk.

"Thank you so much for calling," Sara said. "You've been a big help."

"Boss alert!" Belinda caught on. "Talk to you later."

"Yes, goodbye, and thank you again."

Sara hung up and looked up at Maurice.

"How far did you get on obtaining permission to use those drawings?" Maurice asked.

"What?" Sara hadn't shifted her mind's gears back to work. "Oh. One down, two to go, one of which will call me back. Too early to call L.A."

"Right. I didn't think of that." Sara was surprised he admitted it. As he went back to his office, Helen came out of hers.

"I need twenty copies of these handouts for a class this afternoon."

"Okay, right away," Sara said, taking the folders.

The copy machine was down the hall in an alcove. She set the machine up to copy and staple the handouts, then stood and waited. About halfway through, the machine stopped, and a message flashed telling her to add paper. She opened the copier's drawer and saw there was quite a bit left, as always, but she dutifully got two reams, opened them and put the paper in the drawer. When she pushed "start," the message said to add toner.

"Why me?" she muttered. "Good thing Helen doesn't need these right away."

"Talking to yourself?" JoAnne laughed behind her.

"Oh, hi. Yeah. Machines are driving me crazy today. They're getting to be more of a pain than people. Think we can sue the manufacturers for

81

harassment?"

JoAnne laughed again. "I heard you were playing with the fax earlier," JoAnne said.

"Yup. The telephone's been a real fun toy today, too." Sara opened the cupboard above the copier and got out the toner.

"Anything new happening?" JoAnne asked. "I noticed you weren't here yesterday."

"You wouldn't believe it."

"What? Tell me!" JoAnne demanded.

"I got burgled. Sunday night, or rather, Monday morning. He tied me up, searched my bedroom. Only took my father's letters. The only thing I had from him." Suddenly tears threatened. It was all too much. What was she doing here, worrying about phone calls, faxes and copies? Angrily, she pushed the toner cartridge into its slot and closed the panel. No more Ms. Nice Gal.

"So, the burglary was connected to your father's death?" JoAnne asked, her voice hoarse with excitement.

"Seems that way. Or else the guy likes to collect letters and will go to any length to get them."

JoAnne looked at her oddly. Sara had forgotten that JoAnne's sense of humor was lacking.

"Oh, I don't think . . . " she looked at Sara sharply. "You were kidding."

Sara nodded and pushed the start button on the copy machine.

"Well, you seem to be taking it all rather well. Don't let me keep you from your games," JoAnne said, probably resentful that she hadn't gotten the joke right away. She waved her fingers at Sara and walked down the hall toward Legal.

"See you at lunch," Sara said. She couldn't believe it wasn't lunchtime yet. Now that the copier had been fed its ration of paper and toner, it finished the job, and Sara hurried back to her desk.

She saw that Maurice was in with Helen, and she walked to the door and knocked on the jamb.

They both looked up at her, and Helen motioned her to come in.

"I hate to ask, but can I have Thursday off?" Sara said, standing there awkwardly. "My father died, and I want to go to his funeral."

They stared at her a minute. "You should be on bereavement leave right now," Helen said. "Sit down. Sara, why did you even come in today? For heaven's sake. Are you all right?"

Sara nodded, suddenly tearful at Helen's kindness. She sank into a visitor's chair and forced herself not to cry.

"He was my biological father," Sara explained, "and I never knew him. Both of us were trying to find each other, and we just about did, when someone mur . . . murdered him."

Her supervisors looked at her, eyes wide, their mouths open from shock.

"I already took bereavement leave for my adopted father, so I didn't think the company would let me do it again. Anyway, work is good. Gets your mind off things. You know."

Helen recovered first. "Still, Sara, I think you should go home. This sounds like a complicated story, and I'm sorry I don't have time right now for the details. If Personnel won't approve bereavement, don't you have any vacation time left?"

Sara shook her head. "Just enough for a few days at Christmas. I'd rather not take them, but I'll take one for the funeral, if I have to."

"This is preposterous," Maurice said.

"Maurice!" Helen exclaimed. "Don't you believe Sara?"

He gave them a disgusted look. "Oh, I don't know. I'll let you handle it, Helen." He stood up and left them.

Sara stared at the floor, afraid to look at Helen.

"Do you want to go home?" Helen asked softly.

"No. Really. I'd rather stay."

"Okay. I'm sure we can keep you busy. If it gets too much for you, let me know. We'll work something out."

Grateful that at least one of her bosses was sympathetic, Sara stood up, thanked Helen, and went back to her desk.

She hadn't counted on the attention she'd get at lunch. The cafeteria looked crowded when she arrived. She found Eileen and JoAnne already there, saving her a seat at their table. As she walked towards them with her tray, people stopped talking and stared at her.

"Does everyone know?" she whispered to Eileen.

"I guess they read the papers and gossip," Eileen answered.

"My supervisors didn't know. But Helen came in late, and no one talks to Maurice unless they have to."

"No kidding," JoAnne said. "Him and Bernie Puntz."

All three shuddered.

JoAnne picked up a French fry and pointed it at Eileen. "So when are you going to tell us more about this new boyfriend of yours? He doesn't work here, does he?"

"No," Eileen said quickly, shaking her head. Her heavy auburn hair screened her face a little, but Sara could see she was blushing slightly.

"So where did you meet him? What does he do for a living?"

"I really don't want to talk about him, yet, JoAnne. It's too soon."

"Never stopped you before," Sara said, smiling.

Eileen stood up abruptly. "I said I don't want to talk about him." She yanked her tray off the table and strutted away.

"Wow," Sara said. "I guess she doesn't want to talk about him! Maybe 'cause all the others got talked about incessantly, and they never worked out."

JoAnne shrugged, but Sara could tell she was miffed. JoAnne liked to know everything.

"Maybe he's such a good catch, she's afraid one of us would try to steal him from her," Sara suggested.

"Maybe Eileen should stop dieting so much and her disposition would improve," JoAnne sniffed.

Sara shook her head, thinking Eileen should stop thinking about how a man would solve all her problems, her inability to get ahead at work, and her lack of money. She changed the subject.

After lunch, the day continued. Sara struggled with machines, the telephone and assorted personnel with their idiosyncrasies and quirks. She couldn't remember a time when she'd been happier to leave at five.

Belinda called at eight, as she had promised. She sounded sad to Sara, but Sara thought maybe she was projecting her own feelings onto her friend.

"Tell me about your burglary," Belinda demanded. "You are all right, aren't you? He didn't hurt you at all?"

"Just my dignity," Sara replied, trying to make light of it as she spun back and forth on the bar stool.

"Come on, this is Belinda. Tell me everything that happened."

Sara did so, glossing over the terror she'd felt, and the humiliation.

"Poor Eileen," Sara said. "She wanted to flirt with the cops so bad, but knew she shouldn't for my sake."

84

"But she has a boyfriend, doesn't she?"

"Belinda, did that ever stop her? Besides he's new. I've never even met him."

"Huh," Belinda commented. "So, have you heard anything from the police?"

"Not a word. It's so frustrating. I don't know if they're even working on anything or if they have any suspects. But enough about me. Tell me what's going on with you."

A pause greeted Sara's question.

"Belinda?"

"I'm here. Oh, Sara, I'm not doing too good, and I don't know what to do about it."

"What do you mean?" Sara asked. She stopped swinging back and forth, her heart thudding with worry.

"Well, I have these vague symptoms, but they seem to be the same ones that some women have after having breast implants. Silicone implants."

Sara bit her tongue. She wanted to say, "I told you not to do it!" But she couldn't now, or ever. Instead she asked, "What symptoms?"

"I'm tired and achy all the time. I have this rash that comes and goes. Today my ankle swelled up for no apparent reason."

"But Belinda, a rash? That's not vague. That proves something, doesn't it?"

"Could be contact dermatitis."

"Come on, Ms.-married-to-a-doctor, what's that?"

Belinda laughed, a shaky sound. "A rash from something you're allergic to that touches your skin."

"My god, you're not allergic to Blinky, are you?"

"That's not funny. Because it's a possibility, I've been told."

"You're kidding."

"'Fraid not. Anyway, it's probably not Blinky 'cause the rash is on my legs, around my ankles. He doesn't touch me there as often as he touches me other places, so seems unlikely he's the cause."

"Well, that's a relief," Sara exclaimed. "It seems as if it's your legs and ankles that are mostly involved. Does that mean anything?"

"I don't know. I went to the library today and looked up everything I could find about implants, but there wasn't much material." She paused, and then said so softly that Sara could barely hear her, "I saw another doctor. He said I should have them removed."

"You saw another doctor?" Sara twisted the telephone cord around and around her finger, suddenly scared for her friend. "Does Blinky know?"

"No," Belinda whispered. "I can't tell him. Oh, Sara, I don't know what to do."

Sara thought a minute. "Did you look up your symptoms, or just things about breast implants at the library? Maybe it's something else entirely."

"I've been concentrating on the implants since I learned they can cause this type of problem."

"Well, what does Blinky say?" Sara asked impatiently. The girl is married to a doctor, after all, she thought. She should be in the best of hands.

"He says there's no scientific proof that the symptoms I'm having are caused by the implants."

He's in denial, Sara thought. "Has he given you any other reasons for your symptoms?" she asked.

"No. No, he hasn't," Belinda said. Sara could tell that she was almost in tears. "Our G.P. said that it's the flu, but I think it's gone on too long."

"But that must be it," Sara reassured her. "Some of those can hang on for what seems forever, you know."

"Maybe you're right, Sara. I'm so glad I called and talked to you."

"Well, me, too. Now let me tell you about Ira."

"Who's Ira?"

"He was Howard's partner."

"Howard?"

"You know," Sara said. "My biological father."

"Oh, of course. So what's with Ira?"

Sara related the visit to the warehouse in Brooklyn.

"That's fascinating," Belinda said when Sara finished. "Do you think he might have done it?"

"Killed Howard?" Sara asked, her heart trip-hammering at the thought. "I don't think so. Really, he had nothing to gain, and everything to lose. He said Howard thought up the ideas. So what will Ira do now? He and my half brother alibi each other, by the way. I guess they could be in on it together," she mused. "The police told me the weapon was an invention of Howard's, apparently."

"Really?" Belinda asked.

"Yeah. But they don't know exactly what it was."

"Wouldn't Ira?"

"I guess so. I don't know if they've asked him, yet. This is all so frustrating! I don't know anything about the investigation."

"Why don't you call and ask?"

"Do you think I should do that?" Sara asked, hopefully.

"Why not? What have you got to lose?"

"What if they think I'm a suspect? Would they tell me anything?"

"Why should they suspect you?"

"The oldest reason," Sara reminded her. "Money. Howard was supposed to change his will and make me sole beneficiary, remember?"

"Do the police know that?"

"I don't know," said Sara, twisting the cord frantically around her finger. "You'd think they would by now, wouldn't you?"

"I guess so," Belinda answered. "But suspect or not, you have every right to be interested in what they know. I don't see why you can't call and ask."

"Okay, I guess I will. By the way, the funeral's on Thursday. In the afternoon. Will you go with me?"

"Oh, Sara, I'm sorry, I can't. That's the day I work all day on the cancer drive, and it's our last meeting before the big gala. I wish I could go with you, though."

"Me, too. We're still on for Saturday at Four Seasons?"

"Definitely. I'll be there with bells on."

"Okay, twinkletoes. I'll talk to you before then, though."

"Of course. I'll want to hear all about the funeral. I guess you'll meet your half brother and stepmother and who knows who else."

"Right. I hadn't even thought that far ahead. Should be interesting," Sara said, but her heart sank at the thought of saying goodbye to the father she'd never known. Maybe her mother had been right all along. She should never have tried to find out about her birth parents. But it was too late now.

CHAPTER 11

The landlady met Sara and Eileen at the bottom of the back stairs as they headed to work Wednesday morning.

"Rent's due," Mrs. Abbot said, blocking their path.

"Good morning," Sara and Eileen chimed together.

Mrs. Abbot had the grace to look abashed, her pale blue eyes avoiding theirs. "Good morning, girls. I know you're in a hurry, but I wanted to remind you of the rent."

As you do every month, Sara thought. "We'll bring you a check tonight, after work, Mrs. Abbot," she said.

"That will be fine. I just didn't want you to forget."

"We won't. Thank you, Mrs. Abbot," Eileen said. She brushed past the woman, and Sara followed her out to the car.

Eileen slammed her door shut and buckled herself up. As she turned the key in the ignition, she said, "Have we ever missed the rent? In the whole time we've lived here?"

"Never," Sara said. She put her purse on the floor and buckled herself in.

"What is that woman's problem, then?" Eileen asked, sounding more annoyed than ever about their landlady. Eileen pulled out of the driveway faster than she usually did and sailed down the street.

"Take it easy," Sara told her, clutching the door handle.

"Sorry," Eileen said, slowing down. "The thing is, Sara, that I'm a little short this month. Can you float me for a couple of weeks, until our next paychecks?" Eileen kept her eyes on the road, avoiding Sara's stare.

Sara sighed. It had happened before, and Eileen always paid her back, but Sara didn't like it. She tried to be careful with her money while Eileen spent all of hers, and then some. She felt like saying something about Eileen redecorating every six months, but held her tongue. What good would it do?

"Of course, I'll lend you the money," Sara said. She thought about Eileen's family, remembering the run down house in Bloomfield Eileen had taken her to a couple of times. Eileen's four younger brothers and sisters had a wide-eyed, hungry look, as if they never got quite enough attention or food. Both her parents worked full time, but Eileen explained that they insisted on sending all the children to private school and barely had enough left to clothe them. Ever since Eileen had started to work, she gave her parents a small amount of money every month to help out.

Eileen had looked enviously at Sara's house when Sara took her there to meet her parents. When Sara showed her the bedroom she hadn't had to share with anyone, Eileen murmured, "You don't know how lucky you were, growing up here."

So, Sara tended to excuse Eileen's flightiness. But sometimes she thought her friend seemed a bit dim. She'd never been promoted at Nort. Started out as one of the receptionists and never moved up.

Eileen parked the car in the employee lot, and they said, "Goodbye," at the front reception desk. In her area, Sara was glad to see that her supervisors weren't in yet. She decided to call the New York police to see if they had any news about Howard's murder.

She took Detective Beecham's card out of her wallet and, with sweaty palms, dialed the number. Fortunately, Nort International had a metro line to New York, so she could phone for free.

Doodling, she waited while the call got transferred several times. When she finally got through to the detective, he said, "Ah, Ms. Putnam. How are you?"

"Fine, thank you," Sara answered. She wanted to ask if he'd slain any spiders lately, but didn't. She drew a picture of a spider on her pad. "Any news?" she asked.

"Not much, I'm afraid," he said. "We did find the murder weapon. I can tell you because it will be in the news. Reporters like it when there's something unusual about a case. The weapon was a prototype for an instrument Mr. Lyndquist was working on."

"Where did you find it?" Sara asked.

"On the stairway--about four flights down. Seemed the murderer didn't

89

like elevators."

Sara gasped, hoping the detective couldn't hear her. Was he trying to get her to say something incriminating? By now, her hand had become so wet with sweat that the phone almost slipped away from her. She clutched it tightly. "Maybe he was afraid of being seen in an elevator," she said, hoping her voice was steady.

"Most likely," Detective Beecham said, his tone noncommittal.

"Did the New Jersey police contact you about my burglary?" Sara asked, changing the subject while she drew an elevator with slashing lines.

"Yes, they did. Are you all right?"

"I'm okay. He took my father's letters. Do you think that's significant?" she asked, drawing a masked man with her pen.

"Possibly. I'd like to know what the letters said. Do you think you'd be able to reconstruct them and send me a copy?"

Sara nodded, doodling small pieces of paper on her pad. "I can try. I read them several times, so I can probably do that."

"Ms. Putnam," Detective Beecham said, his tone more serious than before. "Is there any way you can *prove* that you are Howard Lyndquist's daughter?"

Sara's hand stopped doodling. "I have my birth certificate. It lists him as my father."

"It lists *a* Howard Lyndquist as your father. I recommend that you get a lawyer. He, or she, may suggest DNA testing."

Mixed emotions flowed through Sara. If this Howard Lyndquist wasn't her father, maybe her father was still alive. But they had similar features. They had to be related. An image of his squarish face came, unbidden. Suddenly she wanted to put her head down on her desk and cry. It just wasn't fair!

Instead, she thanked Detective Beecham for his advice, promised to mail him the reconstructed letters immediately, and hung up the phone. As soon as she did so, she felt she should have asked him more questions, although she couldn't think of any right now. Next time she'd write them all down before calling.

Maurice walked in then, and she quickly hid her doodling page by flipping a new one over her pad. They exchanged good mornings, and he went to his desk without further conversation.

She sat and thought for a few minutes. The weapon had been a prototype--a prototype of what, she suddenly wondered. Why hadn't she asked? She felt like slapping herself. There had to have been only one or two, if it was a prototype, hadn't there? How had the murderer gotten the weapon? He must have taken it from the warehouse. Unless Howard or Ira took them home. Even so, the murderer had to be someone Howard or Ira knew, who had access to the weapon either at the warehouse or in their homes.

Now she needed a lawyer. But she didn't know any, and she didn't like the idea of looking in the yellow pages. She called Belinda. Belinda should know of someone good, now that she was married to Blinky.

Belinda answered on the fourth ring. Her voice sounded sleepy.

"Did I wake you?" Sara asked.

"What time is it?"

"Nine."

"Yeah," Belinda said, "I've been oversleeping lately."

"I'm sorry. Are you feeling all right?"

"Yeah, just sleepy."

"Gee, just lay on the guilt, Lin."

"Well, a girl's got to have some fun."

"Very funny." Sara said, drawing Belinda asleep, z's over her head, on her new page.

"Was the purpose of this call to wake me up, or did you have something else in mind?" Belinda said, yawning.

"I need a lawyer."

"What? Are you in trouble?" Belinda sounded wide-awake now, and scared.

"No, I need one to help me prove that I'm Howard Lyndquist's daughter."

"Why?"

Good question, Sara thought. "So I can be sure. So I can stop searching and wondering. So I can get on with my life."

"So you can inherit?" Belinda asked.

"I don't know. I just need one to be sure that all my ducks are in a row."

"Well, what about Henry?" Belinda said, yawning again.

"Who's Henry?" Sara asked, bewildered.

"You know. Henry Randall. The lawyer I introduced you to at the party. He's the only one I know who's taking new clients who aren't dripping in money. He's still young and building up his practice. He's right in Montclair, too, so he'd be convenient for you."

"That Henry," Sara said, remembering the untalkative, good-looking lawyer now. "I didn't like him."

"You don't have to like him. He's the only one I know of, Sara."

Sara frowned. "He's really good?"

"I've never heard anything negative about him. Everyone recommends him."

"Oh, all right. Do you have his number handy?"

"Just a minute," Belinda said.

Sara heard her put the phone down. A minute later she came back on the line and gave Sara Henry's number and address.

Helen came in as Sara was writing them down. Sara quickly said, "Goodbye," and hung up the phone, flipping over another page in her notebook.

Helen stopped at Sara's desk. "How are you doing?" she asked.

"I'm okay," Sara replied.

"I've thought about your wanting tomorrow off. What time is the funeral?"

"Two o'clock, in Brooklyn."

"Well, why don't you come in for half a day and make up the time evenings for the next week? I checked with Personnel, and they weren't comfortable about giving you a second bereavement leave for a second father."

Sara nodded. It made sense, especially for a large corporation. Couldn't set any precedents. "That will be fine," she told Helen.

After both Maurice and Helen were occupied giving classes, Sara called Henry Randall's office. She asked if he had any Saturday or evening appointments, and his secretary gave her one for Saturday morning at nine. After hanging up, Sara breathed a sigh of relief. That wasn't so bad, she thought, turning to her computer to get some work done.

At lunchtime, Sara called the New Jersey police and asked about the status of the burglary. One of the partners, and she couldn't remember which was which now, told her that they had made little progress, but they were working on it. After she hung up, she bet herself that they'd never find him.

She shuddered, remembering being tied up and helpless on her bed. She'd had to sleep on the living room couch ever since. Firmly, she told herself she'd try sleeping in her own bed tonight.

After work, Sara met Eileen in the lobby. Eileen mentioned that they were out of milk and bread, so they needed to stop at the convenience store and get some. Sara nodded.

"You know, Mike was held up the other night while I was there. I forgot to tell you."

"No!" Eileen exclaimed, turning her head to look at Sara. The car veered toward the middle of the road as she continued to stare at Sara.

"Look out!" Sara grabbed the wheel. They barely missed hitting an oncoming car that sounded its horn for a long time as it sped away. Sara watched it, the driver waving his fist in the air.

"Sorry," Eileen muttered. "Tell me about the robbery."

Sara related what had happened, leaving out the part where she took the gun. She felt foolish now for having done that, especially after her burglar had thrown it back into her nightstand with such disdain.

"I can't believe it," Eileen said. "And that very night that awful man came and tied you up and took your father's letters." She parked the car in front of the convenience store and put her hand on Sara's arm. "You've been having a rough time."

Sara swallowed the lump in her throat and willed herself not to cry. No self-pity allowed, she told herself. She couldn't look at Eileen. "I'll be all right."

"I know you will," Eileen said, opening her car door. "You're tough."

Sara nodded and followed her friend into the store. Mike greeted them, and suddenly Sara felt shyness overcome her. Should she say anything about the robbery? Pretend it never happened? What would the etiquette books tell her to do?

She walked up to the counter. "How are you?" she asked. "Any more interesting incidents since I was here last?"

He gave her a rueful smile. "Only the usual crazies. The kids playing football with the bread, the homeless guy peeing in the corner, thinking it's the rest room. Nothing unusual."

"I see," Sara said, smiling. "Any luck finding a new job?"

"Naw, but I enrolled in junior college."

"Well, good for you!"

Eileen approached the counter with milk and some other items. When she didn't get out her wallet, Sara realized she expected Sara to pay. After

Mike rang up their purchases and Sara paid, they said, "Goodbye," and Eileen carried the packages out to her car. I suppose, Sara thought, she thinks carrying them will help me forgive her for not paying for them, even though she's late with money for the grocery kitty, too.

Back at their apartment, they had sandwiches for supper. Eileen washed the dishes while Sara sorted some clothes to take to the laundry. The doorbell sounded. Eileen yelled, "You expecting anyone?"

"No," Sara said. "Are you?"

Eileen came into Sara's bedroom, shaking her head, wiping her hands on a towel. The doorbell sounded again.

"Probably some salesman," Eileen said.

Sara sighed. "I'll get it."

She had to go all the way downstairs to find out who it was. She found Lucille standing on the doorstep.

"Mom!" Sara exclaimed. "What are you doing here?" The minute the words were out of her mouth, she realized how rude they sounded. But her mother never came by unannounced.

"Hello, Sara. May I come in?" Lucille's face didn't change from its usual calm expression.

"Of course," Sara said, holding open the door. Sara led the way upstairs. "Look who's here," she said to Eileen, her voice too hearty.

"Hello, Mrs. Putnam," Eileen said. "How are you?"

"I'm fine, dear. And you?"

"Just fine. What a pleasant surprise. May I get you something to drink?"

"No, dear, thank you." Lucille put her purse on the floor next to the couch and stood there looking at Sara.

"Sit down, Mom." Sara said.

Lucille sat.

Eileen stood a moment, looking at mother and daughter. Then she said, "I'll go in my bedroom so you two can talk."

"Thank you," Lucille said.

Sara sat down in the armchair opposite her mother. "Are you all right?" she asked, and realized she was worried about Lucille. Could she be sick?

"I'm fine. Are you all right?"

"Yes. Of course. Why wouldn't I be?"

Lucille reached down and pulled a newspaper out of her purse. "It's a sad day when a mother has to learn that her daughter has been burglarized from the *Newark News*," she said.

"It was in the paper?" Sara exclaimed.

"Monday's. Today is Wednesday, and since I didn't hear from you, I decided I should come myself to see how you are."

"Oh," Sara said in a tiny voice. "I should have called you."

"Yes, you should have," Lucille said as she put the paper away in her purse. "Several of my friends have been asking about you. I, of course, could not give them any answers."

Was she more concerned about what her friends thought, Sara wondered, than she was about me?

"I wasn't hurt," Sara said. "I've been so busy since, I didn't think to call you."

Lucille gazed at her, shaking her head. "I'm the only mother you've ever known, Sara. I expect you to tell me when situations such as this happen to you."

You taught me well to keep my feelings hidden, didn't you? Sara wanted to say it out loud, but didn't dare. Instead, she said, "I'm all right. Really. He tied me up, but didn't hurt me. The only thing he took was my father's letters."

"Your father? Oh, you mean Howard Lyndquist. I can't get used to you calling him your father."

"Sorry," Sara said automatically.

"Why would anyone want to take those letters? What good would they do?"

Sara told her about her conversation with Ira.

"You mean," Lucille said, "that Howard Lyndquist wanted to make you his sole heir?" She looked astonished, and Sara suppressed a smile at the reaction.

"Apparently."

Lucille stood up, a look of horror crossing her face. "But, Sara, that means your life is in danger."

"No, Mom. Sit down," Sara said gently. "There's no will. Since he didn't change it, I don't inherit."

Lucille sat down stiffly on the couch again. She seemed to have aged ten years. "But, dear, even if he didn't change his will, you are entitled to half if you can prove that you are his daughter. Don't you see, those letters helped prove that, and now they're gone."

Sara could feel her heartbeat quicken. Why hadn't the burglar killed her? He must not have been the killer, or he would have.

"The police suggested I get DNA testing done to prove that I'm Howard's daughter. I'm seeing a lawyer on Saturday."

Lucille shook her head in dismay. "You'd be safer to forget the whole thing, Sara. This is preposterous." She stood up again and picked up the cow on the end table. "Where did you get this hideous thing?" she asked absently. She looked around the room. "And the rest of these barnyard animals?"

Sara gave a shaky laugh. "Eileen redecorated."

"Again? My goodness." She put the cow down and turned to Sara. "For your safety, I think you should renounce publicly any interest in Howard Lyndquist's estate. You don't need it. After all, you will inherit from me eventually." Her face had become smooth again.

Sara suppressed a gasp. She'd never thought about that. Never thought of Lucille dead. She'll live to be a hundred, Sara reassured herself. Impulsively, she stood up and hugged her mother. Lucille stiffened at first, but then she relaxed and hugged Sara back.

"Sit down," Sara said, taking Lucille's arm and tugging her to the couch where she sat next to her. "Listen. I know you don't understand this, but I need to know who my biological parents were. This takes nothing away from everything you and Marsh did for me. It's just another dimension of my life. I don't think there's any danger to me. Something would have happened by now. Without a will, there's no way I can inherit it all, and I may not be able to get anything. I may not want anything. Right now, I don't. I don't feel as if I'm entitled to anything. But I want to be sure Howard Lyndquist, inventor, was my father. That way, I can close the book on that part of my life and go on. You won't lose me. If anything, I appreciate what you did for me more now."

Lucille seemed unable to respond to Sara's emotional outburst. "Which lawyer did you choose?" she asked.

"What?" Sara exclaimed. For a minute she couldn't remember. "A guy named Henry. Someone Belinda recommended."

"Why not Marshall's lawyer, Louis Metcalf? What's wrong with him?"

"I forgot all about him. I guess he didn't make much of an impression on me. I've already set up this appointment with Henry. Mr. Metcalf is probably booked up for weeks, anyway."

Lucille sighed audibly. Sara resisted putting her arm around her shoulders. Lucille would feel trapped by too much show of emotion.

"It seems I can do nothing for you," Lucille said and stood up again. "Please let me know if anything else untoward happens, Sara. I want you to know that I think it's a mistake for you to have that DNA testing." A look of distaste crossed her face, gone in an instant. She patted Sara on the shoulder. "You always were stubborn. I guess there's nothing I can do about it now." She walked towards the door.

"I'll walk you down," Sara said, almost sorry to see her mother go.

After they said goodbye at the back door, Sara started back up the stairs. Eugene stood on his landing, obviously waiting for her. "Hello, Sara," he said shyly.

"Hi, Eugene," Sara answered wearily. All she wanted to do was get into a hot bathtub, then crawl into bed.

"That was your mom, wasn't it?" Eugene asked.

"Yes," Sara said.

"Do you know there's a man outside a lot who seems to be watching for you?" Eugene asked, his eyes round.

Sara started. "No. What man? What does he look like?"

"Just like a man. I can see him from my sitting room window sometimes. You want to look?"

Sara really didn't wish to go into Eugene's part of the house, but she thought she'd better. She nodded, and Eugene led the way into his sitting room. Sara looked around with some curiosity. Eugene worked on models of cars. Two dozen or so were scattered around the room, and a card table covered with newspapers held a work in progress. The room was decorated with Victorian-style furniture that looked as if it had come from someone's attic or from a bordello. A red velvet couch was against one wall. Next to it sat an end table with a lamp with a cream fringed shade. Two gilt chairs were on the opposite wall, a needlepoint footstool in front of one. The front bay window had heavy drapes of a cream, silk-like material and sheer curtains.

Eugene led the way to the window. "He usually stands under that tree," Eugene said, pointing. "When you come out, he leaves. I don't know where he goes."

Sara squinted into the darkness. Nothing moved. "Perhaps to a car parked around the corner," Sara mused. Suddenly she remembered the car that followed her and JoAnne when they drove to Brooklyn. "Have you seen a blue Chevy in the neighborhood lately?"

Eugene laughed. "Several," he said, moving away from the window. "They're not exactly unusual."

Sara sighed and stared at the tree. Suddenly, a shape moved away from the deeper shadows and became a human figure. Sara could see the head lift as if looking up at the top of the house. A shiver traveled down her spine, and she felt suddenly cold. Slowly, the figure which she could now see was a man, left the shelter of the tree and walked away. Sara watched until she could no longer see him, a feeling of dread washing through her.

CHAPTER 12

A dull drizzle fell Thursday morning as Sara drove to Brooklyn for her "real" father's funeral. Her stomach knotted up when thunder rumbled in the distance, and the wipers clicked and groaned on the windshield.

She got through both tunnels okay, white-knuckled the whole time. Following Ira's directions carefully, she arrived at the warehouse without incident. The rain made a steady patter on the car. Ira stood at the front door, a black umbrella clutched in his hand, his black raincoat with its small attached cape flapping in the wind. He looked like someone out of a horror movie, Sara thought, then quickly put the idea out of her mind. She pulled up behind his hearse and waited for Ira to come down the steps, the umbrella almost gusting away from him. He opened the passenger door, breathless.

"What a day to bury a friend and partner," he exclaimed as he sat down, shaking the umbrella out the open door, closing it, and pulling it and his feet inside, bringing in the smell of rain and wet clothing.

Sara nodded as Ira slammed the door shut. She backed carefully away from the hearse, then asked, "Which way?"

"Go down to the next corner and make a right," Ira said, taking a large white handkerchief out of his pocket and honking into it.

Sara kept her eyes on the road. "At least it's warm," she said.

"August tends to be," Ira said, stuffing the handkerchief back into his pocket.

"I meant it could be February or something."

"Oh. Right. See what you mean. Have any trouble finding the place this time?"

"No. You gave good directions."

"Have to be good at directions to be an inventor. Your father, now, was so precise. He would have told you the exact miles between turns. Dotted every I, crossed every T, that man did."

"Really?" Sara asked, hoping for more details. She'd file that one away, ponder on it later. Wonder if she was a bit that way, too, especially at her job, and maybe even with her painting.

"Yes, I never had any problems following his instructions for building whatever he was interested in at the moment."

"What else was different about him?"

"Let's see. Well, even though he was exacting in his work, he wasn't too neat personally, if you know what I mean."

"He was sloppy?"

"Not exactly. Just careless, indifferent about details."

"What did he like to eat and drink?" Sara asked.

"Turn right up here at that stoplight," Ira said, pointing with his long finger. "He loved Italian food. Just loved it. That and exotic teas. Don't seem to go together, do they?"

Sara laughed a little. "No, not really. Do you like those things, too?"

Ira seemed surprised by the personal question. "I like German food and coffee. Beer, too. Very traditional."

Sara looked at him sideways. Did he realize how funny that statement sounded coming from him?

"Turn left up here," Ira told her, again pointing. "See the driveway for the funeral home?"

Sara nodded, a lump suddenly forming in her throat. She found a place to park and pulled in, barely noting the Colonial style building, the hearse and limo in the side driveway. She did notice the local television station truck, though, and some reporters in trench coats standing outside the funeral home. The rain pounded harder, throwing angry, fat drops onto the asphalt.

"I'll come around with the umbrella," Ira said, and he poked his long legs out of the car.

As they climbed up the stairs, Sara couldn't help thinking about how they must look together. He, long, slender, all in black with his hair standing almost straight out from his face. She, short in comparison, also all in black, including a small hat she'd found in the back of her closet, black heels and bag.

They entered the funeral home through heavy white double doors. A man in a somber black suit stood inside. "Lyndquist?" he asked.

Ira nodded and closed the umbrella while Sara shivered in the air-conditioned lobby.

The man handed them a sheet of paper and directed them down the hall to the chapel. Sara glanced at the page and was surprised to see a program. She wondered briefly who had decided on the hymns and other details. The son? The ex-wife?

They paused in the doorway to a large room with a coffin opposite the door. Several people turned to look at Sara and Ira. A flashbulb blinded her, and Sara blinked.

Beside the coffin, a woman stood taking pictures of the deceased. Sara felt her mouth open in surprise. What would the woman do with the developed photos? Show them to friends and relatives, she guessed. But when? At birthday parties? Other funerals? When visitors showed up from out of town? How would she start the process? Sara could imagine her saying, "Now that reminds me. Let me get the pictures of Uncle Howie. These are so interesting. Don't you think they did a good job with the makeup? He looks so lifelike. As if he could get up out of the coffin and go dancing. What do you think?"

Sara shivered again, this time not from the cold air. As if someone had walked over her own grave. She remembered her mother, Lucille, saying that when anyone shuddered.

Ira took her arm and led her into the room. She was surprised to see Detective Beecham standing at the back wall. But then, she thought, what better place for him to see lots of suspects all in one place?

Reluctance gripped her as she and Ira got closer and closer to the coffin. Why had she come? She hadn't had to. No one would have thought anything of it if she'd gone to work as if nothing had happened. She didn't know him, would never know him now. Would only remember him from the party and from this ghastly drama. She felt suddenly hyperaware of everything. How each foot struck the rug as she walked. The hushed voices around her. Ira's long fingers, firm but gentle, on her arm. The people in front of the coffin drifted away, except for the woman taking pictures. She continued to snap as Sara and Ira approached. Sara wanted to yell at her to stop, but she felt that her voice would come out as a croak.

As they reached the coffin, the woman noticed them for the first time and snapped their picture. Sara glared at her, and Ira waved his hand as if shooing away a fly. The woman stepped around them, got behind them, and took one more shot. The flash had left red spots in front of Sara's eyes, and it seemed as if the coffin moved up and down as she tried to blink them away.

They stopped in front of the casket. Sara stared at the man whom she'd only seen once before. He looked serene, untroubled, with no sign of how he had died. Sara studied him, aware that she'd never see him again, noting his square chin and brown hair streaked with gray. Maybe she should ask the woman for a copy of the pictures. She pushed the thought aside. She didn't want to remember him this way. But what was better? Him drunk at Belinda's party? Or dead on the staircase?

Tears formed, and the back of her throat prickled. She knew she wasn't sad so much about his being dead, because she hadn't known him at all. She longed for what might have been. With one last look, she turned aside. She needed to sit down.

Ira steered her towards a pew in the second row which had been reserved with a black ribbon with a rosette. He removed the ribbon and motioned her in. She wasn't sure she wanted to be so close to the front.

A hush came over the crowd, and everyone turned to look at a side entrance. A veiled woman, all in black, entered holding onto the arm of a young man. My brother? Sara wondered. She searched his face for any resemblance to herself, or to Howard. He had light brown hair, cut short, blue eyes, and only the Lyndquist squarish face seemed familiar. He stared at her as intently as she looked at him. He stood only two or three inches taller than she. Sara let out a relieved breath of air. He couldn't have been her burglar. He had been at least six feet. All this time she'd been thinking it might have been her brother who did that to her, and she hated the idea of feeling violated like that by him, even though she didn't know him yet.

"That's Miriam, Howard's ex-wife, and Kevin, your brother," Ira said.

Sara nodded, wishing she could see Miriam's face better. "How old is Kevin?" she asked.

"Just turned eighteen," Ira told her. So, he was three years younger than she.

As soon as they were seated, a man standing next to the coffin began to sing. Sara felt goose bumps on her arms and more tears starting because his voice sounded so beautiful. You can't cry, she told herself. You don't want

102

to make a fool of yourself. She felt relief when the man stopped.

The rest of the service passed in a blur. When it was over, Miriam and Kevin left by the side door. Ira and Sara exited the pew. The woman with the camera began snapping photos. Again, Sara had an urge to tell her to stop, but instead, she tucked her head down and walked with Ira down the aisle, back to the lobby. There, Miriam and Kevin stood waiting. Sara followed Ira over and found herself shaking hands with Miriam, murmuring condolences. She wished once more that she could see her face better, but the veil almost completely concealed it. She wore a black silk dress and black satin pumps. Pearls encircled her throat, and a huge diamond ring graced the third finger of her right hand. She wore a heavy scent, expensive, something Sara had smelled before, but she couldn't place where. Maybe in a magazine ad, she thought, where you scratch and sniff.

"You're coming to the house?" Miriam asked Ira. "You're welcome, too, Sara. After the burial." Her voice held no emotion. Sara didn't know what to think.

"Of course we'll come," Ira told her. "How are you holding up, boy?" he asked Kevin.

"Okay, I guess," Kevin said. "It's nice to finally meet you," he told Sara. He sounded more curious than pleased, though.

Surprised, she mumbled, "Nice to meet you, too."

Other people waited behind them. Sara could almost feel them pushing against her, wanting to hear every word.

Sara and Ira sprinted through the rain to her car and waited. It took only a short time for the coffin to be loaded and the others to come out. Miriam and Kevin stepped into a limo behind the hearse, and Sara got in line behind them. They snaked their way to a nearby cemetery, Sara wishing she were at work but knowing that later she'd be glad she did this.

"Nice service," Ira remarked.

Sara nodded. She only had her adopted father's funeral to compare it with. No one took pictures. Her mother didn't wear a veil, lots of perfume, or a huge diamond ring. No singing, either, even such good singing. Just a plain simple service.

"Who was the woman taking pictures?" she asked.

"That was Aunt Gladys. She always does that. A bit of an odd duck."

Look who's talking, Sara thought.

"What did you think of Miriam?" Ira asked.

"She seemed nice. Couldn't see her face. Is she beautiful?"

"Yes," Ira said with an audible catch in his throat.

Sara glanced at him. Was he in love with his old partner's ex-wife? He stared straight ahead at the limo in front of them. Sara turned her head away, frightened by what she saw in his face. Grief and anger. And determination.

They pulled into the cemetery's winding drive. The hearse and limo slowed down even more. Finally, they came to a plot with a canvas covering over the open grave and folding chairs set around. The rain had stopped, but the trees dripped water, and Sara could tell that the ground was sodden. Sara turned off the ignition, and they waited for the men to remove the casket and place it beside the grave.

The limo driver opened the door, and Kevin stepped out, then extended his hand for his mother. She climbed out gracefully, showing a bit of knee, Sara noticed. Sara refrained from looking at Ira.

The service at the gravesite was mercifully short. Afterwards, Sara again caught a glimpse of Detective Beecham standing well away from the mourners under a tree, the rainwater dripping off his hat and obscuring the expression on his face. His presence felt like an intrusion, and she wondered how Miriam and Ira perceived it. But the ubiquitous reporters were also there, also an invasion of privacy.

Sara followed the limo to Miriam's house, an old Colonial set on large lawns with ancient trees along the driveway.

"Wow," she exclaimed, "this is nice." It's almost a twin to the funeral home, she thought with surprise.

"The old family estate," Ira said. "Miriam's family had lots of money. She helped your father get started. Bought the warehouse for him, gave him seed money until some inventions started paying off. Even paid my salary in the beginning."

"If she had all that, why was she trying to get more from the divorce?"

"She felt she deserved it. Without her, he might not have made it. Takes money to make money, as the old saying goes." Ira opened his door and stepped out onto the soaked driveway. Sara followed him up the walk.

Inside, they found Miriam and Kevin standing in a huge front hallway greeting their guests. The veiled hat had been removed, and Sara got to see Miriam's face for the first time. A classic beauty, she didn't look more than thirty-five, although Sara knew she had to be at least forty-five. Her piercing blue eyes were set off with high cheekbones, a longish patrician nose, and a generous mouth painted mauve. Her bleached blond hair swept away from her face, showing delicate ears with dangling pearls in the pierced holes. Again, Sara noticed the perfume and wished she knew what kind it was.

Miriam held out her hand and gently pulled Sara toward her so she could speak into her ear. "Let's have a chat later, shall we? Don't go running off until we have a chance to talk, will you?"

Sara nodded, speechless, deciding she was glad she'd come. Then she was shaking Kevin's hand again, and he said, "Let's try to talk privately later, shall we?"

Sara looked at Miriam, who was hugging Ira. Briefly, she wondered if mother and son knew that each wanted to talk to her alone.

She felt the press of the people behind them, so she followed some other guests towards a large room that she guessed was the living room. Beyond she could see the dining room, the table laden with food. Aunt Gladys had already begun to take pictures. Aghast but also amused, Sara watched her take several of the food from different angles. A sudden image of Gladys' house flashed through Sara's mind. She could see pictures mounted on every wall, grouped according to occasion. Would she put a funeral next to a birthday party? Next to a wedding? Or did she only take pictures at funerals?

The other funny thing about it all was that everyone waited respectfully until Gladys finished with her photo session before disturbing the table. As Sara filled a plate with cookies, pound cake, mixed nuts and some chips and dip, she hoped that Gladys wouldn't take her picture with her mouth stuffed with food. Sara moved as far away from the wild photo-taker as she could get.

Somehow she and Ira got separated, and Sara found herself standing next to an elderly lady dressed all in black, including a small hat with a tiny veil. The woman turned to Sara and said in a loud voice, "So you're the daughter, are you? I do see a slight family resemblance. Did he leave you anything, then?"

Sara stared at the woman a moment, speechless. "I, yes, that is, I'm the daughter," she stammered, feeling distaste overcome her face after repeating, "the daughter."

"You'll have to speak up," the old woman said loudly. "I'm deaf. Are you, or aren't you the daughter?"

Sara looked around helplessly. Everyone in their vicinity had stopped all pretense of not looking and listening to Sara and the old lady. Sara stared into the woman's faded blue eyes.

"I am Sara Putnam," she practically yelled. "Who are you?"

The old lady blinked. "I happen to be Millicent DuPruis, Miriam's great aunt. Did--"

"Nice to meet you." Sara grinned, and held out her hand.

Millicent drew back a moment, then gave Sara two fingertips to shake. Sara grinned as widely as she could. "So," she asked, "did your father leave you anything? I assume he's dead by now?"

Millicent blinked again, and took a step backward as if slapped. Sara caught the grins on several of the faces watching them as she walked away.

She searched for Ira, wondering how long he'd want to stay. She was beginning to feel decidedly uncomfortable at having all the eyes in the room on her. She didn't dare make eye contact with anyone as she didn't want to get into anymore discomfiting conversations.

Feeling a light touch on her arm, she turned to see Kevin. "Would this be a good time to talk?" he whispered.

Sara nodded. Kevin led the way to the front foyer and then to the library. He closed the door behind them, and Sara felt a slight sense of alarm. Even though Ira had alibied Kevin, Sara couldn't trust him, especially since she didn't know him at all. He didn't *look* dangerous. But then, neither did some serial murderers. But this is my half brother, she thought. I want him to be nice. I want to get to know him, to like him, even.

Kevin indicated a chair in front of a desk in the corner. Sara sat on the edge while Kevin settled himself next to her in a matching chair.

"It's too bad we have to meet under these circumstances," he began. "I knew that my father was searching for you, had been for years. But he never found you until Saturday night."

Sara nodded, wondering what Kevin really wanted.

"It's true, then? You never saw or talked to him before?"

Oh, Sara thought. He wants to know if Howard and I were in contact and if there's another will. Even if there were, I wouldn't tell him here, alone in this room with him.

"I never set eyes on him before Saturday. He sent me some letters, to my mother's address. She didn't give them to me until Sunday. The day after he was . . . killed. Until this past weekend, I didn't even know if he

106

was alive or not."

Kevin nodded. "I guess you don't have a will or anything." He looked away for a second, then seemed compelled to stare at her as if he could see inside her to the truth.

"No. I have nothing. Even the letters are gone, stolen during a burglary at my apartment the other night."

"Really?" Kevin said, raising an eyebrow. "How terrible for you."

His voice sounded false, and she sensed that he already knew about the robbery. But how? Personal knowledge, like he hired the burglar? Or secondhand knowledge from the police or another source?

Sara shivered. She was sitting and talking with a man with an excellent motive for murdering their father, or having him murdered. Get to it, Sara girl, she told herself. You may never have as good an opportunity again.

"I understand you and our father were not getting along too well recently."

"Who told you that? Ira?"

Sara nodded.

"He's very honest," Kevin acknowledged. "It's true. Dad and I were having a major disagreement about what I should do with the rest of my life. He wanted me to go into the family business. I felt I didn't have the talent. He thought any son of his would have to have inherited his gifts. I thought I should make my own way, do what I *wanted* to do, not what he felt I should do."

"And that is?"

"Journalism. I want to write."

"He didn't think that was a good profession?"

"For anyone else. But not for *his* son," Kevin said, bitterness in his tone.

Sara sighed. "Well, he and I never had a chance to have a disagreement."

Kevin leaned toward her, put his hand out as if to pat her arm, then drew it back. Somehow the gesture made her feel as if she could believe him, that he couldn't be evil enough to murder his own father. Not someone who showed compassion so spontaneously. But that was silly. It could all be an act. Pull yourself together, Sara told herself. Don't jump to conclusions. Then she remembered the falseness in his voice when he expressed surprise about the robbery. A poor liar. If he'd killed Howard,

107

he wouldn't be able to hide the fact from the police. She wondered if they'd ever be able to have any semblance of a normal relationship like most brothers and sisters. Regretfully, she supposed not.

Sara stood up. "I guess we don't have much else to talk about."

Kevin got slowly to his feet. "Sara, I have two more things to ask you."

Sara waited without saying anything.

"You didn't kill him, did you?"

Shock ran through her. "Why would I? What possible reason would I have to murder him? I wanted to talk to him, get to know him!" Tears formed at the corners of her eyes, and she swiped at them angrily. "You have a hell of a nerve, you know that?"

"You had the same motive I did. You can inherit. All you have to do is contest the will."

Sara stared at him, her mouth slightly open. "I never even thought of that! I don't feel as if I'm entitled to anything from him. We didn't even know each other."

"But you were his legitimate daughter. At least I expect you can prove that you are."

But could she?

"Which leads me to my second question," Kevin said.

Sara watched him warily. "Which is?"

"Are you going to contest the will?"

Sara shook her head. "I have no earthly idea. How can I know now what I'm going to do? What's in the will, anyway? Do you know?"

"The one my mom has lists me as sole beneficiary."

"Of course," Sara said. She could hear the bitterness seeping into her tone. "I'm the child he forgot. Even in death."

"But he was trying to find you."

"Only because he got mad at you. I could only be a second-best child. Look, I think I'd better go. I want to go home."

Kevin gestured toward the door, and Sara walked quickly to it.

When she pulled it open, she found Miriam standing there. Sara wondered how long she'd been in the hall, what she'd heard. "There you are," Miriam said, not acting at all flustered. "I've been looking all over for the both of you." She walked towards Sara who had to back up to get out of her way. Miriam turned to close the door, then went and seated herself behind the desk. "Please sit down so we can talk a minute, Sara. You'd better stay, Kevin, since this concerns you."

Like obedient children, Sara and Kevin sat.

"Now, Sara, tell us what you're going to do about the will. Howard left everything to Kevin. Since you seem to think you're Howard's daughter, I want to know what you're going to do."

"I honestly don't know, yet," Sara said. "How much money are we talking about, anyway?" She held her breath waiting for the answer.

Miriam looked at Kevin. "Between four and five million," she stated, her voice reluctant.

Sara gasped. Then she looked steadily at Miriam. "Maybe I will contest it. That sounds as if there's enough to go around."

"I'd strongly advise against it," Miriam said, her tone menacing. "You have no idea what you'd be getting yourself into. My advice to you is to leave here today and never look back. Forget all about Howard Lyndquist. Do I make myself clear?"

Sara stood up and glared at her. "No. Nothing is clear."

Kevin stood up, too. "Sara, you'd better do what Mom suggests."

"Are you threatening me?" Sara demanded, looking from Miriam to Kevin.

Kevin remained silent.

His mother answered for both of them. "Yes. Yes, we are."

CHAPTER 13

Saturday morning, Sara groaned when the alarm clock buzzed at seven-thirty. Why had she made the appointment with that lawyer, Henry, for so early? Then she remembered. She had a lunch date with Belinda at Four Seasons.

What should she wear? She might not have time to change between the meeting and the luncheon, so she chose her best summer dress and sling-back sandals. She dabbed on her most expensive perfume, as well.

She parked her car and climbed the stairs to the converted-to-offices Victorian, her stomach in knots. As Sara rung the bell, she tried to analyze her feelings. She could come to no conclusions before the door opened. She was astonished to see Henry standing there in khaki shorts, button-down blue Oxford shirt open at the neck, and tan sandals.

"Hello," he greeted her, smiling professionally. "You must be Sara Putnam?" He opened the door wider to let her enter.

So, he didn't remember her. Sara sighed and followed him down a narrow hall to a large office.

"Have a seat. Can I get you some coffee?"

Sara shook her head and sat in the tufted oxblood leather chair.

He settled himself behind his enormous partner's desk and studied her a moment. "I know you. Where have we met before?"

Sara crossed her legs, tugging at her skirt as she did so. "At the Smithfield's anniversary party. Belinda introduced us."

"Of course!" he exclaimed. "What can I do for you today?" He reached for a yellow pad and his pen.

This man is just full of chitchat, Sara thought ruefully. Even informally dressed, he couldn't relax. She noticed that every black hair on his head was in place, and it occurred to her that he might pluck stray eyebrow hairs away from the bridge of his nose. Those eyebrows were almost too perfect.

"It's rather hard to explain," Sara began.

Henry nodded. "Problems brought to a lawyer frequently are."

Was he trying to be kind? Or was this just part of his lawyerly persona?

"Were you still at the party when the police came?" Sara shifted in her chair, trying to get comfortable.

He stared at her a moment. "No. I'd already left."

"Well, I found the man who was murdered, and I have strong reason to believe he was my father. My biological father."

Henry made a note on his pad, then looked up at her, waiting.

Damn the man, Sara thought. She wished she'd never come. This was worse than going to the dentist. "Have you heard anything about the case?" she asked desperately.

"Just what I read in the *Times*."

"They didn't say much," Sara fumed. "I guess I should start at the beginning." She decided to hell with it and told him the whole story, leaving nothing out. Once she got started, she found it easy. Henry made copious notes, hardly looking up.

"Detective Beecham suggested that I might want some DNA testing and said that I'd need a lawyer. So, here I am."

Finally, Henry looked up. "This is quite a jumble." He scratched his chin. "Are you sure you wouldn't like some coffee? Or how about some bottled water?"

"Bottled water?"

"Perrier?"

Sara shook her head. She had no idea what he was talking about. "Okay." She did feel thirsty all of a sudden. She glanced at her watch. She'd been talking for almost an hour.

He stood up, and she admired his legs as he strode out of his office. She glanced around, noting the bookcases filled with legal texts, a couple of file folders on his desk, a globe in the corner.

Henry came back with two glasses and handed her one with sparkling water and ice cubes. He took his own to his desk and sat down. Sara lowered her eyes to her own glass and took a sip. It tasted pretty good, she decided.

She took another swallow.

"Okay," Henry said. "Let's go over a few points. Then give me the details of exactly what you want me to do. You said that you have no written proof that Howard Lyndquist is your biological father, except for a birth certificate."

Sara nodded.

Howard made a check mark on his yellow pad. "Okay. You've heard or read about DNA testing? It's rather new."

"That I have heard about," Sara said. "It's fascinating."

"Yes, it is." Henry smiled, showing white, even teeth.

Sara realized it was the first time she'd seen him smile. "Can you arrange for the testing?"

He nodded. "Yes. I assume that's one of the things you want me to do?"

Sara reached for her water and took a sip. "Please. And will you be able to find out what's in the will?"

"No problem there. Are you thinking of contesting?"

"I don't know! It feels so strange. It doesn't seem right to contest it, but it seems silly not to."

"If you are his daughter, and that would be legal daughter, remember, not even illegitimate, since he was married to your mother, then you are entitled to your share. There is nothing wrong with that."

"I know," Sara said softly. "If there was no one else, no one who knew him as his father, I wouldn't think twice about it. Kevin probably didn't even know I existed until a while ago. I wonder how long he has known," she mused.

"I don't see what difference that makes," Henry said impatiently. "Shall I proceed as if you are going to contest?"

Sara nodded slowly. "I guess so. Yes," she decided. "Why not?"

"Indeed," Henry remarked. He gave her an another appraising look. Now that he knew she was an heiress, could he be interested in her?

A sudden chill slid down Sara's spine. "Wait a minute," she said. "If someone killed Howard because he was going to make me his heir, will my life be in danger if I contest the will?"

"I suppose that might be a consideration. But wasn't he going to make you *sole* heir? He might have been killed for an entirely different reason, anyway, you know. Most likely was. He was an inventor? Maybe someone thought he infringed on a patent. Maybe someone wanted to patent something Mr. Lyndquist had invented. It could have been over a woman, for all we know."

"I never thought of that. After I found out about his wanting to find me and change the will, I assumed that that was the reason. But you're right. It could have been anything. Anything at all." Sara looked at Henry with a bit more respect.

Henry stood up. "Okay then. I'll get an order for the DNA testing and get to work on the will. I'll give you a call in a day or two. You may pay my clerk a retainer on your way out."

"What?" Sara asked, confused. "Where?" She hadn't known anyone else was in the building.

"Down the hall, to your left," Henry said indifferently. He had begun to study his notes once more, his hand on the telephone.

* * * * *

Sara always took the bus to the city because she hated to drive there, and even worse, she hated to park there.

Buses were usually on time, and a stop was just up the street, so after she got home from the lawyer's office, she walked and waited. She had never minded the diesel smell and even liked the sound of the door closing with a whoosh behind her. After depositing the correct change, the bus took off, and she lurched to a seat and settled back to relax.

Her fellow passengers were a mixed lot, ranging from a couple who looked like street people to a woman in a man-tailored suit.

She felt like a young girl again as they approached the city. She always got excited, as if something wonderful would happen any minute.

Now when Sara entered New York, it almost always meant she was going to see Belinda. She could not remember a time when she had not known her best friend. Some of her earliest memories were of them playing together, going to school together, fighting and making up, being best friends. They giggled in the halls and the girls' room at school; they double dated and told each other everything. If they weren't together, they were talking on the phone to each other.

Belinda knew things about Sara that Sara's own mother didn't know, and vice versa. Belinda liked sports and played on the softball, basketball,

113

and soccer teams while Sara loved art and spent every spare minute taking lessons or painting.

When Belinda got married, Sara was maid of honor. Now she wondered about that marriage. Would the stress of what was happening to Belinda's health put too much strain on it?

Sara sighed. Today, as the bus entered the Port Authority Building, she felt a kind of dread. She wasn't a young girl any longer. She and Belinda had adult problems now.

She left the bus and took the escalator upstairs, careful to keep her purse hugged to her side and her eyes watchful. Out front she hailed a cab and told the driver, "Four Seasons."

He nodded and pulled on the meter. She tried not to watch him drive-- it was too scary.

They pulled up in front of the restaurant, and she gave him the fare and a tip.

Belinda's limo drove in behind her. Sara waited for the ritual of the chauffeur opening the door, one of Belinda's long, slim legs, then the other, coming out, then her head ducking down and appearing, the chauffeur taking her arm, and her emerging like a Jill-in-the-box. Today Belinda seemed to appear extra slowly, and when she straightened up, Sara saw a grimace of what looked like pain. The two friends hugged, then entered the restaurant. The maitre d' greeted them with a smile and led them to a booth.

After they sat down and ordered cocktails, Sara put her napkin in her lap and studied her friend.

Belinda's usually bright black hair looked dull, as did her deep brown eyes. She appeared to have lost weight. Fidgeting with the silverware, she would not look Sara in the eye.

Sara touched her hand. "Tell me. Did you talk to Blinky about your visit to the other doctor?"

The waiter came with their drinks and took their order.

When he left, Sara squeezed Belinda's hand. "Just tell me." She took a sip of her Vodka Collins.

Belinda took two sips of hers. "I couldn't. I can't. Oh, Sara, I don't know what to do."

Sara's stomach did a nosedive. Belinda seemed unable to go on. "How do you feel?" Sara asked softly.

"Not good," Belinda whispered. "I'm getting worse. I ache all over.

Jan Christensen

My throat hurts. I've had a couple of places on my feet swell up. Then it goes away." She took a long swallow of her cocktail and started playing with the silverware again.

"You're not only worried about your health, you're worried about how Blinky will react."

Belinda nodded, a single tear sliding down her cheek. Angrily, she wiped it away. "I don't know how I'll ever be able to tell him."

You might not have to, Sara thought as she studied her friend. "If the symptoms get bad enough, he'll know without your saying anything," Sara told her.

The waiter approached and asked if they wanted another drink. Sara nodded. The food came. They both looked at the expensive meals and knew they wouldn't eat.

Sara picked up her fork and poked at the chicken breast on her plate. Why, of all the things she could have picked, had she chosen the breast? Belinda didn't seem to notice. She probed her fish as if looking for bones. Sara speared an asparagus tip and put it in her mouth, chewed and had trouble swallowing it.

"This doctor you saw. He said it's definitely the implants causing all these symptoms?"

"Well, I didn't have the swellings when I saw him. He sounded pretty positive, though. I have so many of the symptoms. It started with fatigue and body aches, and the doctors all said it was psychological when they couldn't find anything physically wrong. The body aches have gotten so bad that I have trouble getting out of bed in the morning. Different lab tests for autoimmune dysfunction sometimes help with a diagnosis, but not always, and I've had them all . . ." her voice trailed off.

"Maybe you should have them again. You're further along with whatever it is. And you're beginning to sound as if you're in the medical profession yourself."

"I know." Belinda poked at her fish again, then moved it around her plate with her fork. She took a long swallow of her drink and Sara did the same, then signaled the waiter for another round. Might as well get smashed--neither of them had to drive anywhere.

"What are you going to do?" Sara asked softly after the drinks were placed in front of them.

"I don't know!" Belinda looked away from Sara and stared into space a

115

moment. "What would you do?"

Sara thought for a moment. "I'll tell you what I'd do. I'd go to a different doctor entirely. Family practitioner or internist. Tell him your symptoms. Don't mention the breast implants except on your history. See if they come up with something else. Or the same thing. What if they're okay? What if you have the surgery, and it's something else entirely? You've been focusing on the implants, blaming them, probably because that's the only surgery you've ever had, and it makes logical sense to blame them, but it might not be them at all. If it's not, and you have the surgery, you'll have even more of a problem with Blinky."

Belinda stared at her a moment. "You're absolutely right. Why didn't I think of that?"

"Because you're too close to the problem." Sara raised her glass, silently toasted her friend and took a sip.

Belinda smiled at her. "I'll do it," she said thoughtfully. "Now, tell me about what's going on in your life. What was the funeral like?"

"Very interesting," Sara replied, rolling her r's. "Aunt Gladys took pictures, my brother asked me all kinds of questions, and my stepmother wanted to know if I planned to contest the will. Other than that, not much happened. Oh, and I think Ira might be in love with Miriam."

"Good heavens," Belinda exclaimed. "Tell me more."

"I think someone's watching me, following me around. It's kind of spooky."

"Did you tell the police?"

"No." Sara was surprised. "I didn't even think of it. What could they do? They might not even believe me."

"Why shouldn't they?"

"I don't know. I always had the impression that the police don't believe anyone much."

"Sara, that's silly. I want you to call them."

"Yes, Mom." Sara laughed.

"Speaking of Moms, how's Lucille? How did she react to your finding your real father?"

Sara grimaced. "Please, don't call him my 'real father,' especially in front of Mother. She's highly offended by the whole thing. Thinks I should have left it alone, never tried to find out anything."

"But why?" Belinda took a sip of her cocktail.

"I should be grateful for what I have. Don't make waves. You know

116

the drill."

The waiter approached with a dessert tray.

"What do you think?" Belinda asked Sara.

"Why not? We sure didn't eat much of this." Sara pointed at their plates.

"Something chocolate, I think," Belinda smiled for the first time since they'd sat down.

"Absolutely," Sara smiled back.

"And then we'll drive you home."

"In the limo? Really?"

"Really." Belinda pointed at a dessert. "Two Death by Chocolate's and two creme de menthes," she said imperiously, then winked at Sara when he turned away.

"And to think," Sara mused, "when we were kids we thought a brownie and a glass of milk were wonderful. We didn't know what wonderful was!"

They were quiet a moment, finishing their cocktails. The woman in the booth opposite had a louder than normal voice and said to her companion, "I told him to keep his damned designer drugs. If I want a mind-altering experience, I go through the automatic car wash a few times. You know how you sit there, knowing the car is stationary, and when the machine goes around, you feel that you're moving? Definitely feels as if it's altering my mind. Seems as if my brain's moving back and forth inside my head."

"Mildred, you're a hot sketch," her companion exclaimed. Her hair was dyed a peculiar shade of blond, Sara noticed, and she wore a sweater of the same color. Sara wondered if she went to the hairdresser with the sweater and asked her to match it.

The waiter brought the desserts and liqueurs. The tension broke, and by silent mutual consent, Sara and Belinda would not talk about their problems again today.

They gathered coats and purses, Sara's head buzzing slightly, and walked slowly outside where the limo waited. Sara glanced at her watch--it was almost three. The chauffeur, a darkly drop-dead handsome man of about thirty-five, rushed to open the door. He had compelling brown eyes, and every time Sara saw him, she tried not to stare or drool all over herself. As they glided safely and smoothly through the city, Sara thought how the cocoon of wealth wasn't able to protect her friend from problems. Belinda had put her head back on the plush cushion and seemed to be dozing, but she opened her eyes as Sara stared at her.

"What?" Belinda asked.

Sara turned her head away and looked out the window. They had already exited the Lincoln tunnel and were almost in Montclair, stopped at a red light. Sara saw three men and a woman in city uniforms crouched around the open door of the large box that housed the controls for the traffic signals.

"Look. How many city employees does it take to change a light bulb?"

"Four," Belinda counted quickly. "Let's see. One to push the buttons, one to watch the lights, one to count the cars. . ."

"And one to hold the door open. Perfectly logical. But why are the traffic lights never set right?"

"Because none of the workers has ever driven a car."

"That explains it!" They laughed as the light turned green. In a few minutes they were at Sara's house. She felt foolish waiting for the chauffeur to go around and open the door for her. Sara asked Belinda, "Are you coming in?"

"Not today. I'm a bit tired."

Sara nodded, a lump forming in her throat. "Call me." The door opened, and the chauffeur took her arm. "Thank you, Charles. Goodbye."

"Goodbye, Ms. Putnam," he replied and touched two fingers to his cap. She took a deep breath and walked up her front walk, turning at the door to watch the limo glide noiselessly down the quiet street. She waved, wondering what Belinda would do, hoping whatever was wrong wasn't serious. Maybe it's just a virus, she reassured herself. Sighing, Sara stepped inside.

CHAPTER 14

Belinda woke to a gentle shaking of her right shoulder.

"Mrs. Smithfield? Mrs. Smithfield, we're home," Charles told her.

She opened her eyes and blinked at her chauffeur. Embarrassment washed through her. She must have been sleeping hard for him to have to shake her.

With as much dignity as she could muster, she straightened up and said, "Thank you, Charles."

He held out his hand to help her out of the limo, and she took it gratefully. But his firm grasp made her wince in pain. Her knuckles felt on fire.

"Will you be needing me any more today?" asked Charles, apparently not noticing that he'd hurt her hand.

Belinda couldn't remember if she and Blinky had any function to attend tonight. They must have because it was a Saturday, she thought as she glanced at her watch. Four-thirty! She stood awkwardly on the sidewalk in front of her building, the doorman holding open the lobby door, and didn't know what to tell the chauffeur. Tears welled up behind her eyes, and she turned her head away. This was ridiculous. She fumbled in her purse for her appointment book, then for a moment couldn't remember the date, not even what month it was. She turned to the back of the book and flipped quickly towards the front until she found some pages with filled-in dates. July. It was July 6, 1985. One week from their anniversary. Now she remembered and found the correct page. Except for the notation about lunch with Sara, it was blank.

Belinda sighed and glanced up at Charles. He seemed to be watching her with some concern, and she quickly looked away from his gorgeous brown eyes. A horn tooted nearby, making her jump and almost drop her appointment book. She became suddenly aware of standing on a busy New York street, people swirling around them, some looking at her curiously as she stood in front of the open limo door. Charles couldn't close it because she was in the way.

"No, Charles, we won't be needing you tonight," she told him. "Thank you." She walked with as much dignity as she could towards the open apartment house door, automatically smiling at the doorman and thanking him as well.

She rode the elevator alone and let herself into the apartment. For some reason, the foyer and living room seemed enormous to her today, and it took an effort to walk through them and down the hall to the bedroom. There, she removed her shoes and drifted to the master bath to wash up. Her fingers still hurt where Charles had grabbed them, and she looked at them carefully, but could see nothing wrong. Her mouth tasted terrible, so she brushed her teeth and used some mouthwash.

She went to look for Blinky and found him in the sitting room reading a medical journal.

"There you are!" he exclaimed and stood up to greet her.

Belinda dissolved into his arms gratefully, loosing herself in the feel of him. They kissed and held each other for a long time.

Finally, Blinky broke away, giving a shaky laugh. "Mustn't start something," he said, regret in his tone. "Can't be late for dinner with Mumsy and Dad." He looked at her appraisingly. "What are you going to wear?"

Belinda gazed at him blankly.

"You forgot!" he said, disappointment plain on his face.

Belinda walked over to the couch, stumbling a little.

Blinky's eyes narrowed. "Have you been drinking?"

"I had lunch with Sara. We had a couple of drinks, but it's more that I'm tired." She rested her head against the back of the couch. How could she still be tired? She'd had a nap in the limo. The limo! She groaned. She'd told Charles they didn't need him tonight.

Blinky sat down opposite her in his chair. "What's the matter?"

"I . . . dismissed Charles."

He shook his head. "You did forget. Belinda, what am I going to do with you? You didn't used to be this way."

120

"What way?" she asked.

"So forgetful. Absentminded. Like with your driver's license."

Two tears ran down her cheeks. Damn, she thought, swiping them away. She never used to feel so sad, either. Her fingers ached, and her left ankle throbbed. The beginnings of a headache had started behind her eyes.

Blinky seemed to be looking at her coldly. She had disappointed him. She wasn't the perfect wife he wanted. Why did she ever think she could be?

"I guess we can use a cab," he said, "although it's a stupid expense."

"Are you calling me stupid?" Belinda asked, suddenly angry. She didn't feel well, hadn't for weeks, and she was married to a doctor who seemed indifferent to that fact. She stood up, put her fisted hands on her hips and glared at her husband.

He got up, too, and took a step towards her, then stopped, studying the expression on her face. His hand reached out to her, but she frowned at him, and he dropped it to his side. "I didn't call you stupid," Blinky pointed out in a reasonable tone. "I said calling a cab was a stupid expense. But it's all right. Not a big deal."

Sometimes she couldn't believe the rich. Since she'd met Blinky, she came in contact with lots of wealthy people, most of their money inherited. They'd spend millions on a painting, then worry about the expense of a cab ride.

"Take it out of my allowance," Belinda said and turned to leave the room. "I'll go change. What time is dinner?"

"Seven, but we need to be there at six, of course," Blinky told her retreating back.

In the bedroom, Belinda put on her basic black dress, her three stands of pearls, pearl drop earrings, and black high heels and re-did her makeup. She wobbled a bit going back to the sitting room, but decided it was because her ankle hurt, not from drinking. Or maybe she was fooling herself.

Blinky put down his journal and gave her an appraising look. As if she were something for sale at Sotheby's, she thought.

"You look very nice," he said.

Damned with faint praise, she thought. "Thank you," she said, glancing at her watch. Five thirty-five. "Should we go now?"

121

He nodded.

The cabdriver deposited them on Park Avenue in front of a building similar to their own, and the elevator whisked them up to the penthouse. Blinky's parents greeted them with typical restraint--tiny hugs and light pecks on the cheek. Mumsy looked at Belinda with a critical eye.

"You look tired, dear," she remarked, as if it were some failing that could be and should be avoided.

Belinda nodded but didn't say anything. Mumsy looked terrific, as usual. She'd had her first face-lift six months ago. Within two weeks of the operation she'd gone back to exercising an hour a day and having her hair and nails done every week. She watched her fat grams and got a full eight hours of sleep every night. She'd made taking care of herself, and her surroundings, a religion. Belinda glanced around the white-toned living room. Winter white carpet, eggshell white couches and chairs, off-white drapes and curtains. The only color bloomed in the flower arrangements and the bright paintings of gardens and birds on the white walls.

Dad, tall and darkly handsome with gray wings in his hair, handed out glasses of white wine just as Blinky's sister, Tiffany, and her husband, Jerry, came in. Pouring more wine for the new arrivals, he asked them, "How was Europe?"

"Just great, Dad," Jerry said with enthusiasm. He smoothed the side of his medium brown hair with his hand, a nervous gesture Belinda had seen him use often. He just missed being handsome because of a too-big nose that was slightly crooked. He had a sensuous mouth, though, and high cheekbones. "Especially Paris. Right, Tif?"

She smiled. "Especially Paris. We're trying to decide when to go back." Tiffany was beautiful in an intense, almost angry way. Of medium height, she looked taller because she moved like a dancer.

"But can you fit it in between saving the whales and hugging trees?" Blinky asked.

Tiffany's green eyes flashed him a cold glance. Belinda shivered. Not in the house ten minutes, and already they were going to fight.

"Sorry we missed your anniversary party," Jerry said quickly. "How did it go?"

"Just fine, except for the murder," Blinky told him.

Tiffany gasped. "Murder? You're kidding, right?"

"I wouldn't kid about something like that," Blinky told her solemnly. "You've met Belinda's friend, Sara. Her father was killed in our stairway.

Stabbed." He took a sip of his wine, watching their reaction over the rim of his glass.

"It was awful," Belinda put in. She hadn't liked the cold-blooded way Blinky presented the facts. "Sara had been looking for her biological father for almost two years, and there he was, murdered before she could get to know him."

"But who did it? Surely not Sara?" Jerry asked.

"No, of course not," Belinda said. "No one knows, yet. There was something about an inheritance. He was an inventor. Maybe someone wanted to steal a patent or something."

Blinky looked at her, surprise in his eyes. "Where'd you hear that?"

Belinda shrugged. "Nowhere. I just thought of it."

"What did he invent?" Dad asked.

"Lots of different things, I understand," Belinda told him. "His most famous invention was the robotic vacuum cleaner."

"I read about that in the paper the other day," Dad said.

"That's right," Blinky said, taking a sip of his wine. Dad poured more for everyone. "The article came out the day before he was murdered."

Tiffany shivered. "How terrible. What was his name?"

"Howard Lyndquist," Belinda and Blinky said together.

"Never heard of him," Jerry said.

"Me, either." Tiffany set her wine glass down on the glass coffee table. "How on earth did he end up on your staircase? Did he attend the party?"

"He crashed it," Blinky replied. "Looking for Sara, apparently, but never did tell her who he was. Got drunk instead. Then left, and got killed on the landing. Sara found him, poor thing."

"That reminds me of something." Belinda turned to Blinky. "Did you hire that clown?"

"What clown?"

"The one at our party."

"No," Blinky said. "I thought you did."

"Another crasher?" Jerry asked.

"Appears that way," Blinky said. "Maybe we should tell the police."

"Did you see him do anything? Any tricks or anything while he was there?" Belinda asked.

Blinky shook his head. "You mean like make animals out of balloons, grab quarters from people's ears?"

"Yes. I did see him make one balloon animal, but that's all. I saw a clown downtown the other day. Seeing him reminded me of the one at our party, and I knew I hadn't hired one, and I was a bit surprised to see him, but never got close enough to chat."

"Do you suppose he was an invited guest who showed up in costume?" Tiffany wondered.

"To an anniversary party?" Blinky asked. "I doubt it. I don't know any of our friends who would do something like that, do you, Belinda?"

Belinda shook her head. "Blinky, maybe he was the murderer!"

"What?" all five of the others exclaimed at once.

A maid entered the room. "Dinner is served," she announced.

"We'll be there in a minute," Mumsy told her. "Belinda, what do you mean the clown could have been the murderer?"

"Disguised. It worked, too. I thought Blinky hired him, Blinky thought I did. He got to be there without anyone knowing who he was. He was gone by the time the body was discovered."

"You might have something there," Blinky acknowledged. "I think we'll have to tell the police about this."

"And tell Sara, too," Belinda said.

"Clowns might seem disguised," Dad told them, "but each one does his or her face up the same way each time, almost like a signature."

"That's right," Mumsy exclaimed. "I read about that somewhere. Do you remember what the clown looked like? I mean, what kind of makeup he wore?"

Belinda and Blinky shook their heads. "Carrot hair, white face, red lips and cheeks. Typical clown. If it was a disguise, he could have used it only the one time," Blinky told them.

"That's true," Dad said. "Maybe we should go in to dinner before it gets cold."

Everyone stood up and proceeded into the dining room. More white greeted them--antique white French Provincial table, chairs, buffet and serving table sat on the Oriental carpet which had a white background. The walls and drapes were also shades of the non-color. Belinda blinked in the candlelight (white candles, of course) and took her seat at Dad's right, Tiffany across from her, and Blinky beside her. Belinda stared with distaste at the half grapefruit with the half cherry in its center on the white plate. She looked for the sugar bowl and put as much of the white stuff on the grapefruit as she could. Her mouth puckered before she could even take a bite. At least the sections had been cut, so it was easy to eat.

"No talk of murder over dinner, now," Mumsy told them. Belinda noticed that she hadn't put any sugar on her fruit.

"You're absolutely right," Dad said, looking at his grapefruit glumly. "Tell us about Europe, Tiffany."

"You've all been there," Tif said, forgetting that Belinda never had. "It's old, and smells funny."

"What do you mean, smells funny?" Blinky asked.

"I don't know. It just smells old to me. Different. Didn't you notice that, Jerry?"

Jerry pushed his half-eaten grapefruit away. He had a sour look. "I don't know what you're talking about." He took a sip of water.

Tiffany shrugged, delicately taking a grapefruit section and putting it into her mouth. "Well, if no one else has noticed, I can't help that. Anyway, we did the usual. The Louvre, the Eiffel Tower, a few castles, including Versailles, and Rome, Florence, then London, and home. Did I leave anything out?" she asked Jerry.

The maid came in and removed the first course, replacing it with a Caesar salad. They all looked a bit happier as they began to eat again.

"Are there groups in Europe that have your interest in the environment and saving animals?" Blinky asked his sister.

"If there were, we didn't find any," Jerry answered.

"You wouldn't even look," Tiffany accused him.

"We were there to vacation, not to save the earth," Jerry said, spearing a lettuce leaf angrily with his fork.

"You can't take a vacation from saving the earth," Tiffany insisted. It sounded like an old, tired argument to Belinda. The maid returned and replaced the salad with plates of roast beef, asparagus, and scalloped potatoes. Except Tiffany didn't have any meat on hers. She had some disgusting looking brown beans instead.

Belinda began to cut her meat and noticed that her fingers hurt so much that she could hardly do so. The fork clattered from her nerveless fingers, and everyone looked at her. She blushed faintly.

"What's wrong with your hand?" Blinky asked.

Everyone stared at her black and blue fingers. Belinda looked at them with horror. How could that happen just from Charles grabbing them a little strongly? She must had knocked her hand on something without remembering.

Gently, Blinky took her sore hand. "Let me see," he said, frowning. He examined her hand closely, let it go, and took her other one. For the first time, Belinda noticed that the knuckles on that hand were a bit swollen.

"Do you have any other swollen joints?" Blinky asked.

Belinda's eyes widened. "My ankle," she whispered.

"Let me see." He shoved his chair away from the table, and Belinda swung her foot around onto his lap. He removed her shoe and looked at her ankle through her stocking. He touched a red spot on her leg with his finger. "Purpura," he breathed.

Belinda was suddenly conscious of everyone watching them. She took her foot out of Blinky's lap and put her shoe back on.

Blinky stared at her, and she saw dread in his eyes.

"What is it?" she asked, hardly able to breathe.

"I'm not sure. But you need to see a Rheumatologist. As soon as possible." He stood up suddenly, turning to his parents. "We should leave. Sorry."

Chairs were pushed back as the others stood, murmuring, concern on their faces. Blinky took Belinda's elbow and steered her out of the room, out the front door and into the elevator before she could think of anything to say.

As they descended, he pulled her to him, hugging her firmly but gently. "I'm sorry, Lin. So sorry I ever doubted you," he said into her ear.

Her heart pounded with fear when he let her go, and they walked out of the elevator, his hand again cupped around her elbow. "What do you think it is?" she asked as he hailed a cab.

"I don't know. But we have to find out. Soon."

CHAPTER 15

The phone ringing beside her bed woke Sara Sunday morning. She squinted at it, and sat up, swinging her legs around so that she perched on the edge of the bed, at the same time grabbing the annoying thing.

"Hello?" she mumbled. Her voice sounded thick with sleep.

"Sara?" Belinda whispered.

"Lin? What's up?"

Belinda didn't answer.

"Belinda? What's wrong?" Sara asked, her chest constricting with fear.

"I don't know." Belinda's voice had gotten a tad stronger. "Oh, Sara, Blinky's acting as if I have some life-threatening illness. I think he's called every doctor he knows in the city."

"Whatever made him change his mind?" Sara asked, rubbing the sleep from her eyes and frowning.

"My fingers. My fingers are black and blue, the knuckles swollen. He's seen my ankle now, too. And the spots on my legs. He just dashed out to get the paper and some doughnuts, so I thought I'd call you. I'm so scared, Sara."

"But what does he *say*?" Sara asked, exasperated at the thought that a doctor didn't know what was wrong with her friend. "Doesn't he *know* what's wrong now?"

"I don't think so. I really don't think he knows. I think he's afraid it might be from the implants, but he doesn't know that either. He has no way of telling, Sara. There haven't been any studies, no real proof that the implants cause these kinds of problems." Belinda's voice got even softer. "He finally told me that he's never seen anything like what I have before.

He said he doesn't know what it is, and he sounded scared, Sara."

Sara didn't know what to say. She had a hard time imagining Blinky scared. "You said he was calling other doctors. Surely one of those will know what it is, and what to do to cure it."

Belinda sighed. "I guess so. He's set up several appointments for me tomorrow. Now both my ankles are swollen, and my knees are starting to act up, too. You know, I can't help but think about the problem I had with the Division of Motor Vehicles. Like it was prophetic. Sara, I'm scared I'm going to die."

"Oh, God, no, Belinda, don't say that!" Sara begged. "Don't even think it." *You can't die*, Sara thought. *I couldn't bear it.* "Some doctor has to know what it is. You have to believe that."

"Sara, I'm sorry. Sorry to lay this on you. But I had to talk to someone, and you're my best friend."

"I know. It's all right. I understand." Sara, fighting back tears, tried to make her voice calm and normal-sounding.

"Listen, Blinky's going to be back any minute. I wanted to let you know I remembered something about the party that might be a help in finding the murderer."

It took Sara a minute to comprehend what Belinda meant. She couldn't get the image of her friend, lying ill and helpless in her luxurious New York apartment, out of her mind.

"There was a clown," Belinda continued. "Did you see him?"

Sara thought back to that night, only a week ago. "Yes, I saw one. Why?"

"Well, neither Blinky nor I hired him. So he crashed. A perfect disguise for a murderer, isn't it?"

Sara gasped. She tried to remember what the clown looked like, exactly, but she couldn't. "Do you remember what he wore?" Sara asked Belinda.

"Just vaguely. Some of the other guests might remember better. Someone who interacted with him, perhaps. I think you should call that detective and tell him about it. The police can interview everyone again and maybe find out more."

"Good idea. I'll do that right away."

"Here comes Blinky. Got to go."

Sara wondered briefly why Belinda didn't want her husband to know she was talking to her, but she guessed Belinda had a reason. "Okay," she said. "Get better, and keep me posted."

"Will do. Bye." She hung up.

Slowly, Sara replaced the receiver and remained sitting on the edge of the bed awhile, thinking. She got up slowly and went to brush her teeth. Before even getting dressed, she found Detective Beecham's card and called the New York Police Department. He wasn't in, so she left a message.

Sara threw on some jeans and an old T-shirt, then went to the kitchen and made coffee. Eileen came out of her bedroom in pajamas and a robe.

"Who was that on the phone so early on a Sunday?" Eileen asked as she got out mugs for the coffee.

"Belinda. She's sick. Really sick. They don't know what's wrong with her."

Eileen's green eyes widened. She sat down on a bar stool and poured coffee into the mugs. "But she's so young. What could it be?"

Sara shrugged and sat down next to her. "I don't know. It sounds like arthritis--her joints are swollen, but she had some kind of rash, too."

"Arthritis is for old people. That can't be it. You don't think it's cancer, do you?"

Sara winced. "Please, Eileen. Don't even say it. She sounded really scared."

"And married to a doctor." Eileen took a sip of coffee and made a face. "Hot. Doesn't he know what's wrong?"

Suddenly, tears welled, and Sara looked away, shaking her head.

"Hey," Eileen said, putting her arm around Sara. "Don't. She'll be all right. They just have to find out what's wrong, then they can fix it. They can fix almost anything nowadays."

Sara sniffed and got up to get a tissue. "You're right, of course," she said, dabbing at her eyes. "It's just so unexpected. Eileen, Belinda thinks it might be related to her implants."

Eileen paused with her mug halfway to her lips. Her eyes widened. "The ones Blinky put in? Ouch! I can see where that might be a huge problem."

Sara nodded. "That's an understatement." She sat back down on the bar stool, and they drank coffee in silence for awhile.

"Well, to change the subject," Eileen finally said, pouring herself some more coffee, "what do you hear about the murder and your burglary? We haven't had a chance to talk since you went to the funeral."

"Nothing. It's so frustrating. Oh, I wanted to ask you if you've seen anyone strange lurking around lately. Eugene says he's noticed a man watching the house since the murder. The day after it happened, I thought someone was following me, too."

Eileen shook her head, her auburn hair flowing around her shoulders. "Haven't seen a thing, and I wouldn't take Eugene too seriously," she said. "So, you've no news from either the Jersey cops or the New York cops?"

"Well, I've called them and asked if they had anything, but either they don't, or they're not sharing it with me."

"How rude of them! Don't they know they're supposed to share? They should have learned that in kindergarten!"

Sara laughed, stood up, and stretched. "Yeah," she said as a loud knocking sounded on their apartment door.

"Sara? Eileen?" their landlady called. "Are you up?"

"Now what?" Sara asked as she strode across the living room and swung open the door. Mrs. Abbot's chins were quivering with excitement. "There's a man downstairs says he knows you. He looks so disreputable, I wasn't sure I should let him in."

"Good morning, Mrs. Abbot," Sara said. Eileen had come up behind her and also said, "Good morning."

Mrs. Abbot nodded. "He said his name is Ira something. He's dressed all in black and looks like a funeral director. He's even driving a hearse! You don't know this man, do you, Sara?"

Sara smiled. "I'm afraid so, Mrs. Abbot. You can show him up, if you want. Or I can come down."

Mrs. Abbot huffed and muttered, "I'll show him up, I suppose. I can't believe you know such a person."

"He's an inventor, Mrs. Abbot. A bit eccentric is all. Perfectly harmless."

"If you say so." Mrs. Abbot turned around and made her way slowly back downstairs.

"I'll get dressed," Eileen said, going to her bedroom.

Sara nodded and glanced around the living room. As usual, everything looked okay, both she and Eileen being neatniks. Sara could hear Ira coming up the stairs, and after he turned at the landing, saw his now-familiar person, dressed the same as when she first saw him.

He grinned when he caught sight of her and started climbing a little faster. "I brought pictures," he called, waving a package.

Sara closed her eyes a moment. She didn't know if she was ready for pictures.

"So soon?" she asked faintly.

He looked like a kid at Christmas. She held the door open for him to enter, and he gazed around the apartment with apparent interest. "How are you?" he asked, remembering his manners.

"Just fine. Yourself?" Sara gestured for him to have a seat. He chose the couch, and she sat opposite him in an armchair.

His white socks peeked out from beneath his black trousers as he crossed his long legs. "I'm okay," he said. "Nice cows."

"What?" Sara looked around the room as if seeing it for the first time. "Oh, my roommate decorated."

"A country girl?"

Sara laughed. "No, she's from New Jersey, like me. We work together."

"There's still country in New Jersey. The Garden State."

"Oh, yes," Sara said. "South and west. I grew up in Caldwell, and she grew up in Bloomfield."

"I see," Ira said. "You want to see the pictures?"

"I'm not sure." Sara stood up. "Can I get you some coffee first?"

"That would be great," Ira told her, getting up and following her to the kitchen. "You don't have to look at them, if you don't want to. I could just leave them here, and you can view them when you feel like it."

Sara nodded, an unexpected lump forming in her throat. Hastily, she began to pour their coffee.

"Did the police tell you about the weapon?" Ira asked.

Sara put the coffee pot down with a thump. "Only that it was something he invented. Do you know what it was?"

Ira took a mug from her and put lots of sugar and some milk in the coffee. They went back to their seats in the living room. "They brought me in to look at it Friday. It's a prototype for a new surgical instrument."

Sara shuddered. "They told me it might be a kitchen implement of some kind. It must have been very sharp.

Ira nodded. "Extremely. We invented it specifically for plastic surgeons, and we were hoping it would cause less scarring."

"What an odd coincidence. The friend of mine who gave the party is married to a plastic surgeon, Dr. Smithfield."

"I know." Ira gave her a piercing look.

"Oh?" Sara studied the man sitting opposite her. Was he here to give her information, or to get some from her? Suddenly she felt a bit queasy. She had to swallow hard to keep the coffee from coming back up.

"You all right?" Ira asked.

She felt surprised at how perceptive he was. She must remember not to underestimate his intelligence, and perhaps his cunning. Or was she getting paranoid?

"I'm fine," she answered him, pretending to take a sip of coffee while scrutinizing him over the rim of her mug.

As if he could read her mind, Ira stood up, his long legs seeming to propel him off the couch. "You don't trust me anymore," he said, distress evident in his tone. He began to pace around the room, cocking his eye at each cow as he walked by. "What did I say? Or do?"

"Of course I trust you!" Sara exclaimed, hoping her voice didn't betray her doubt. She set her mug down and stood up, too, as she remembered something. "How's Miriam, by the way?"

She watched for his reaction.

He'd been facing her, but he spun around quickly and picked up the same cow her mother had the other day. She couldn't see his face.

"I haven't seen her since the funeral." Ira put the bovine back on the table and turned around. He smiled at her, trying to be ingratiating, she thought.

Sara sat down again. "Tell me more about the knife. How many prototypes did you make?"

Ira crumpled back onto the sofa. "The police asked me the same thing. We made a dozen."

"That many!" Sara exclaimed.

Ira nodded. "We gave eight to plastic surgeons to try. We kept three at the warehouse, and Howard had one at home. He liked to keep current models with him, if they weren't too large, so he could examine them before bed. He frequently had inspirations during dreams or first thing upon wakening."

"Have they all been accounted for?"

"Two are missing from the warehouse." Ira crossed his legs again and leaned back. "The other piece of interesting information is that your friend, Dr. Smithfield, had a prototype."

"What?"

Ira uncrossed his legs and leaned forward. "He's a leading plastic surgeon in New York City. Of course, we asked the most prominent ones we could find to test them."

Sara felt the beginnings of a headache behind her eyes which she rubbed absently. "Can Blinky account for his scalpel?" she asked.

"Blinky?"

"Dr. Smithfield. That's his nickname. Apparently his sister couldn't say 'Bancroft' when they were little, so he became Blinky."

"Interesting," Ira murmured. "He kept it all this time?"

"Just family and friends use it, of course."

"Of course. I don't know if he can account for his prototype. The police didn't let me in on that bit of information, or whether any of the other doctors can, for that matter."

"But I don't see any reason for Blinky to harm my father."
Sara's mind rushed through the facts she knew, and couldn't think of any possible explanation. "Did you and Howard talk to these surgeons much, get to know them at all?"

Ira shook his head and ran his hand through his bushy hair. "Not really. As I said, they were chosen because of their reputations. What worries me more is that one is still unaccounted for."

Sara had almost forgotten he'd said two were missing. "Maybe my father had them with him?"

"Doubtful. Why should he? He had one at home, and the ones in the warehouse. He didn't need to carry them around."

"Unless he thought he needed a weapon."

Ira jumped up again. Sara wished he'd stop doing that. Her head pounded even harder.

"I never thought of that! Maybe he was being threatened. But those scalpels were awfully sharp to carry around casually. He could have put them in cases, though." He stopped talking and pacing and thought for a moment. "I'll have to mention that to the police. See if they found anything on him that might have been used as a sheath. The killer could have taken the second one with him." He stared at Sara. "This gets more and more complicated."

"It does. The next question is, who had access to the warehouse? Who could have taken the missing scalpels?"

"Not that many people, really. Howard and myself. Kevin. Some vendors. I gave a list to the police, but neither Howard nor I interacted with any of them socially, so I don't know of any reason for them to do it. Actually, they'll be harmed by his death--lose business."

"That's all?" Sara asked. "No one else came in?"

"Well, Miriam came by once in a great while, but I haven't seen her lately."

"How long ago? Since the scalpels were made?"

Ira sat down again and thought for a minute, then nodded. "I think so. Maybe right afterwards."

"Anyone else?" Sara got up, her mug in her hand. "More coffee?"

Ira stood up again, too. "Please," he said and followed her to the kitchen.

"Kevin has a couple of friends who like to come by and see what we're up to. None have been over in several weeks. I do remember one other person, though. Kevin's girlfriend. He took her for a tour through the whole building a month or so ago. Really spent a long time, too."

"He has a girlfriend?" Sara asked, handing Ira his mug.

He stirred in milk and sugar. "Yes. I can't remember her name. Pretty."

"She wasn't at the funeral?"

"No. No," Ira said slowly as he walked back to the living room and sat down. "Maybe she couldn't get time off from work."

Sara sat down, too, and placed her mug on the side table. "What do you know about her?"

"Not much. I don't think Kevin has known her that long. He doesn't talk about her much. But when he does, he seems smitten."

"So, you don't know what she does or where she works or anything?"

"No." Ira took a sip of coffee. "He just talks about where they go on dates, things like that."

Sara decided to drop it. What reason would Kevin's new girlfriend have to kill Howard anyway? "You can't think of anyone else who's been there lately?"

Ira shook his head.

"Did the doctors come in to pick up the scalpels, or did you deliver them? How did that work?"

"I personally delivered them to each office. Howard didn't like to get involved in things like that. I gave the doctors questionnaires to fill out about their results."

"When did you do this? How long ago? Have any of the doctors returned the questionnaires, yet?"

Ira smiled at her. "You're beginning to ask as many questions as the police."

Sara looked down at her lap. "Sorry. I guess I really need to know what happened and why."

"Don't be sorry." He stood up, came over to her, and patted her shoulder. "You have very good reasons to want to know what happened."

"Thanks," Sara murmured.

Ira paced a minute, thinking, then sat down and drank more coffee. "I'm trying to remember. It's early July now, and we took those scalpels around in March. We told them to have the questionnaires back in six months. So, no, I don't think anyone has returned one as yet."

"Okay," Sara said. "To change the subject a bit, do you know anyone who dresses up as a clown sometimes? One showed up at the party, apparently no one the Smithfields invited. A perfect disguise."

Ira shook his head, looking dejected.

Sara couldn't think of any more questions to ask about the murder. She noticed the look on Ira's face and suddenly felt sorry for him. After all, he'd lost his best friend and partner. "How are you doing?" she asked softly.

He looked up at her, his eyes as startled as a deer's caught in headlights. "I'm okay," he said, shrugging his shoulders.

"You're sure?" She wondered if he had anyone, any friends, relatives. She realized she didn't know a thing about him, really.

He smiled at her. "You're a nice girl. I'll be fine."

"Are you working on any new inventions?"

"No. I've been concentrating on the murder trap. Large enough to hold the person who murdered my friend and partner. Metaphorically speaking."

"After you find the murderer, what will you do?" Sara asked, really wanting to know.

"I'm not sure. I could retire. Work in my rose garden. Drive the neighbors wild with my eccentricities."

Sara laughed, delighted that he knew himself to be eccentric. Did he think it went with being an inventor?

"Do you think you could find a new partner?"

Ira shook his head. "I doubt it." He stood up. "Well, I've taken

135

enough of your time. Thanks for the coffee."

"Thank you for bringing the pictures by, even though I haven't looked at them yet." Sara got up, and they walked to the door. "Let me go down with you and show you the back way in. Then you can avoid my charming landlady if you come visit me again."

Sara led the way down. Eugene came out of his part of the house and met them on the landing. Sara wondered how he could do that so often. Maybe he could hear her coming, she thought, as a stair creaked under her foot. Sara introduced him to Ira, and they continued downstairs.

"You're an inventor?" Eugene asked, excitement clear in his voice.

"Yes," Ira answered as they went out the back door.

"Here's our doorbell," Sara said, pointing.

They began to walk towards the front of the house. As they came to the front sidewalk, Eugene exclaimed, "There he is! The guy who's been watching the house!"

"Let's get him!" Sara yelled and took off running.

She could see the surprised expression on the man's face as he saw her coming towards him. He turned and ran away from them. She heard Ira and Eugene's footsteps pounding behind her, and she picked up speed. But the man ran faster. As they rounded the corner, they saw him jump into a late model Ford and speed away. The three of them stood panting on the sidewalk.

"Can you see the license number?" Sara asked, squinting.

"It looks as if it's covered with something," Eugene said as the car drove off, tires squealing.

"Mud," Ira said. "Guy looked familiar, though. I think he's a friend of Kevin's." He looked like he wished the words back when he saw the expression on Sara's face.

CHAPTER 16

"Come on," Sara said. "We need to call the police."

They started walking back to the house. Sara still felt a bit out of breath, and Ira was puffing noticeably. Eugene seemed completely recovered from their sprint.

They trudged up the stairs. Eugene paused on the landing.

"Come with us, Eugene," Sara suggested. "You can tell the cops what you know about the house being watched."

He blushed and nodded his head. Sara realized that he'd never been in their apartment before.

They entered the living room, and Sara told them to have a seat while she got the phone numbers for the police. In her bedroom, she could hear Eileen moving around in hers, opening and closing drawers, things thumping on the floor. She must be rearranging again, Sara thought with a smile. She found the business cards with the numbers for both the New Jersey and New York police and took them out to the kitchen with her.

Eugene stood with a bemused look on his face in the middle of the room. Ira had sat back down on the couch, but stood up again as soon as she entered the living room.

"The phone's in the kitchen," she told them. "Let's go in there so if they have any questions for either of you, you can talk to them."

Both men nodded and followed her. The kitchen felt tiny with all three of them crowded into the small space. Sara dialed the New Jersey station first.

One of the men who had come to her apartment after the burglary answered. She couldn't remember his name or if he was the blond or the brown-haired one, but it didn't matter. She explained what had happened, and he asked to speak first to Eugene, then to Ira. After they told the policeman all they knew, Ira said to Sara, "He wants to talk to you."

Eugene and Ira left the kitchen, and Sara said, "Hello, again," into the receiver.

"Ms. Putnam, I suggest you call Detective Beecham and let him know about this development. We will follow up on this end, but there is a problem here of jurisdiction."

"I understand," Sara said. "I planned to call him, anyway."

"Good. Now, this man you saw today. Did he in any way remind you of your burglar? Height, weight, the way he moved?"

"I don't know." Sara thought as hard as she could. "I don't think so. I only saw him from a distance, and it's hard to judge height and weight that way. And he was running today. The burglar moved around slowly. I'm sorry. I really can't say."

"That's all right. If you think of anything else, anything at all, you give us a call. Keep your doors and windows locked. You might consider a burglar alarm."

Or a bodyguard, Sara thought. Maybe she could recruit Eugene.

"I'll call you if anything else happens, and I'll certainly think about putting in alarms."

"Good. Thank you for calling."

They hung up, and Sara went to the living room to find the others. Eugene was looking through the pictures she'd left on the coffee table, Ira explaining them in a low voice. They looked up guiltily when they saw her.

"I'm going to call Detective Beecham now. If you'd come with me . . ."

Hastily, Eugene set the pictures down, and he and Ira followed her back to the kitchen.

The Detective was unavailable. She left a message and hung up.

Ira looked at his watch. "I'd better be going. Tell the Detective to call me if he has any questions. I'll be at the warehouse. I'm trying to sort out papers for the lawyers and do some other things to wrap up a few of our inventions that were almost finished."

Sara nodded. "I understand."

She followed him to the door, Eugene behind her. Ira left, and Eugene stood there awkwardly. If he had a hat in his hand, Sara thought, he'd be twisting it.

"If you'll excuse me, Eugene, I have a lot to do today."

He nodded, his Adam's apple bobbing up and down. "Sure," he said. "I'll go now. You call me if you need me."

She put her hand on his arm. "I'll do that."

He looked at his arm as if it were burned. He didn't move until she took it away. Blushing, he left, bumping into the doorframe on his way out.

Sara smiled and closed and locked the door after him. She stood there a minute, wondering what to do. She turned around and saw the pictures on the coffee table. Slowly, she walked over to them and sat down on the couch. They had fanned out a bit when Eugene dropped them.

The first one to catch her eye showed her father in his coffin. She quickly put it aside. Next came pictures of the gravesite. Everyone's head was bowed against the rain, and she couldn't pick out any people in particular, except Miriam and Kevin, Ira and herself.

The next several shots were of the food. Sara smiled as she looked at these photos, wondering who had so artfully arranged it. Miriam? The following pictures were of guests. She recognized the old woman who had questioned her about who she was. There were shots of Ira, Miriam and Kevin, and even of herself. A picture of three young men standing in a corner, talking, caught her eye. Probably friends of Kevin's, she thought. She didn't remember seeing them there. The one in the middle looked a lot like the guy they had just chased down the street. She peered at him more closely. Yes, she was sure. And the guy next to him--he had the same posture and build as her burglar. Could it be?

"What're you doing?" Eileen asked, startling Sara so badly that she dropped the photos.

Sara looked up at Eileen who had gotten dressed in jeans and a T-shirt, penny loafers on her feet. She'd gathered her beautiful auburn hair into a ponytail and had a smudge of dirt on one cheek.

Sara blinked. "These are photos of the funeral. Ira brought them by. Where have you been? I could have introduced you."

"Oh, I got into one of my cleaning-out-and-straightening-up moods. Pictures of a funeral? How macabre."

Sara nodded. "You're not kidding."

Eileen sat down on the couch next to her. "Let me see. I bet the police would like to look at these."

"You're right!" Sara exclaimed. "Maybe there's a clue here. Besides the picture of this guy." She put her finger on the watcher. "He's been watching the house. We caught him as I let Ira out, and chased him. He's a friend of Kevin's. This one looks as if he could be the burglar. Eileen, it's beginning to look more and more as if Kevin did it. His friends are helping him. He wants to inherit it all."

Eileen looked puzzled. "I thought he had an alibi."

"Ira," Sara said softly. "I like Ira, but could he be protecting Kevin? Coming over here to find out what I know, what I'm going to do?"

"What *are* you going to do?" Eileen asked, shuffling absently through the pictures.

"Well, I hired a lawyer. He's going to get a DNA test done, and then I'm going to see about getting my share. After all, if this Howard Lyndquist is my father, then I'm his legitimate daughter, and I'm entitled."

Eileen put the pictures down on the table. "Of course you are. You sound so defensive."

Sara sighed. "I know. Somehow I just don't feel right about it. He rejected me. Why should I think I'm entitled to anything?"

"But he was trying to find you."

"Only because he was mad at Kevin."

Eileen put her hand over Sara's. "You might look at it the other way."

"How's that?" Sara asked.

"Like he owes you. He neglected you all those years. Now you can get something back."

Sara gasped. Of course Eileen would think that way. "I never thought of that," Sara said. "Do you think Kevin did it?"

Eileen shrugged. "How would I know? He's the most obvious suspect, I guess. What about his mother, though? She'd be mad at Howard if he planned to disinherit their son, wouldn't she? What's she like? Do you think she's capable of murder?"

Sara laughed, a hollow sound. "Probably. One of those rich bitches used to getting her way. Since I don't know any murderers, it's hard to say. That is," she said slowly, suddenly coming to an intense realization, "I probably know one, but I don't know who it is."

Eileen shivered. "Maybe we should get a burglar alarm. A watchdog."

"I don't think Mrs. Abbot would let us have a dog. The cops did suggest we get an alarm."

"How much do you think that would cost?" Eileen asked.

"I haven't got a clue. Probably too much. Could they just do the apartment? What about the rest of the house?"

Eileen shook her head. "I don't know. I guess we could call someone and ask." She sounded reluctant as she picked up a picture of Kevin and studied it.

After all, Sara thought, it isn't Eileen's problem. She sighed. If they got an alarm, Sara supposed she would have to pay for the whole thing.

The phone rang, startling them both. "I'll get it," Sara said. "It might be Detective Beecham."

His gruff voice came through the receiver and asked her how she was doing. She told him all that had happened.

When she finished, silence hummed on the line for a moment. Finally, he said, "I hate to ask you, but it would help a lot if you came in to the station and gave me a signed statement. I'd like to see the pictures, especially the one of Kevin's three friends. Would that be possible?"

"Today?" Sara asked, looking at the clock on the microwave. Two in the afternoon. Where had the time gone? She hadn't had any lunch, either. At the thought, her stomach rumbled.

"Well, if you come in today, you won't have to miss work."

That was true.

"All right," Sara said reluctantly. "Where is the station?"

He told her, and they hung up after she promised to be there as soon as she could.

"Damn," she muttered as she got bread, ham and cheese out to make a quick sandwich.

"What's wrong?" Eileen asked.

"I have to go into the City to see Detective Beecham. Where's the bus schedule, do you know?"

"Should be in that drawer," Eileen said, pointing.

Sara fished around in the junk and came up with the schedule. Only a year old, she noticed. Should be okay. While eating her sandwich and drinking a glass of milk, she found the Montclair to NYC schedule. They only ran every hour and a half on Sundays. She breathed a sigh of relief. She had forty-five minutes left to catch one. Just enough time.

After changing into a skirt and blouse, Sara grabbed up the pictures and left for the bus stop.

The ride in was uneventful on the almost empty bus. At the Port Authority she rushed outside and hailed a cab. The cabby looked at her twice when she told him her destination. Sara ignored him.

141

The station, an old brick building, loomed over the sidewalk like some medieval castle without turrets. Sara's heart pounded faster than usual as she climbed the stone steps and entered the gloomy lobby. Several people milled about, and others sprawled on benches along the walls. In the center of the room stood a large reception desk, raised up so high that Sara had to crane her neck to see the policeman standing, or perhaps he sat on a stool, at the center of the desk.

He looked down at her. "May I help you?"

Sara swallowed. "I'm here to see Detective Beecham. He's expecting me."

"Your name?"

"Sara Putnam."

"I'll let him know you're here. You can have a seat."

Sara looked at the benches, all of them occupied by people she'd expect to be at a police station, and decided to stand.

After awhile a young policewoman approached her.

"Ms. Putnam?"

"Yes."

"This way, please." She led Sara through a maze of hallways, up some stairs, down more halls and finally to an open area filled with desks. At the end of the area, she saw an office with frosted glass windows all around it.

"Here we are," the policewoman said, knocking on the door.

"Will someone take me back to the front? I'll never find my way out." Sara had visions of spending the rest of her life in this warren, not a pretty thought.

The woman nodded as a voice commanded, "Come in."

Opening the door, the policewoman waved Sara into the office. Detective Beecham sat behind a massive, old scarred desk, papers piled neatly into high stacks all around.

"Ah, Ms. Putnam," he said, standing up and holding out his hand.

Sara stepped forward to shake it as the policewoman left, closing the door behind her.

"Have a seat." Detective Beecham sat down.

Sara perched herself in the visitor's chair, an old wooden one with a carved seat.

"You have the pictures?"

Sara nodded, took them out of her purse, and stood up again to hand them to him.

142

He glanced through them. "These are good. Who took them?"

"Aunt Gladys," Sara told him as she sat back down.

"Who's she?"

Sara shrugged. "I'm not sure. Ira told me, 'Aunt Gladys,' when I asked him."

"Okay. Doesn't matter, right now, anyway. If I need to know later, I can find out. Now show me the one with the man you saw outside your house. This also has the one you believe might be your burglar?"

"Yes." Sara stood up again, feeling like a yo-yo, and came around the desk. Detective Beecham spread the pictures out, covering everything, including the stacks of paper. Sara pointed to the picture with the three young men.

"Okay. Which is which?"

Sara told him.

Detective Beecham grunted. "Anything else in any of these pictures strike you?"

"No. Nothing."

After giving them all another look, the detective gathered them up. "Do you know if these are all the ones taken? Or did they just give you certain ones? How many are there, anyway?" He began to count.

"I don't know." She waited for him to count all forty-four of them. "Ira didn't say."

"Do you mind if I have some copies made in our lab while you wait? It won't take more than half an hour." He picked up the phone and told someone to come to his office.

Sara's "okay" got drowned out by the Detective's talking on the phone.

A knock sounded on the door and an officer came in, picked up the photos and left with hardly a glace at Sara.

"So, Miss Putnam, tell me a little bit about yourself." Detective Beecham leaned back in his creaky chair and gave her his undivided attention.

Unnerved, Sara stuttered, "W-what do you w-want to know?"

He smiled. "Everything."

Sara wondered if this was an official part of his investigation. Was she a suspect? Don't be naive, she told herself. Of course I'm a suspect.

"Well," she said hesitantly, "I suppose you want to know about my adoption and everything."

143

He nodded encouragingly, picking up a pen and twisting it through his fingers.

"I've learned in the last two years that I was four when a neighbor brought me home one day and found my mother, um, dead. A suicide, they said. She drank and did pills."

"This was in New Jersey? What town?" Detective Beecham stopped twirling the pen and got ready to write.

"Caldwell."

He nodded. "I'll look up the old records. See what I can find out."

"Why?" Sara asked.

"Unnatural death. And her husband murdered years later. Probably no connection." He waved his hand.

"Oh," Sara said in a tiny voice, her mind spinning.

"So, anyway, the neighbor found your mother. Then what happened?"

"Yes, well. I don't remember any of this, you understand, but I'm told they placed me in a foster home, and Lucille and Marshall Putnam adopted me."

"An older child. Why was that, do you think?" He went back to twisting the pen around his fingers.

Sara twisted her mouth in response. "Lucille is a perfectionist. I think she didn't want a messy baby."

"You call her Lucille?"

Sara shook her head. "In my mind lots of times. She's not too terribly motherly."

"I see."

Sara leaned forward in her chair. "No, you don't," she said with some heat. "She did everything right. There is nothing at all to criticize in how she brought me up. So when I say she did it with no passion, no emotion, no angst, maybe you understand a little, but it's impossible to grasp the effect that had on me. Fortunately, Marsh seemed more human. But I've always felt that emotions were messy and unacceptable. So, I never questioned them about my birth parents. Until Marsh died. Then I got scared--a terrible emotion. What if something happened to Lucille, and I didn't know anything about my other parents? So, I set out to find out about them. Lucille was no help. As you know, she hid the letters from Howard until after *he* died."

"What I'm particularly interested in," Detective Beecham told her, "is how Lucille and Marshall Putnam adopted you. Did they know your birth parents by chance?"

"I don't know the details of that," Sara said slowly. "Maybe they did." Possibilities began swirling in her head. Suddenly, she wanted to talk to Lucille again. Up close and personal.

Detective Beecham made another note on his pad. "Lucille's maiden name?" he asked.

"What?" Sara was startled. "I don't remember."

"It wasn't Lyndquist?"

She gasped.

"Or what was your birth mother's maiden name? Any connection there?"

Sara's mind whirled. She stood up and began to walk around the small office. "You think they might have been related some way. I never thought of that. It would be too fantastic. But possible." She sank back down onto the hard wooden chair like a deflated balloon while Detective Beecham continued to make some notes on his pad.

CHAPTER 17

"I'll research some records myself, of course," Detective Beecham said. "But you might have better luck talking to your mother."

Sara nodded, still in a daze.

A knock sounded on the door, and the officer who had taken the photos to copy stuck his head inside. "They're done," he said.

Detective Beecham held out his hand. The officer came in, handed him all the pictures, and left without another word.

After separating the copies, Detective Beecham held hers out to her. As she stood up to get them, he said, "If Mrs. Putnam isn't forthcoming with you, I'll pay her a little visit myself."

As she took the pictures from him, Sara couldn't help smiling at the thought of the Detective and her mother sparring. "You can even be there," Detective Beecham said, returning her smile with a grin. "You might be able to help."

Sara stuffed the photos into her purse.

Detective Beecham stood up and held out his hand. "I'll be in touch. Call me if anything at all comes up. Be sure to lock up tight, both apartment and car." He let go of her hand and gave her a grave look.

"I will. Thank you. Can someone show me how to get to the front?" she asked, embarrassed a little.

"Of course." He came around the desk and followed her out of his office. "Ernie," he called to an officer. "Take this young lady downstairs, will you? Don't be embarrassed," he said to Sara. "No one can find their way out the first time. I spent a week in here when I came to work in this

146

building--slept at my desk."

Sara smiled at him, not believing a word. But he was nice.

Ernie took her to the front entry and left her to find a cab on her own. She glanced at her watch as she waited. Four-thirty. She wanted to go see Belinda for a few minutes. Finally she saw an unoccupied taxi, and it even came over when she raised her arm. She jumped inside and gave the driver Belinda's address.

At the Park Avenue apartment house, Sara left the cab and went inside. The bank of elevators faced her, shiny gold doors shut. She stood irresolutely in front of them, her heart pounding with its usual fear. The thought of the stairs was equally scary, though. She didn't want to see the spot where her father had been murdered, and it was a long walk up. Surely the elevators in this building would be maintained in perfect order. She remembered in vivid detail being stuck in the hospital elevator when she visited Marshall for the last time. It had taken them over two hours to get it going again, and she had ended up in a ball in the corner, shaking so hard with fright that they almost admitted her to the hospital for shock.

Come on, she told herself. Nothing to be scared of. What are the chances of getting stuck in an elevator twice in one lifetime? Depends on how often you use an elevator, her pessimistic voice answered.

At that moment, a woman of about Lucille's age entered the lobby with a small poodle in her arms, red leash dangling. She was the stereotypical New York matron out walking her dog on Park Avenue. She had bright blond hair in tight ringlets close to her head, wore an expensive red pantsuit, and jewelry had been placed everywhere she could put it, including on the dog. Sara blinked at the dazzle.

"Hello, dear," the woman said. She looked at the elevator buttons. "Are you going up?" she asked. The dog growled low in his throat at Sara.

Neither of the buttons was lit, Sara realized, and she quickly pushed the up one as she nodded at the woman, keeping her distance from the dog who snarled some more.

The elevator doors slid silently open, and they all got in, Sara trying not to hyperventilate.

"What floor, dear?" the woman asked when Sara made no move to punch the buttons.

"Twelve," Sara managed to say.

The woman pushed twelve and fourteen, and the elevator rose

soundlessly upwards. Then it almost immediately stopped. Sara gasped.

"We're stuck," she moaned, grabbing onto the brass railing on the elevator wall.

"Don't be silly, dear," the woman said as the doors opened to reveal another middle-aged woman holding a miniature Schnauzer. As she stepped inside, the dogs began growling and snapping at each other, both trying to wiggle from their owner's arms.

The doors closed again, and they began to rise.

"We're going up!" exclaimed the second woman who had bright red hair, wore an emerald pantsuit and gold shoes, and jewelry everywhere. Unlike the first women, who was rail-thin, the second one could stand to lose about fifteen pounds.

Sara and the first woman just looked at her. "I need to go down," she exclaimed and pushed the stop button.

The car lurched, and Sara grabbed the bar again, moaning some more. The dogs continued to wiggle and snarl while both women started to talk at once.

"What did you do? You can't do that," the first woman said.

"Mitsy needs to go bad," the redhead said. "I've got to get her out." She pushed the ground floor button.

Nothing happened.

Sara's head whirled as she gasped for breath. She began to imagine being stuck with these two women and their dogs for hours in this elevator. She looked at the panel frantically to see if there was a symbol for a phone. There was one, but no guarantee that it would work.

Both women looked at the button panel, frowning slightly.

The redhead pushed the ground floor button again. For a moment, nothing happened, then the car began to move.

The blond pushed the stop button.

Sara almost screamed. "What are you doing?" she managed to gasp.

"We were here first. This elevator is going up." She pushed twelve and fourteen again.

The redhead shoved the blond, trying to get in front of the panel. Both dogs began to bark in earnest.

Sara thought she was going crazy. "Get out of the way!" she screamed at the women, elbowing them aside to stand in front of the button panel. "Don't either of you touch that stop button again, or I'll take both dogs away from you and put them on the floor to fight it out. Do you understand me?"

The women looked at her as if she were a lunatic. Who's the crazy one here, Sara wondered? The elevator came to a stop once more, and Sara looked at the panel frantically. Bright red letters read, "12." The doors opened, and Sara stumbled out onto solid flooring. Flooring that would not move. She turned to watch the doors close on the two women fighting for control of the panel.

On shaking legs, Sara crossed the hall to Belinda's apartment and rang the bell. After what felt like a long time, Blinky opened the door. He looked at Sara as if he didn't recognize her. Then he seemed to collect himself.

"Hello, Sara. Come in. Belinda will be glad to see you."

As shook up as she was from her experience in the elevator, Sara couldn't help noticing how terrible Blinky looked. He'd aged ten years in the last week. His fine features looked droopy, emphasized by the dark bags under his eyes. His hair was disheveled, as if he'd been out in a fierce wind. Sara even noticed that his hands shook a bit as he closed and locked the door behind her.

"She's in the other room," he said, leading the way. "How are you?" He never forgot his manners.

"Okay," Sara answered as they came to the sitting room.

Belinda reclined on the couch, covered to her chin with a blue quilt. Her beauty was unmarked, and she actually looked a lot better than her husband. Her black hair shone in the lamplight, and her smile lit up her face when she saw Sara.

"What a wonderful surprise! Sara, come sit down."

Sara noticed she didn't take her hands out from under the quilt. As Sara sat in a chair opposite her friend, Blinky murmured something about what would she like to drink?

"She drinks Vodka Collins," Belinda told him. "I don't suppose I can have one?"

"Better not," Blinky told her. "How about some milk?"

"Ugh. Lemonade be all right?"

Blinky tried to smile at her. "That would be acceptable."

Belinda nodded. "Good."

"You look fine," Sara murmured as Blinky left the room.

Slowly, Belinda removed her hand from underneath the quilt. "I keep it hidden. Blinky looks stricken every time he catches sight of it."

Sara suppressed a gasp as she stared at her friend's fingers. All four on her right hand were black and blue and so swollen at the joints that Sara could see Belinda would not be able to remove her rings.

"How did that happen?" Sara asked.

Belinda quickly hid her hand beneath the cover again. "Charles grabbed my hand to help me out of the limo. He didn't grip that hard, really. I don't know why I got so bruised."

"What does Blinky say?" Sara asked.

"Blinky says that she's going to be fine," Blinky said as he entered the room again with drinks on a tray. "Some heavy-duty antibiotics should fix her right up."

Belinda smiled up at him. "He's already started me on some. Pills that could choke a horse." She took her left hand from beneath the cover to take the lemonade Blinky held out to her.

Sara looked at that hand, and although it was not black and blue, the knuckles were as swollen as those on her right one. Her glance slid to Blinky. It looked as if he was trying not to stare at Belinda's hand.

"So," Belinda said after taking a sip of her lemonade and setting it down on the coffee table. "Did you come all the way into the City just to see me?"

"I would have," Sara said, "but I also had to talk to Detective Beecham about the case. There have been some new developments."

"Tell me," Belinda demanded. Sara did, and when she finished, Belinda asked, "Did you tell him about the clown?"

"Oh, no, I forgot." Sara was furious at herself. "So much else happened . . ."

"Well, call him now and tell him," Belinda suggested. "Phone's over there." She nodded her head to a corner of the room instead of pointing with her misshapen hand.

Sara found the detective's card in her purse, got up and walked to the phone and dialed his number. She heard Blinky ask Belinda how she felt. Belinda nodded impatiently, as if now tired of so much attention. Detective Beecham wasn't in. She left a message for him to call her between eight and eleven when she figured she'd be home.

"Have you had dinner?" Belinda asked.

"No." Sara laughed a little as she sat back down. "A late lunch. This has been a strange day."

"Hilda left a roast in the oven, and some new potatoes. Eat with us before you go back home."

Sara looked at Blinky. "Please join us," he said formally. His eyes seemed to plead with her to stay. He probably didn't know what to say to Belinda any more, Sara realized. She would act as a buffer.

"I'd love to." Sara stood up. "What can I do to help?"

Blinky smiled at her as he also got up. "You stay there and rest," he told Belinda. "We'll call you when everything's set up."

"Yes, Master," Belinda said, but gave him a dazzling smile.

"Are you hungry?" he asked.

"A little," Belinda said, but not convincingly, at least to Sara's ears. Blinky seemed reassured, however. He and Sara walked to the kitchen where the smell of the meat roasting made Sara realize that she had been hungry all along.

Two places had already been set, Sara guessed by the housekeeper. Blinky grabbed another place mat and some silverware, handed them to Sara so she could put them out, as he took the roast out of the oven.

"If you'll get the potatoes, green beans, and the salad in the refrigerator, I'll carve the roast," Blinky said, reaching for an electric knife.

They worked in companionable silence except for the whine of the knife until all was ready. Sara followed Blinky to get Belinda and their dirty drink glasses. When Belinda tossed the quilt aside, Sara saw that she was dressed in khaki slacks and a red turtleneck.

Belinda stood up, but immediately fell back onto the couch with a soft, "Oh."

Blinky rushed to her. "What's wrong?"

"I . . . I don't know. Oh, my knees and ankles hurt."

"Let me see," Blinky said. He helped her lie back down on the couch, hunkered down beside her, and pulled up one pants leg.

Sara suppressed a gasp when she saw the almost purple, dime-size dots on the lower part of Belinda's leg and her swollen ankle and knee. She also saw a strange lump on the top of Belinda's foot. Sara looked at Blinky for an explanation.

He shook his head and pulled up the other pant leg.

"What are those spots?" Belinda asked in a trembling voice.

"Purpura," Blinky answered gruffly.

"What's that? What does it mean, Blinky?"

"There're not anything to really worry about. Just a symptom. They'll go away when we get you-better. I'm not sure." He looked totally defeated.

"You still don't know what's wrong?" Belinda asked.

He looked at Sara, then back at Belinda, and shook his head. He stood up and said, "I think we need to get you to the hospital."

Belinda's eyes widened with fear. "Won't the pills you gave me help?"

He sighed. "Belinda, I don't know what's wrong. We need other doctors, other specialists, to look at you."

"What other specialists? What do you *think* it is?" She held out her hand to him, and he grasped it. When she winced, he let go as if he held a hot poker.

"Sorry," he mumbled. "I'm not sure, but it looks like some arthritic disease. Perhaps caused by the implants."

She gave him a stricken look. "Oh, no, Blinky, I'm sorry." She began to cry softly, reaching for the quilt to cover her face.

"Belinda, don't. Please, don't be sorry for me, for God's sake. We need to get you well."

"Will you have to take them out?" she whispered.

He reached out his hand as if to grab hers, then remembered. He turned away from her, but Sara could see his anguished face, and her heart went out to him, as well as to Belinda. Blinky stumbled over to a chair and sat down, putting his face in his hands. Sara, weak-kneed, decided to sit, also.

After he'd collected himself somewhat, Blinky looked up and said, "I don't know the answer to your question, Lin. This isn't my field. We need to get you into the hospital so other specialists can come and look at you. That will be the quickest way to find some answers."

"Let me go put the food in the refrigerator," Sara said, "then I'll go with you. Take Belinda to the bedroom and let her tell you what to pack. She'll need a few things."

Both of them looked at her gratefully.

Belinda tried to stand up again, but her legs wouldn't hold her. Blinky picked her up in his arms and carried her to the bedroom while Sara went to the kitchen and put the food away.

They met in the front hall, Blinky carrying Belinda. Sara took the small overnight bag from him, and they left the apartment, Sara locking up. It seemed to take the elevator forever to come, and Sara prayed it would be empty, then chided herself for being afraid of an elevator ride when her friend was facing something much more frightening. When it arrived, it yawned emptily at them, and they rode downstairs in silence. Outside, Sara hailed a cab with little difficulty, and Blinky told the driver, "Presbyterian Hospital." Blinky sat up front so Belinda wouldn't be squeezed in the back.

"You all right?" Sara murmured in Belinda's ear.

Her friend's eyes were huge as they were caught shining in the street lights they passed. "I guess so. I'm just so surprised, you know?"

"Yeah," Sara said. She felt the same way. Surprised and scared, but she didn't say that to Belinda.

They arrived at the hospital, and as Sara watched Blinky pay the cabby and commandeer a wheelchair to take Belinda inside and get her admitted, she felt a deep sense of helplessness, of the inability to control events. Belinda remained silent in the wheelchair unless asked a direct question, and Sara could tell she was feeling the same sensation of powerlessness.

Soon Blinky was wheeling Belinda to another elevator, Sara following with the overnight bag. "What floor?" she asked Blinky as they waited.

"Third," he said.

Sara put the bag in Belinda's lap. "I'm going to walk up, okay? I've had enough elevators for one day. What's the room number?"

Blinky told her, and Sara waved at them as she found the stairwell and began climbing. Good for my figure, she told herself as she trudged upwards, not even out of breath when she arrived. Blinky and Belinda were getting off the elevator as Sara pushed open the stairwell door.

"Good timing," she said inanely. Next to a waiting room, they found 309 and went inside. Only one bed, so it was private, Sara noticed. Of course, Blinky was affiliated here.

"Can you help her get into a nightgown while I go see who's on duty tonight?" Blinky asked Sara.

"Of course," Sara replied.

"I'll send a nurse, too," Blinky said. He bent to kiss Belinda's cheek. "We'll be moving you to a VIP suite when one becomes available. Be back as soon as I can."

He seemed relieved, Sara thought as she watched him leave the room. Belinda sat perched on the bed.

"Let's get the turtleneck and bra off first," she said, reaching to pull up her shirt. But she had to let her hands fall uselessly to her sides. "Hurts too much. Can you do it?"

"Sure," Sara said, stepping up to the bed. "Let me get out your nightgown." She opened the suitcase and pulled out a beautiful rose-colored waltz length gown.

Belinda raised her arms, and Sara pulled off the turtleneck and unclasped her bra. Well, she thought, her breasts are gorgeous, but I guess this isn't a good time to compliment her on them. She slipped the nightgown over Belinda's arms and shoulders and adjusted it around her.

"Can you stand for a second holding on to me so we can pull down your pants?" Sara asked.

"I can try." Belinda eased herself off the bed, holding onto Sara's shoulder. Quickly, Sara tugged her pants down and let the gown fall over Belinda's legs. Belinda got back on the bed, and Sara removed slacks from Belinda's swollen ankles, then raised her legs up gently so that her friend could stretch out.

A nurse entered the room with a package and a clipboard. "Good evening, ladies," she said cheerfully, setting down the tray. "I need to ask you some questions and give you some supplies." She punctured a shrink-wrapped package, pulling the plastic away from the contents. She took out a bedpan, a vomit basin, pitcher, glass, disposable needle holder, and a box of tissues and arranged them around the room. "Here we go. Now, some of the questions I need to ask are a bit personal. Do you want your friend, to wait outside, or is she your sister?"

Belinda shook her head. "She's my friend, Sara Putnam. I don't mind if she stays. We've known each other forever, so she knows everything there is to know." She gave Sara a wan smile.

"All right, then." The nurse went down a list of questions about previous illnesses and operations, immunizations, allergies, and Belinda's family's health history.

Blinky came back into the room as the nurse asked her last question. He said hello to everyone, then announced, "Dr. Archer will be here momentarily. He's a dermatologist."

"A what?" Belinda asked.

"Dermatologist," Blinky answered. "Skin doctor. I know you've never had a blemish in your life, but I want him to look at those purpura."

The door opened, and a short man in green scrubs entered, a mask dangling around his neck. Partially bald, his blond hair was clipped short so that he almost looked totally hairless. He had full lips, soft brown eyes, and a stubby nose.

154

"Dr. Smithfield," he said, coming in and shaking hands with Blinky. "I hear your wife is not feeling too well." He turned and gave Belinda a piercing look, as if it were her own fault.

"Thank you for coming so quickly, Dr. Archer," Blinky said. "This is my wife, Belinda. And her friend, Sara Putnam."

Dr. Archer nodded at them and approached the bed. "A rash on your legs?" he asked. Then he looked at Sara. "Perhaps you could step outside while I examine the patient." He took some rubber gloves from his pocket and started to pull them on.

Sara glanced at Belinda. She looked really scared. Sara wanted to stay, but decided it would be best not to argue. "I'll be in the waiting room," she said and left.

The waiting room was small with two vinyl couches and three chairs of the same dull yellow material. The walls were painted a pale blue, and tattered magazines lay on the three tables. Fluorescent lights glared overhead, but the decorator had also bought some ugly white stone table lamps and some inoffensive landscapes to adorn the walls. Sara plopped herself down wearily into one of the chairs and looked at her watch. Eight-forty.

Her stomach growled, startling her. With all the excitement, she'd forgotten her hunger. She shrugged and picked up a magazine. Nothing she could do about it right now. She'd barely read the Table of Contents when she saw Dr. Archer and Blinky come out of Belinda's room. They stood in the hallway and talked in low tones.

Dr. Archer left, and Blinky walked into the waiting room and sank down onto the chair next to Sara.

"You might as well go home," he said. "Until we learn more, Belinda will be restricted on visitors."

"What did Dr. Archer say it was?"

"He doesn't know. Never seen anything like it before. He's afraid she may be septic, so everyone going into her room will have to put on protective clothing, and visitors will be limited to hospital personnel and family."

"What do you mean, septic?" Sara asked.

"Contagious, with a raging infection throughout her system. We'll give her antibiotics I.V. and watch her carefully. Call in other specialists. Dr. Resendez, a rheumatologist, will be here soon. We'll see what he has to say.

We have to protect both her and everyone else who comes in contact with her." He looked at Sara bleakly. "This isn't going to be easy to figure out. Whatever it is, it's no common disease. God, Sara, I'm so afraid it has something to do with the implants. But it might not. I just don't know."

Sara put her hand on his arm. "Wait until you find out more before you go blaming yourself, Blinky. After all, you couldn't know. And she's the one who made the decision to have them."

Blinky ran his hand through his hair, mussing it up even more than it already was. "Don't you see? I don't know what I'll do if it's the implants. She'll have to have them removed. She might be horribly disfigured. Worse than from a mastectomy. Worse than you or she can imagine."

He stood up. "First we have to figure out what to do about her symptoms right now." He began to pace the small room. "Septic. I wanted to die when he said that. Not that I hadn't been thinking it already, you understand."

Sara got up, too, and grabbed his arm. "You have to get control of yourself, Blinky. She needs you. Stop thinking of all the bad things it could be. Maybe it is just an infection and the antibiotics will take care of it. Isn't that the theory you're going on right now?"

He stopped pacing and nodded at her. "You're right. If it's an infection, it has nothing to do with the implants. They would cause an autoimmune response." At Sara's puzzled look, he said, "That's where the body's immune system attacks itself and causes different diseases. Like arthritis."

"Oh," Sara said. "But if it's an infection, the implants would have nothing to do with it."

"Right. Maybe we should increase the antibiotics." He looked around as if the answer were somewhere in the room.

A man in a gray suit approached them and held out his hand to Blinky. "Dr. Smithfield?"

Blinky nodded.

"I'm Dr. Andros Resendez. I understand you have a very sick wife. I've come to take a look. What room is she in?"

The two doctors left Sara in the waiting room. She sat back down in the chair and let the tears come, feeling more helpless than ever.

CHAPTER 18

Belinda punched her pillow feebly when Blinky and that awful skin doctor left the room. Septic! As in septic tank. It sounded so gross. She felt unclean, contaminated, by the way he'd used gloves to examine her. She could still smell the latex odor inside her nose.

He'd talked to Blinky, not to her. As if she were a piece of meat on a slab. Meat that had gone bad three days ago.

A brisk knock sounded on the door, then it swung open. A woman entered, wrapped in green pants, shirt, cap and a mask. She wore gloves, too. Only her brown eyes twinkled at Belinda.

"Trick or treat," she said cheerfully. "And boy, do I have a treat for you. Antibiotics I.V." She held up a bag of clear liquid for Belinda to see.

"How exciting," Belinda said. "Do I get a choice of flavors?"

"'Fraid not. The pharmacist isn't that creative." She came over to the I.V. pole standing next to the bed and hung the bag.

"You do look as if you're from outer space, you know," Belinda told her.

"I know. I don't get to dress up like this often. By the way, I'm your private nurse. Dr. Smithfield asked for me. They don't want too many people coming in."

"Because I might give them something." Belinda scowled.

"Well, but for your own protection, too. You don't need to be exposed to anything else." The nurse patted her arm with her gloved hand. Somehow it wasn't offensive the way the doctor had been.

Belinda looked at her name tag. Jenny Fowler. She seemed nice.

"I'm going to have to prick you now," Jenny said. "Let me see the top of your hand."

Belinda pulled her right hand, the one nearest the I.V. pole, out from under the covers.

Jenny's eyes widened. "Oh, you poor dear. Does that hurt?"

"Not too bad," Belinda said.

"Let me see the other one. I really don't want to use your right."

Belinda showed her her left hand, and Jenny nodded. She walked the I.V. pole around to the other side of the bed. "Let's use that one," she said, taking Belinda's hand gently into her own. She found the vein without any trouble and soon had Belinda hooked up. Jenny was adjusting the drip when Blinky entered the room.

He had suited up, also. All she could see were his eyes and the two frown lines between his brows. Her heart ached for him. He was so worried. She could feel his sense of helplessness, his utter confusion. He wasn't used to uncertainty. Everything had always been smooth and easy for Bancroft A. Smithfield II, M.D. Until now.

He nodded at the nurse, then came over to the bed. He didn't touch her. Where could he touch her? Both hands were unavailable, and he couldn't kiss her through the mask.

"Did the aliens treat you well, I hope?" Belinda asked.

Smile lines crinkled at the corners of his eyes. "Admirably. They examined me thoroughly, decided I wasn't good enough for them, and tossed me from their spaceship."

Jenny checked supplies around the room, nodded her head approvingly, then sat down in a visitor's chair.

"You met Jenny, I see," Blinky remarked as he sat down next to her. "How do you feel?"

"Is that a question from the doctor or from the husband?" Belinda asked.

He thought for a moment. "Who would get the more honest answer?"

Belinda smiled ruefully. "The doctor."

"I thought so." He stood up and walked to the side of the bed. "As your doctor, I want to know how you feel."

"Mainly tired," Belinda admitted. "My joints hurt a bit."

"A bit? Or a lot, Belinda? Be honest."

"A lot. They seem to get worse by the hour."

Blinky nodded and turned away from her.

"I think," Belinda said, "that you need to stop being my doctor and just be my husband." She could hear the strain in her own voice. "Where's Sara, by the way?"

It took him a moment to turn around. "I sent her home. For now, only medical personnel and family can see you."

"But she is my family, here, anyway," Belinda protested. "Everyone else is in Florida."

"I know that. You don't want her exposed any more than she's already been, Belinda. I'd hesitate to let your family in, either."

"Oh." The sound escaped her lips in a sigh. "How long, Blinky? How long will this go on?"

He started to run his fingers through his hair. When they encountered the cap, he put his arm down to his side. He looked defeated. "I don't know, Lin. Shouldn't be more than a few days. Dr. Resendez is looking through your chart right now and should be here any minute."

"What kind of doctor is he?"

"Rheumatologist. He knows about arthritis. Your symptoms are clearly arthritic."

"Clearly? You mean you know what it is?"

"No. There are over a hundred arthritic diseases. Some extremely rare. He might know, though."

"Might? Blinky! I don't understand. I thought doctors could always at least tell you what you had!"

Blinky looked away from her and went to sit down again, his shoulders slumped. "Not always, Belinda. It could take awhile."

Belinda turned her head, feeling the tears slide down her cheeks. This couldn't be happening to her. She saw the fluid dripping slowly through the tube. Everything seemed to hurt. She wanted to ask him about her chances of dying, but she couldn't do it. Would he even know since he didn't know what she had? A feeling of dread came over her, suffocating her. She felt her lungs gasping for breath from the fright. She was aware of every part of her body as never before. Her ankles ached, and her knees. Her bruised hand felt a different kind of pain, more sharp, and the I.V. site prickled. Her throat hurt slightly, and there was a pressure around her eyes and sinuses as if from unshed tears. She wanted to go home. She wanted this to be over.

Jenny got up and wiped away Belinda's tears just as a short knock sounded on the door. It opened to show a man in protective wear standing there.

"Mrs. Smithfield?" he asked.

"Yes," Belinda answered.

He stepped inside, the door closing automatically behind him. "I'm Dr. Resendez. How are you feeling?" He approached the bed, his shoes squeaking slightly on the tile floor.

Belinda sighed. "Okay."

"Really?"

She could tell he smiled because of the crinkles around his eyes.

"Then why are you here?" he asked.

She smiled back at him tremulously. "I came because I like to see people dressed up in funny costumes. It's a hobby of mine."

He laughed out loud. Touching her hand with the I.V. lightly, he looked into her eyes. He walked around to the other side of the bed and looked closely at her right hand. The smile went away. "That hurt?"

She nodded.

"I understand you have some purpura and some swelling of knees and ankles. Hello, Jenny, Bancroft."

Jenny and Blinky murmured, "Hello." Jenny stepped away from the bed and stood in the corner of the room, her hands clasped in front of her.

"May I see your legs?" Dr. Resendez asked.

Belinda pushed the sheet down. Her gown had ridden up slightly so that her knees were in plain view. He touched one lightly, then examined both ankles. When he finished, he slowly pulled the sheet back up.

He took a chair, placed it close to the bed, and sat down. Taking out pen and notebook, he said, "Please tell me everything, starting as soon as you noticed any symptoms."

Belinda tried to remember exactly when they did start. She wasn't even sure of the month. She told him as best as she could.

When she finished, the doctor snapped his notebook shut, put away his pen and sighed. "I'm afraid I don't have any quick answers for you. There are several possibilities." He stood up. "We'll know more after all the blood work is done. I'll order that right away. I'll be back tomorrow morning after I get some preliminary reports."

"What do you think it might be?" Belinda pleaded, her voice strained.

He shook his head. "Don't want to speculate just yet." He patted her forearm. "Tomorrow."

He said a general, "Goodbye," then left, the door whooshing after him.

Blinky stood up, stretched. "Sorry, darling," he said, coming over to the bed. "Listen, I'm going to leave now. You need to rest." He leaned down and whispered, "I'll miss you."

Tears welled again. She took a deep breath. They'd never slept apart since their marriage. A year. They'd had a year. Was that all they'd get? A sudden image of a computer screen popped into her head. Next to her name, it said, "DECEASED."

She caught her breath.

"Are you in pain?" Blinky asked. "I can't prescribe anything until we have a diagnosis. It might screw up the blood work."

"I'll be all right. Go on home." She had to think of something else, something besides this hospital room, her aching joints, her panic. Suddenly, she wanted him to leave. He was suffocating her with his concern. She chided herself for being unfair.

He touched her cheek lingeringly before he turned and left. For a moment, the room remained silent. Another knock came on the door, and a tech entered with a tray and took five vials of blood from her. She gritted her teeth, thinking he'd never finish.

When he left, Jenny asked, "Can I help you to the toilet?"

With Jenny's help, she managed to hobble to the bathroom, dragging the I.V. pole behind her like some alien monster.

When she'd gotten settled back in bed, Jenny asked, "Can I get you a sleeping pill, Mrs. Smithfield?"

Belinda shook her head. "Call me Belinda. It's easier. I'd rather not use a pill."

"Let me know if you change your mind," Jenny said. She straightened the bedcovers, then went and sat down.

* * * * *

The sound of voices woke Belinda the next morning. She had no idea what time it was because the heavy drapes remained drawn. She looked around the room and saw two protective-suited people standing near the door.

Jenny noticed she was awake and approached the bed. "Good morning. This is Mrs. Hawkes. She'll be taking care of you during the daytime. Six to six. I'll be back this evening."

Belinda nodded.

"How are you, dear?" Mrs. Hawkes asked. She had sharp brown eyes, and by the wrinkles in her forehead, Belinda decided she was considerably older than Jenny.

"Okay," Belinda answered. "Thirsty."

"I'll see you later," Jenny said, her voice cheerful.

Mrs. Hawkes poured some water from the pitcher into a glass. She got out the bent straw and brought the drink to Belinda's lips.

Belinda sipped gratefully. When she finished, she noticed she needed to use the bathroom again.

As Mrs. Hawkes helped her to the toilet, Belinda realized that her feet and knees felt worse. She wondered why the drip antibiotics weren't helping.

Someone delivered a breakfast tray. Mrs. Hawkes took it at the door, brought it over to the bedside tray and opened everything up for Belinda.

She started to eat, her hand clumsy with its swollen fingers, but after a few bites, her appetite left her. She drank the juice and coffee, then pushed the tray aside.

Mrs. Hawkes sat in a corner reading a magazine. She didn't look up until a knock sounded on the door. Another suited stranger stepped inside. Belinda realized she probably wouldn't recognize any of these people when they were allowed to come in wearing regular clothes.

By his height and bushy eyebrows, Belinda assumed the person now approaching her bed was male. His low, grumbling voice confirmed it.

"Mrs. Smithfield? I'm Dr. Cassandra. I understand you're not feeling too well."

Belinda nodded. She was tired of talking about it. He had her chart, and he began reading through it. "Hmm," he said. "Interesting. You have a sore throat? Let me see." He pulled a tongue depressor out of his pocket and unwrapped it, tossing the wrapper towards the trash. He missed but didn't bother to pick it up. He asked her to say, "Ah," then checked her ears, pulled down her lower lids and looked into her eyes. "You have a slight nasal drip, some sinus congestion. Nothing serious there."

"What about the rest?" Belinda asked. "The rash, swollen joints?"

"Rash? Oh, you mean the purpura. Haven't a clue." He shook his head and gathered up her chart. "Sorry. Not in my field. Some other doctors will be visiting you soon." He nodded to the nurse and left.

"Well," Belinda objected, "he was real helpful."

Mrs. Hawkes didn't say anything as she bent down to put the tongue depressor wrapper into the trash. She was straightening up the bed tray when another knock came on the door, and it swung open.

"Mrs. Smithfield?" A person stood in the doorway peering at her over his or her mask.

"Yes," Belinda said.

"I'm Dr. Phillips. Understand you are not feeling too well."

Belinda nodded, wondering why this person didn't come in and close the door.

"Could I see one of your legs?" Dr. Phillips asked.

Belinda pushed the sheet down. The doctor nodded. "Interesting," he said. "Thank you." The door whooshed behind him, and Mrs. Hawkes helped Belinda pull the sheet back up.

"Who was he?" Belinda asked, irritated. "Why wouldn't he even come into the room?"

Mrs. Hawkes shrugged and turned away. "Dr. Phillips is an orthopedist. He probably didn't think what you had is in his line, and he didn't want to get too near you in case you're contagious."

"What?" Belinda spit out. She felt rage racing through her body. "He's a doctor!"

"Orthopedics don't treat cases like yours. Probably Dr. Smithfield asked him, as a courtesy, to have a look at you. Just to cover all bases."

Through the hazy red rage, Belinda was aware that Mrs. Hawkes wasn't too happy about defending Dr. Phillips. After all, Belinda thought, she's here touching me all day long. Sudden gratitude came over her, replacing her wrath.

"Thank you, Mrs. Hawkes."

Belinda saw the surprise in the woman's eyes. She nodded, then the corners of her eyes crinkled. She patted Belinda's arm. "You're welcome. Can I get you anything? Some juice, perhaps?"

"That would be nice," Belinda said.

Mrs. Hawkes used the call button to ask someone to bring some juice, then she sat down in her chair. Belinda didn't realize she'd been dozing until a sharp knock on the door woke her with a start.

"Room service," a cheerful voice announced. Another suited figure entered with two containers of juice. "Pick your poison. Apple or grape?"

"Dr. Quillen?" Mrs. Hawkes asked, standing up and quickly going over

163

to him to take the juice.

"The same. I understand we have a lady here who has confounded all the experts, and I'm been asked to shed some light." He approached the bed and studied Belinda for a moment. "Not feeling too perky, are we?"

Belinda smiled and shook her head.

He took her left hand, careful to avoid the I.V. needle. "That should help." He gestured towards the drip with his other hand. He let go of her hand in order to pull up a visitor's chair. Perched on the edge, he said, "Tell me about it."

Belinda sighed. "I need to make a recording of this."

"No. No, it's better to keep telling it. You might remember something important that you didn't mention before. Start at the beginning, go slowly, and tell the good doctor everything you remember."

Belinda recounted all her symptoms. As she was talking, Blinky came in. The two doctors greeted each other, then Dr. Quillen indicated that Belinda should continue.

When she was finished, Dr. Quillen said, "Now, I understand Dr. Visa here did some surgery on you about two years ago."

"Dr. Visa?" Belinda asked, looking at Blinky.

"Short for plastic surgeon," Dr. Quillen said. She could tell he was smiling.

Belinda didn't know how to react. She said the first thing that came to mind. "What kind of doctor are you?"

The smile disappeared. "Internal medicine. I specialize in diagnosing. We do have a tough case here. But you already know that. Tell me about your surgery."

"It was routine," Blinky said. "Nothing unusual happened. Everything went smoothly, and she had a normal recovery."

"No problems with the implants? You didn't have to throw away two or three that leaked before you found one that didn't?"

Blinky shook his head.

"Did they become encapsulated? Did you have to pound on the young lady's chest?"

"No, Hank. Everything was routine, I tell you."

"Okay." Dr. Quillen turned back to Belinda.

"Now, you tell me. How did it seem to you?"

Belinda looked at Blinky but couldn't read his expression under the mask. "I . . . I thought everything went fine," she said. "Just the way Blinky told me it would."

"After you started these symptoms? What did Dr. Visa do then?"

"He sent me to see Dr. Anderson, our family doctor. He thought it was the flu, told me to rest, drink plenty of fluids and come back in two weeks if I wasn't better."

"You went back to see him?"

Belinda nodded.

"Then what did he do?"

"Well, I felt somewhat better then. He did some blood work, didn't find anything, and told me sometimes it took awhile to get over the flu."

"Hmm. Okay. Now, did you see any other doctors?"

Belinda looked at Blinky and blushed.

Dr. Quillen looked back and forth at the two of them. "Perhaps you'd rather your husband step outside a minute."

"No. No, that's all right. I'm sorry, Blinky." She couldn't help the tears, and she rubbed at them angrily with her bruised, swollen fingers.

Blinky took a step towards her, but made no move to touch her. "It's all right, Belinda. Just tell us what happened."

"I . . . I went to see someone else. Another plastic surgeon. Dr. Alverado. Do you know him?"

The other two doctors nodded. "He's well-respected," Dr. Quillen said. "What did he tell you?"

"He . . . he told me the implants were . . . were making me sick. He said I should have them removed."

"Oh, God," Blinky said, stumbling backwards as if hit in the chest. He found the chair behind his back with his hands and sat down.

Belinda began to cry harder. "I'm . . . I'm s . . . sorry, Blinky. I was scared. I didn't know what to do!"

"It's all right," Dr. Quillen said. "What you did was natural, normal. Anyway, I think Dr. Alverado was wrong."

"What?" Belinda and Blinky said at the same time.

Dr. Quillen nodded. "I'm not sure what you have as yet, but I'm pretty sure it has nothing to do with the implants. From what I've read and the few patients I've seen with leaking implants, the symptoms start at the chest and shoulders, near the implants. Makes sense, doesn't it?"

Belinda nodded, wide-eyed.

"Okay, now. You are having problems mainly with your hands and feet, and your knees. Far away from the implants. So, I think we're dealing with a different issue here. Now, who have you seen so far?" He listed the five doctors. "That's all? I mean since you were admitted here. And me."

Belinda nodded and looked at Blinky. She hated the mask--she couldn't tell what he was thinking. Was he mad at her, relieved?

"Okay," Dr. Quillen continued. "We need to get every other specialist we can think of in here. Someone must have seen a case like this before somewhere."

"So," Belinda sighed. "You don't know what it is, either."

He shook his head. "I've thought of some possibilities, but it's too early to say." His tone was regretful. "Let's continue with the drip antibiotics and see what happens." He stood up and turned to Blinky. "If I think of anyone you haven't listed to see her, I'll let you know." He patted Belinda on the upper arm. "Hang tough, young lady. It shouldn't be much longer before we have some answers. Want to step out into the hall with me, Bancroft? I think we should consider a subclavian, and a few other things. See you later, Belinda. Hang in there."

The two doctors left, and Belinda lay still, thinking. Despite Dr. Quillan's reassurances, a feeling of hopelessness overcame her again. What if they never did find out what she had? She felt that she was getting worse, not better. Every day for the past week or so, she'd gotten a new symptom. She sensed that Blinky was surprised that the antibiotics hadn't made any improvement. If they couldn't help her, what could?

Mrs. Hawks came over to the bedside. "Can I get you anything, dear?"

A new body, Belinda almost said. But she already had that. New breasts, anyway. Dr. Quillen said they weren't the problem. At least she had that to be grateful for. If he was right. It seemed as if several doctors had been wrong already. He'd sounded so positive. They all did. Positive they'd have the answer any second. Meanwhile, here she lay. She felt so tired and helpless. So tired.

CHAPTER 19

Sara dragged herself out of bed Monday morning, her mind feeling like mush. As she drove to work, Eileen had to tell her to watch out twice-- once for a red light, and again for an oncoming car.

"Sorry," Sara said automatically each time.

"What's wrong with you?" Eileen asked, irritation in her tone.

"I'm sorry," Sara said again, looking over at Eileen.

"Look out!" Eileen screeched.

Sara turned the wheel just in time to avoid hitting a parked car.

"Jeez Louise," Eileen exclaimed. "You want me to drive?"

"No, no, I promise to pay more attention," Sara mumbled, forcing herself to watch the road, to concentrate.

"What's the matter?" Eileen demanded again.

"It's Belinda. She's really sick--they admitted her last night." Sara told Eileen all that had happened the evening before. She hadn't had a chance when she'd gotten home. Eileen had already been in bed.

"You can't even go visit her?" Eileen asked. "That's awful. I'm really sorry, Sara."

"Yeah," Sara said. "Me, too. Not only that, I have to go see my mother with some questions Detective Beecham brought up."

"Like what?" Eileen asked.

"Like did my mother know Howard Lyndquist personally? Or perhaps, was she related to him?"

"Wow! Do you think that's possible?"

"Maybe." Sara sighed. "Maybe not. But he thought it odd that Lucille adopted me as an older child and that she maybe knew who my parents

were. A bit unusual. If I can't find out anything, he's going to talk to her.
I'd like to see that! Oh, and he's also going to search my birth and adoption
records."

"Wow," Eileen said again. "Sara! Here we are! Gee, you almost missed
the entrance."

"Sorry. How about you drive home?"

"Sounds like a great idea to me."

Sara found a parking spot, and they walked inside. "See you at lunch,"
she said and wandered off to her office area.

Maurice was already there. As usual, he looked at his watch when he
saw her. Sara sat down at her desk and tried to concentrate on work.
Helen came in, then she and Maurice left to give a training session in
another part of the building.

Sara didn't think much of it when Bernie approached, his big ears pink
around the edges.

"Hi," he greeted her, then parked his butt on the edge of her desk.

He sat too close for her comfort level, but she said, "Hi," back.

"How about having lunch with me?" he asked, grinning at her.

"I'm sorry, I already have plans," she told him, feeling the heat rise to
her face.

"Come on, we haven't had a chance to talk since you transferred out of
Accounting."

"Really, Bernie, I can't. I have a lot of work here, if you don't mind."

"But I do mind," he said, leaning close to her. "Come on, have lunch
with me today. I promise it will be worth your while."

"What do you mean?" she asked, wanting to back away from him, but
her chair was already pushed as far as possible against the other section of
her desk.

"Look, I know you're probably just going to eat with Eileen and the
girls," he whispered. "I can show you a better time than that. We'll even go
out to a restaurant instead of eating in that awful cafeteria."

What don't you understand about NO, Sara wondered. Maybe she hadn't
been firm enough.

"Sorry, Bernie. Not today," she said.

"Tomorrow then," he said in a gotcha tone. "I'll be here at noon to
take you downstairs." He leaned back and looked at her. "I really need to
talk to you."

Sara sighed. Better to get it over with. "Okay, Bernie, you win. We'll do it today."

He grinned at her. "That's my girl."

Sara winced.

He got off her desk and waved. "See you at noon."

"Yeah," Sara muttered, "whatever."

* * * * *

Noon came too soon. Sara looked up to see Bernie standing in front of her. She'd called Eileen and told her not to expect her in the cafeteria. As they walked out together, Sara hoped she wouldn't see anyone she knew. But there was JoAnne coming towards them.

Sara could see the surprise and speculation on her face. They all greeted each other, then JoAnne asked, "You guys going out for lunch?" She looked pointedly at Sara's purse.

"Yes, we are," Bernie said. He smiled at JoAnne. "If you'll excuse us, we need to hurry in order to get a good table."

"Of course," JoAnne said. She raised an eyebrow at Sara. "Have a good time."

Bernie took Sara's hand, much to her humiliation. She tried to pull away, but he held on tight. He walked her briskly out the door and over to his Mercedes. He even held the passenger door open for her.

"You like Italian?" he asked as he drove out of the parking lot.

"Yes," Sara said.

"Good." He didn't say anything else until they pulled up in front of a restaurant Sara had never been to before, even though it was only a couple of blocks from the office. Maybe it was new.

After greeting Bernie by name, the headwaiter showed them to a corner table. "Is this all right, sir?"

"Fine, fine," Bernie said and slipped him a bill.

Sara was surprised at how suavely he did it.

The headwaiter seated Sara, righted some glasses and poured water. "Your waiter will be here presently," he said, and left.

Sara looked around. Red flocked wallpaper, gold carpet, white linen tablecloths and napkins. Very nice, she thought.

"I recommend the spinach ravioli," Bernie said. "Or, if you don't like spinach, the cheese manicotti with Alfredo sauce."

169

Sara nodded but looked at the large red menu with a tassel on the bottom. She decided on the ravioli so she wouldn't have to have a long conversation about why she chose something else. She knew that's what would happen if she did.

After ordering, Bernie tried to entertain her with a couple of jokes. She laughed politely. Then he told an off-color one. After he gave the punch line, she looked at him with a straight face and lied, "I don't get it."

Just then, the waiter brought their lunch, so Bernie couldn't respond. Sara began to eat, avoiding eye contact with the horrible little man.

"Here's the deal," Bernie said, taking a sip of wine. "I want you to be one of the first to know, I've been promoted to V.P. of Accounting." Under the table, his leg pressed against hers while he looked into her eyes. Deeply, she supposed. Did getting promoted turn him on?

Sara frowned and moved her leg away from his. Then she smiled brightly at him. "Congratulations. How exciting." She realized her voice sounded flat.

He nodded as if she'd been sincere. "I get a corner office and everything."

Her smile began to hurt her face. She took a sip of wine.

"Since Roger is taking Gretchen with him, I also get to pick my secretary." He gave her a significant look.

"Really?" She played with the wine glass, turning it around and around in her fingers nervously.

"I'll bet you can't guess who's my first choice." He grinned at her. She felt as if his protruding teeth were ready to tear at her flesh.

"Leslie?" she asked. After all, she was departmental secretary.

Bernie shook his head. "Guess again." His leg pressed against hers again.

Sara shuddered and shook her head.

Bernie raised his glass as if to toast her. "Why, you, Sara, of course."

"Why me?" she squeaked.

His leg pressed harder. "I think you know why. You play your cards right, and the job is yours."

Play her cards right? She wanted to throw her wine in his face and leave. But she sat rooted to her chair, thoughts swirling. She needed her job. He was related, if only by marriage, to the owners. What would the consequences be if she turned him down? Could he, would he, get her fired? A sick feeling invaded her stomach, and she felt the ravioli rising.

She swallowed hard. If only she had that inheritance. She wouldn't be sitting here at the mercy of this creep.

"So, what do you say, Sara?" Bernie interrupted her thoughts.

"I . . . I don't know what to say. I'm flattered, of course. But I like Training and Development. Really." Her voice sounded desperate, even to herself.

Bernie's grin faded. "But you'll take the job," he said flatly.

No, Sara thought, I won't be pushed like this. "What do I have to do to get it, Bernie? What happens if I refuse?"

He looked flustered. Then mad. "You're not that naive. Come on, Sara."

"Whatever do you mean?" She widened her eyes at him, then patted her lips with her napkin.

He grabbed her hand. "I want you, Sara. I want you as my secretary so I can see you every day. Is that so awful?"

She jerked her hand away, knocking over her half-full wine glass. A red stain marred the white tablecloth.

Bernie swore and waved for the waiter. When his head was turned, Sara knocked his glass over, making sure the red liquid landed in his lap.

"Oops, clumsy me. So sorry," she said.

Bernie jumped up, swore some more, and mopped his lap with a napkin. The waiter and headwaiter came over, both solicitous. Sara tried not to grin.

"Sir, if you'll come to the men's room," the headwaiter said, "we'll use some club soda to get that stain out."

Bernie followed the man through the restaurant, holding the napkin in front of the stain.

Sara couldn't help giggling as she left the building. It was such a nice day, she decided to walk back to the office.

Fortunately, Maurice wasn't there to look at his watch when she came in fifteen minutes late. She settled herself at her computer and began to type a new training module from Helen's handwritten scrawl. Around two, she answered the phone.

"Where'd you go?" Bernie demanded.

"I . . . I needed to get back to work. I was late as it was."

"When you're out with me, you don't have to worry about the time."

Panic started in her stomach. She felt her face flush, and her hands

171

began to shake. He wasn't going to give up. He was as relentless as a pit bull.

"We'll try again tomorrow," Bernie said. "I'll come by your desk at noon." He hung up.

Sara pulled the receiver away from her ear and stared at it a moment before setting it thoughtfully back in its cradle. She felt as if the walls were closing in on her. She forced herself to get back to her typing.

* * * * *

That evening Sara called Lucille and asked if she could come by the house. They set the time for seven-thirty.

As Sara pulled into the driveway, she remembered the last time she'd been here. She'd thought she had all the answers then. Now she had more questions than ever.

When Sara entered through the back door, she found Lucille in the kitchen fixing a tray of hot cocoa and banana bread.

"There you are!" Lucille looked at the clock. Just like Maurice, Sara thought.

"Hi," Sara said. "Let me help you with that." She followed her mother to the sunroom and set the tray on the coffee table.

"How are things?" Lucille asked as they settled themselves.

"Not too good," Sara answered. She told her mother about Belinda.

When she finished, Lucille said, "That's terrible. I feel for her and Bancroft, and for you, Sara. I know how close the two of you are."

Sara held back tears at her mother's words. She ached to be with Belinda right now. But Blinky said he'd call her with any news, and he wouldn't let them see each other until the quarantine was lifted.

For some reason, she told Lucille about Bernie. When she got to the part about spilling the wine, her mother began laughing. "That's the way you should handle him," she said, still laughing. "Keep on being a klutz. Embarrass him. Soon he'll be the one who doesn't want to be around you."

Sara looked at Lucille in amazement. What a great idea! Why hadn't she thought of it? Practical Lucille. Suddenly she wondered if Lucille was lonely. Marsh had been gone for two years now. But Lucille never talked about such things.

"Thank you," Sara said.

Lucille smiled at her. "Come upstairs. I want to show you the skirt I'm

172

making for the Autumn Festival."

They went upstairs to Sara's old bedroom, now the sewing room. Sara thought it might be a good place to ask her mother some questions about her adoption.

Sara admired the material with a leaf print in autumn tones. "Very pretty," she told Lucille.

Her mother sat down in the sewing chair, and Sara slouched onto the old sofa that used to be in the living room.

"You knew my mother, didn't you?" Sara asked abruptly, hoping to shock Lucille into a confession. Confession of what, she didn't know.

"What makes you think that?" As always, Lucille's expression didn't give anything away.

"I'm not the only one who thinks so. I had to explain to a detective at the N.Y. police department about being Howard Lyndquist's daughter. He thought you might be more than just my adoptive mother."

"For example?" Lucille asked, still giving nothing away.

"My aunt? Howard's sister, maybe? Even just a friend or neighbor. He's going to search the records."

"Really?" Lucille said, her voice faint.

"He's going to find something, isn't he?" Sara asked, her heart thumping.

Lucille stared at the skirt, eyes unfocused. She fingered the material. "I don't know."

"There's something you haven't told me. I know there is!" Sara sat up straight on the sagging sofa and leaned towards Lucille. "Please, Mom. I need to know. Please tell me."

Abruptly, Lucille stood up, her movements jerky. She'd gone pale and wouldn't look at Sara. "I can't . . . ."

Sara stood up and took Lucille's arm, gripping it hard. "You must. I have to know!"

Lucille looked into Sara's pleading eyes, then drooped a little. "All right." She shook off Sara's hand and collapsed onto the couch. "Gloria, your mother, was my sister."

She began to cry, horrible wracking sobs that tore at Sara. She sat down next to Lucille and put her arms around her. "Tell me," she whispered. "You'll feel better if you tell me."

While Sara held her and patted her back. Lucille's sobbing diminished and finally stopped. Sara got up to get her a box of tissues. "You're my aunt, as well as the mother who raised me," Sara said with awe. "That's wonderful. You can tell me all kinds of family history."

Lucille blotted her eyes, then looked at Sara with gratitude. "You don't hate me, then?"

Sara shook her head. "You had reasons. I know you had reasons not to tell me. But I'm an adult now, Mom." She almost said she had a right to know, but bit it back. Instead, she said, "I'd like to know everything."

Lucille dabbed at her eyes some more and blew her nose. "It's not a nice story, Sara. That's why I've kept it from you." She stood up to throw the tissues away. "Howard, your natural father, was a miserable excuse for a man. How I hated him." She sank back down onto the couch.

Unbidden, the thought came to Sara, *Enough to kill him?* Then she remembered Ira talking about him, about how wonderful he was. Where was the truth?

"What did he do?" Sara asked.

"He drove Gloria to suicide."

Sara gasped. "How?"

Lucille's mouth compressed into two straight lines of disapproval. "He was arrogant, self-centered and demanding. Everything had to be done his way, and at first Gloria gave into his every whim. She was so in love with him. Then they had you." Lucille's face softened as she looked at Sara.

"But," she continued, "Howard's demands didn't diminish. If anything, they got worse. Gloria could hardly make it through the day. She was exhausted. Her doctor gave her some pills to pep her up. Then she had trouble sleeping, so she'd have a drink or two before bed. You were a sweet baby." Lucille touched Sara's cheek. "But like all babies, you cried during the night and needed a lot of care."

"What was Gloria like, though?" Sara asked. "I mean before she met Howard, before she had me?"

"Fragile. Gloria was always delicate. Artistic. She wanted to be a painter. After she married Howard, she didn't have time because of his demands. He said they didn't have money for oil paints and canvases. He took all the money he could get his hands on to buy things for his inventions. He gave no thought to her needs, her talent. For all we know, hers could have been greater than his."

"That's why you always encouraged me," Sara said.

"Yes. And that's why I never wanted you to have any contact with him.

174

What if he stifled you as he had Gloria?"

"But didn't he leave her?"

Lucille nodded. "Walked out on her, filed for divorce. You were about two. She didn't have the strength to fight him. Didn't get a lawyer, didn't get alimony or child support. She was defeated, done. That's why he walked. She couldn't give him any more. I began to take care of you most of the time. I'd come and get you, bring you home to me and Marshall. By then we knew we couldn't have children. Marshall adored you. So did I," Lucille said softly.

When she stopped talking, the light bulb turned on in Sara's head. "You found her, didn't you? You were the neighbor bringing me home who found her." She couldn't stop the tears streaming down her cheeks. Lucille's anguished face answered her. They fell into each other's arms, both crying.

After awhile, they drew apart, wiped their eyes and blew their noses. "I don't remember it," Sara said. "I don't remember a thing."

"You've probably blocked it out," Lucille said, her voice hoarse. "It's just as well. I hope you understand now why I couldn't tell you when Howard was alive. After he died, I was afraid you'd hate me. I was afraid that if the two of you ever met, he'd take you over as he did Gloria and I'd lose you, too. That's why I hid the letters. You don't hate me, do you, Sara?"

Sara's heart seemed to turn in her chest. She had never seen Lucille so vulnerable, not even after Marshall died. "You did what you thought was right for me. How could I hate you for that?"

"Thank you. Thank God." Lucille dabbed at her eyes one last time, then put the tissue aside. "You're the only thing left of Gloria. I couldn't bear losing you."

Sara had never known that Lucille cared so much. The thought came, though, unwanted, that her adoptive mother had an excellent motive for killing Howard Lyndquist.

CHAPTER 20

When Sara arrived home to an empty apartment after being with Lucille all evening, she called the Smithfield's and spoke into the answering machine. After she said a few words, Blinky picked up.

"How is she?" Sara asked.

"About the same," Blinky answered, sounding exhausted.

"Can I come see her?"

"Not yet. I've had a couple of doctors take a look, but no one knows what it could be, and we haven't lifted the quarantine. Someone will know eventually, though."

"Have you called her folks in Florida?"

"She doesn't want me to until we know more. Makes sense. No use worrying them. Since they're elderly, I don't want them to be in physical contact with her until we have a diagnosis."

Sara pictured Belinda's parents in her mind. Her mother had been in her forties when Belinda, their only child, was born. Although totally unexpected, they greeted her with joy and tended to spoil her. Hence her preoccupation with her looks. Although Sara sometimes felt jealousy because Belinda seemed to get everything she wanted and Sara's mother thought out every purchase carefully, Belinda was so much fun to be around that Sara had been drawn to her since they were in first grade.

"I promise," Blinky was saying, "to let you know as soon as you can visit her. She wants to see you as much as you want to be there."

"Okay, Blinky. Thanks. Have a good night."

"You, too." He mumbled, "Goodbye," and they hung up.

Sara sighed with exhaustion as she began to undress. As she soaked in a hot bath, Sara decided she wanted to talk to Kevin again. Her new-found brother might have some answers to puzzling questions about their father. For example, why did Ira describe him as remarkable, and Lucille say he was a low scoundrel?

When she finished her bath, she glanced at the clock and decided it was still early enough to call Kevin. She realized she didn't have his number-- didn't even know if he lived with his mother, so she couldn't call Information.

She had Ira's number at the warehouse, though. He'd know, if he was there this late. Plus, she could ask him a few pointed questions.

He picked up on the third ring.

"Ira, it's Sara."

"Hello!" He sounded pleased to hear from her.

"How are you doing?" she asked, picturing him in the warehouse, tinkering with some weird invention.

"Fine. Fine. Yourself?"

"I'm okay. I just learned that my mother is really my aunt. Quite a shock. I don't suppose you knew?"

"What? What do you mean?" He sounded surprised.

She explained it to him.

"Honestly, Sara, I never knew about this. I met your father after he'd married Miriam and had enough money to hire an assistant. I didn't even know he had a daughter by his first marriage until about six months ago. That was when he got so angry with Kevin and started searching for you."

"All right. What I'd really like, Ira, is to talk to Kevin. Does he live at home with Miriam? Or does he have his own place?"

"Still lives at home, but he has a private number." Ira gave it to her. "Why do you want to talk to him?"

"I need to know more about our father from his point of view. You paint a nice picture of him. My mother, I mean Lucille, doesn't."

"I would guess not." He cleared his throat. "He could be a hard man. He was driven, you understand. That trait's not easy on wives, or children."

"Or assistants?"

"But I quickly became a partner. So, I guess I'm somewhat similar."

Sara smiled. Two men could not have looked different. Her father, even drunk, looked like a staid businessman, just letting his hair down. But

Ira. Ira looked like a mad scientist. A chill shivered down her back. Was he mad enough to murder?

This was really unproductive, she thought. She bounced from one person to the next, suspecting them all. Paranoid.

"I looked at the pictures, by the way," she said. "I took a set to the police."

"I know," Ira said. "They called Aunt Gladys and asked her if those were the whole set. Rattled her something terrible to have to talk to the cops."

Sara laughed. "I imagine. My goodness, I'm not related to her, am I? I just realized I probably have relatives out there in Brooklyn that I don't even know about."

"No. She's Miriam's aunt. There are no other relatives, except a cousin or two who defected to California. Oh, and I think an aunt of your father's in Florida. No one here, though."

"Oh," Sara said, disappointed. "Except Kevin. I guess I should call him now." She looked at the clock. "You don't think it's too late?"

Ira laughed. "No, he's a night owl. I'm sure you won't wake him."

"Okay. Ira, thanks. I'll talk to you later?" She wondered if and when.

"I'd like that. Don't be a stranger."

"Thanks. Bye." She hung up, a warm glow running through her. She really liked Ira.

When she tried Kevin's number, she got a machine. She didn't particularly want to leave a message, so she hung up. The phone rang immediately, and startled, she jerked.

Detective Beecham said, "Hello, Ms. Putnam. I understand you called last night. I'm sorry, I haven't had time to get back to you until now."

Sara grimaced, imagining him out in the city at murder scenes. "That's all right," she said. "I remembered something after I left the station yesterday afternoon. Actually, Belinda Smithfield told me about it."

"Uh huh?"

"There was a clown at the party. Neither Belinda nor Blinky had hired one. They found this out later, you know, when she asked him about it. She thought he'd hired him, and Blinky thought she had."

"I see. I'll need to talk to them."

"That might be difficult. Belinda's in the hospital, quite ill, and he's upset. We thought maybe you'd get a description from other guests. I barely remember seeing this guy, myself. Someone there must have gotten a good look, though."

"Okay. Thanks for calling. This might be one of our better leads."

"Great!" Sara said.

After they hung up, tiredness swept through her. She'd had quite a day. Her last thoughts before falling asleep were about Lucille being her aunt.

* * * * *

At a long table near her desk, Sara finished collating the latest training module. When she looked up she saw Bernie standing in front of her desk. She glanced at her watch. Exactly noon.

"Hi, Sara. Ready for lunch?"

Sara sighed, squared the pages, and went to get her purse.

As they walked down the hall, Bernie said, "Obviously, I forgive you for spilling the wine."

Well, she thought, thanks a lot!

"I talked to your friend, JoAnne, yesterday afternoon. She told me about your father's murder. I didn't realize you were going through such a tough time."

"Thank you," she said, surprised at the concern in his voice, wondering if it was genuine.

He punched the elevator button, and they waited. Moving close to her, he whispered in her ear, "You can tell me all about it at lunch."

The elevator arrived and Maurice and Helen got off, giving Bernie and Sara sharp looks. Sara could feel Bernie's breath on her cheek. Her face flushed from both embarrassment and anger. Everyone said, "Hello."

Bernie took her arm and steered her into the elevator. When they turned to face the front, Sara saw her supervisors watching the door close. Alone in the elevator, Sara shook off Bernie's hand and moved as far away from him as she could.

As they approached the huge glass front doors, Sara saw the Vice President of Personnel, Vice President of Purchasing, and the President of Nort International coming towards them on the walk.

"Oh, I forgot something!" Sara exclaimed. "Would you hold this?" She thrust her purse at Bernie, turned quickly around, and headed for the ladies' room, trying not to giggle.

While she grinned at herself in the mirror, she pictured Bernie standing there in front of all those high-ranking men with a purse in his hands. Had he hastily thrust it behind him? Or was it over his arm? Clasped in his hands in front of him? Any way he held it, she could imagine the raised eyebrows, perhaps the jokes.

She waited for five minutes by her watch. Then she peeked out the door and saw Bernie standing down the hall, her purse on the floor next to him.

As she approached, he asked, "Where did you go? Next time, take your purse with you."

"Sorry, I just remembered something I had to do." She picked up her purse, and they left the building. Sara thought she detected some pink around Bernie's ears.

During lunch at an Indian restaurant, she told him about her father. He seemed fascinated by the story. He even took out his daily planner and began to make a list of the people involved.

"Let's see, there's your brother--half brother--who stood to lose his inheritance. Your mother--really your aunt--who didn't want this man to have any influence in your life. Your half brother's mother who didn't want her son to lose his inheritance. The doctor who had easy access to the murder weapon and at whose apartment the murder happened--don't have a motive for him, yet. Then, of course, there's you," he looked up from his Daytimer and grinned at her. "You stood to gain from his death, and if you really found out what he did to your mother before his murder instead of after, as you claim--"

"Bernie!" she protested.

"Kidding. Just kidding. I'm sure you didn't do it." His leg found hers under the table. "So, who else? Oh, yes, his partner, Ira, was it? Motive undetermined." He made a note. "Anyone else?"

Sara moved her leg away from his and shook her head. "I can't think of anyone, but I don't know everyone he knew. Could have been someone I've never heard of. Someone he did business with. Some secret girlfriend he had."

"True," Bernie said. He shut his book with a snap. "It's fascinating. Just like you." His eyes bored into hers.

Sara looked away.

"You going to come work for me?"

"I . . . I need a little time, Bernie. This is a bad period to make a decision like that." She looked at him, trying to look sincere. "You

180

understand."

"Of course." His eyes caressed her face.

Sara felt violated. She began to crumble a piece of bread with her hands. A feeling of disgust sent tremors through her stomach. She hoped she wouldn't lose her lunch. Although that would be the ultimate humiliation for Bernie, she supposed. Upchucking into his lap would certainly be even more dramatic than the wine. Then the feeling passed, and she looked up from the bread crumbs to see him signaling for the check.

After she settled back at her desk, she called Kevin's number. He'd probably be out, she thought. At work? She didn't even know if he worked. He answered on the third ring.

"Kevin? This is Sara Putnam."

"Well, Sara," he said, sounding surprised. "What can I do for you?"

"I . . . I thought we might talk. Maybe we could meet somewhere this evening? In Manhattan?"

"I'd be delighted."

She couldn't tell if he meant it or was being sarcastic. They settled on seven-thirty at an Italian restaurant they both knew, then hung up. Sara sat a moment, her stomach uneasy again. At this rate, she'd get an ulcer.

* * * * *

Sara sat in Gino's staring at the Chianti bottle with the dry streams of different colored wax trailing down it. She looked at her watch. Almost eight. Was she going to be stood up? She ordered another glass of wine. She'd give him until eight-fifteen.

At eight-ten he stood in front of her. "Hi." He pulled out a chair and sat down.

She felt the uneasiness in her stomach again, shyly returning his "Hi." Her brother! She couldn't believe she had a brother. She wanted to like him, for him to like her. Studying his face, she saw a slight resemblance, more in the shape than anything. He had darker hair and eyes than she did.

He ordered a Scotch. After the waiter left, he said, "I understand you've ordered some DNA testing."

"You don't believe in small talk, do you?" She tried to smile, but it felt forced. She took a sip of wine, watching him over the rim.

181

"No point that I can see in this situation," he answered, nodding at the waiter as he placed the Scotch on the table.

"Really." Sara put her glass down with a plunk.

"Ready to order?" the waiter asked.

They did so quickly, then Kevin said, "So, tell me about the DNA testing."

"What's to tell? I need to be sure my rights are taken care of. Our loving father didn't seem to be very fair in that regard."

Kevin nodded. "Have to agree with you there. He should have split it down the middle and been done with it."

"What?" Sara asked, surprised. "I thought you wanted it all," she blurted out.

He smiled at her and shrugged. "Not really. I plan to make my own way, you know. I didn't like the idea of having it taken from me because I didn't conform to his ideas of what I should do with my life. I can tell you that."

"Well, that's understandable," Sara said, moving her arms out of the way for the waiter to put down her salad.

"I'm glad you think so," Kevin muttered.

"Of course I do!" She decided to change the subject a bit. "Do you know how he treated my mother?"

Kevin put down the fork he had just raised to his lips. "No. I know how he treated mine. Like a bank. It might be that you were better off never knowing him, you know."

Sara stared at him, wide-eyed. "I never thought of that," she said softly. "I always wanted to know what my 'real' parents were like, and of course I assumed they'd be perfect."

"Of course."

"I had a long talk with my adoptive mother last night. She's my aunt-- my mother's sister. Maybe you knew?"

He shook his head.

"Anyway, she told me how Howard Lyndquist treated my mother who was apparently artistic and delicate."

Kevin grimaced. "I can imagine."

"Oh?"

"He could be devastating. Cutting. Had to have his own way all the time."

"So, what were his good points?" Sara laughed nervously and took a sip of wine.

Kevin looked surprised by the question. "I don't know. I guess I always concentrated on his bad ones. That's terrible. Let's see. He had a good sense of humor, also cutting, but sharp. And he was brilliant, naturally, incisive. He could get to the heart of a problem in a heartbeat."

"Nicely put," Sara commented.

"Thank you."

"Was he kind to animals and small children?"

Kevin smiled and toasted her silently with his Scotch. "Usually. He wasn't a monster or anything. Just hard."

Sara nodded. "I still wish I had known him," she murmured. "So, you want to be a journalist."

"True."

"No desire to invent anything?"

"No."

"Me, neither. I do paint. I understand my mother did, too, and Howard didn't encourage her in any way. Wouldn't buy her paints and canvases because he needed the money for his inventions."

"Sounds like Dad," Kevin admitted.

The waiter cleared their salad dishes and set down their spaghetti. They began to eat without talking. What else can I ask him, Sara wondered. She was beginning to like him more and more. But what about his friend, the lurker?

"How much did you pay your friend to watch my house?" she asked, hoping to startle him into a confession.

"I admit to nothing." He twirled some spaghetti expertly on his fork and put it into his mouth, giving her a wide-eyed innocent look.

"Oh, and you don't admit that another one stole my father's letters?"

Kevin shook his head and twirled more spaghetti.

"Well, I find it intrusive and . . . and just awful that you did something like that."

"Not saying that I did, but what might you do in my place?"

Sara thought for a moment. "I'm not sure. Certainly nothing illegal. How does your mother feel about all this? Does she believe as you do, that we should split it down the middle?"

Kevin laughed. "The Bank? No. I should get it all, and she should manage it for me."

"What about Ira?"

"What about him?"

"Well, shouldn't he get some consideration?"

"You mean money?"

Sara nodded.

"He's a partner, so he gets to keep half the business, but that has nothing to do with inheritance."

"I see. He and our father got along?"

Kevin smiled at her. "You're trying to find out who murdered dear, old Dad. Well, Ira had the least motive. He loses by his death, at least financially. Actually, I think you had the best motive."

"Me?" Sara squawked.

"Sure. You gain financially from his death. He was nothing to you alive. I bet you found out how he treated your mother before he was murdered. Or at least, you can't prove otherwise."

"But . . . but, I didn't . . . I couldn't." Sara couldn't talk. She looked at Kevin, stricken.

"Well, I don't know you well enough to know either way, now do I?" He waved the waiter over. "You don't want dessert, do you?"

She shook her head, feeling tears behind her eyes. She refused to cry.

"The check, please," Kevin said. "Maybe this meeting wasn't such a good idea. Until this is settled, we'll be nothing but adversaries."

"I think you have some of our father's cruelty inside you, Kevin," Sara said bitterly.

"Maybe I do. But then, maybe you do, too. Enough to kill him, perhaps."

"You're turning this all around. I didn't even know who he was until the night he died."

"You say." Kevin smiled up at the waiter who handed him the bill. The waiter looked at them a moment before he moved away.

Feeling attacked, Sara stood up. "It's true, Kevin."

"Right." He looked at the bill. "Your half comes to fifteen dollars. Plus tip."

Tears blurring her vision, Sara fumbled in her purse. She found a twenty and threw it at him. Then she stalked out of the restaurant, away from The Bank, Jr.

CHAPTER 21

Sara arrived back at her apartment late but found Eileen still up, sprawled on the couch, watching a horror movie. Sara stood in the doorway, looking around slowly.

"What on earth did you do?" she asked. All the cows were gone. In their places stood strange objects made of cubes, triangles and rectangles in bright, primary colors. A statue on the stereo speaker was of a nude woman, painted matte black, balanced on her shoulders, hands holding up her rear end, with a white globe ball lamp on her toes. A black panther stalked across the coffee table. A couple, also black, kissed on the end table.

"Art Deco," Eileen explained. "Isn't it great?"

Sara set her purse down on the bar. "I guess so," she said dubiously, wondering where Eileen got the money. Maybe her new boyfriend helped.

"Where did you go?" Eileen asked.

"To see my loving brother."

Eileen pushed the mute button and looked at Sara sharply. "You sound bitter."

"I am. He practically accused me of murdering our father."

Eileen smiled. "Really? He doesn't know you very well, does he?"

"What do you mean?"

"I can't picture you doing it, is all." She shook her head, her long red hair swinging. "You don't have enough passion, enough fire, to do it."

Sara didn't know whether to be insulted or not. She plopped herself down on a chair.

"You're too much like Lucille," Eileen continued. "Controlled. I won't

185

say bloodless." She cocked her head at Sara. "Of course, the passion may be hidden, buried, ready to come out when provoked."

Sara smiled. "You've been watching too much TV. The point is, I did not kill Howard Lyndquist. Kevin has some nerve. He had as much, if not more, motive than I did."

"Well, other than that, what did you think of Kevin?" Eileen asked. She sat perfectly still, waiting for the answer.

"I don't know," Sara muttered. "He calls his mother The Bank. I think he's The Bank, Jr."

Eileen didn't laugh.

Sara shrugged. Sometimes Eileen's sense of humor got lost in the mists. "Anyway, he claimed he's not money hungry. Wants to make his own way. I'm not sure I believe him."

"Why not?"

"You have to look at the time frame of this murder. Howard was killed after he declared that if he found me, he was going to disinherit Kevin. I think that makes Kevin or his mother the prime suspects."

"What about Lucille? I thought you thought she might be a suspect. And Ira."

"Not the best. As you say, Lucille doesn't have much fire. And Ira lost by Howard's death, as far as I can see. No, my money's on Kevin now. Or Miriam, or both of them together. Yes, that sounds the most likely."

"Huh," Eileen muttered and pushed the button to make the sound come back.

Sara wondered vaguely if there'd been any phone calls while she was out. Eileen always turned the phones off when she got engrossed in one of her movies. They should probably get an answering machine--it was the 80s, after all. Sara sighed. "I'm going to bed," she said. "Keep it low, will you? All that screaming tends to keep me awake."

"Sure," Eileen said.

* * * * *

Eileen drove them to work the next morning. As they pulled out of the driveway, Sara asked, "Is that a new perfume?"

"Yeah. Do you like it? My boyfriend gave it to me."

"Nice," Sara said. "Speaking of men, do you know Bernie Puntz in Accounting?"

Eileen turned pale. "Yes. Why?"

"He asked me to be his new secretary. He's been made V.P. of Accounting."

"I know."

"What do you mean, you know? That he's been made V.P. or that he asked me to be his secretary?"

"Both."

"Wow. The grapevine's working overtime. Anyway, I was wondering if you've ever heard anything about him, uh, you know, maybe getting women to do things for him, that is sexually, in order to stay with the company."

Suddenly, Eileen swerved over to the shoulder and stopped the car.

"What's wrong?" Sara asked, alarmed.

Eileen was shaking.

"Eileen, tell me? Are you all right?"

"Bernie Puntz. Is he hitting on you, too?"

"Well, yes. Too? You mean--"

Eileen began to cry, and Sara realized she'd never seen her friend cry before. She put her arms around her and patted her back. "Are you all right? What's going on?"

"I'm . . . I'm sorry." Eileen gulped, trying to stop sobbing. "It's just been so awful. God, I hate him!"

"What did he do to you?" Sara asked, her heart pounding, her mouth suddenly dry.

"He made me . . . made me go out with him, have sex with him to keep my job. You know I have to have my job. I help my parents out, and . . . and he gives me some money, too, you know to help me out, but I feel so awful! So cheap. And now he's doing it to you? He still sees me once or twice a week. I can't believe it!"

"Eileen, how long has this been going on? Why didn't you report him?"

"Who's going to believe me? It started about six months ago. No one believes the woman. You know that. But if he did it to more than just me . . ." she looked up at Sara, her green eyes wide. "If he did it to you, too, we could both say . . . But no, we're friends, no one would believe us. I don't know how much longer I can stand it."

Sara couldn't take it all in. She'd never thought about Bernie doing the same thing to anyone else. But it made sense.

"Look," she said to Eileen. "We need to check around, see if he did it to anyone besides you. If he didn't, we'll have to trap him."

"But how?"

"I don't know," Sara said, getting out of the car and coming around to the driver's side. "I'll drive. You need to fix your makeup for work. Come on. We'll get the bastard."

* * * * *

At ten o'clock, Sara decided to take her morning break. She walked up two flights to JoAnne's new office on the lawyer's floor. JoAnne, on the phone, waved her in, looking surprised to see her. Sara closed the door behind her.

JoAnne cut the conversation short, and smiled at Sara. "What's up?" she asked.

Sara plunked herself down in a visitor's chair. "Bernie Puntz."

JoAnne made a distasteful face. "That creep? What's he done?"

"What you'd expect, if you thought about it. Sexual harassment."

JoAnne's eyes widened, and her expression became avid. "Who?" she breathed.

"First Eileen. Now me."

JoAnne slumped back in her chair as if hit in the chest. "No!"

Sara nodded. "And we need you to help us prove it."

"Me? How?" JoAnne perked up, leaning forward with her elbows on her desk.

"Well, I was hoping you had some kind of recorder that I could hide when I talk to him. I'd get him to be really specific about what he wants."

JoAnne stood up, excited. "You need a body mic! We have a couple of those."

"What's a body Mike? Sounds almost as obscene as Bernie."

"No, not the name! Mic short for microphone."

"Ah. How does it work?"

"It's tiny. We tape it to your body. When Mr. Puntz or you talk, the recorder records. It's very sensitive to sound." JoAnne paced around the room.

"Great. Can you get one for me?"

"Those have to be signed out. When do you need it? Maybe I can sneak it out for a couple of hours."

"We have a lunch date at noon. Just need it for an hour or so then."

"Wait here." JoAnne left the room.

She came back in a few minutes with a bulky manila envelope. "Got it!" She closed her office door.

"Great." Sara stood up and watched JoAnne pour the contents of the envelope onto her desk. "The only problem is, Sara, it's illegal to tape a conversation without the other party knowing about it. So, you couldn't use this in court. But it sure would get the higher-ups' attention. I'll dig around, see if I can find anyone else he's harassed. The more accusers, the more clout."

"Makes sense," Sara said. "How does this all work?"

JoAnne showed her. They taped the recorder to her side above her waist and hid the microphone between her breasts. JoAnne showed her how to turn the machine on when the time came. "This feels weird," Sara said, suddenly becoming frightened. "What if he finds out I'm doing this?"

"What can he do? Get so mad he stops harassing you?"

"Fire me." Sara felt week-kneed and sat down heavily. "Maybe I shouldn't . . . "

"Sara, with your skills, you can always get another job. Stop worrying. Look at it as an adventure. And think about Eileen. She'd have a much harder time finding another position that you would. We've got to get her out of this mess."

"You're right," Sara said. "She's been acting strange lately. I should have questioned her earlier. She sleepwalks, redecorates the apartment every five minutes, and goes on these crazy diets all the time."

"She's stressed to the max. You're doing the right thing."

Sara sighed. "I know." She glanced at her watch. "I better get back to my desk. Thanks, JoAnne."

"Come back here right after your lunch with the creep, and we'll play the tape. I'll eat at my desk so I don't miss you."

"Thanks," Sara said again.

She walked back to her office, totally aware of the pieces of metal strapped to her body. She moved carefully so she wouldn't dislodge anything while she worked the rest of the morning.

At noon, Bernie came by her desk to take her out. She realized she couldn't turn on the recorder while he watched. It would be too obvious. Panicking, she wondered what she could do. When they left the elevator on the ground floor, she remembered the ladies room and excused herself, taking her purse with her this time. She entered a stall and pushed the on button for the recorder.

Bernie chose a Chinese restaurant with a buffet. Was it her imagination, or were the restaurants getting cheaper and cheaper the more he took her out? No white linen here--just bare wood tables with place mats and paper napkins. She found it awkward balancing a plate and a cup of wonton soup without knocking the recorder on her side. She breathed a sigh of relief when she got back to their table.

Bernie found her leg with his. This was getting old, she thought. She felt sweat pop out on her forehead, and she took a sip of water to cool herself down. Everything else was hot--the tea, the soup, the food on her plate. Bernie didn't suggest ordering any wine. Just as well, she thought. It would make her even warmer.

"Good sweet and sour pork," Bernie remarked, shoving the stuff into his mouth.

"Mmm," Sara answered, not looking at him.

"So, Sara, are you coming to work for me?"

Sara put her fork down and locked her eyes onto his. "What happens if I don't, Bernie?" She held her breath, waiting for his answer.

"Use your imagination, Sara," Bernie said sharply.

"What do you mean? I don't know what you mean," Sara said desperately. She lowered her gaze, aware that her face felt hot. He mustn't guess she was trying to trap him.

"Of course you do, Sara," he said in a condescending tone. He waved a waiter over for more tea.

After the waiter left, Bernie pressed her leg even harder with his own. "Look, Sara," he said. "You are one of the best secretaries at Nort International. Of course I want you in my department."

"I like where I am, Bernie."

"But this job has more prestige and more pay."

"Accounting doesn't do it for me, Bernie. I like Training and Development. It's more interesting."

Bernie sighed. "You'll like Accounting just fine. Trust me."

Sara laughed. "Women are never supposed to trust a man who says, 'Trust me.'"

Bernie smiled at her, but it looked forced. "Sara, I must really insist that you take this job."

"Or else what, Bernie?" She looked at him with her eyes wide.

He grabbed her hand and squeezed.

"Ow," she said, "That hurts. Let go!"

"Listen, Sara, I'm tired of your games. If you don't transfer to Accounting, I'm afraid your days at Nort are numbered."

"You mean you'd get me fired because I won't come work for you? Can you do that?" She tried to keep her eyes wide with surprise, even though her stomach was sinking and she felt a bit dizzy. She tugged her hand away from his.

"Sara, you know that's not all I want." His leg pressed, pressed. He licked his chapped lips, and she saw the gleam of his buck teeth.

Sara shuddered. Thoughts of Eileen--beautiful Eileen--and this . . . this jerk together filled her mind. Her skin crawled, and she almost choked. She covered it with a cough and took a sip of water.

"Tell me what you want," Sara demanded, desperate to get him on tape.

"Sara, Sara," he crooned. "You know I want you. You have such wonderful skin." He rubbed her arm, raising goose bumps of disgust and horror. "I'll bet you have other wonderful parts," he began. Then he told her graphically what he wanted to do to her.

Sara had never heard such language directed at her before, and she first blushed, then blanched as he continued. She sat rooted as his words assaulted her. It felt as if he were hitting her in the face with them. She flinched, then ducked her head in shame. She felt violated, raped. The room disappeared, and all that remained were her and Bernie wrapped in this ugliness, this vile sewer of loathsome defilement. She wanted to throw things at him, slap him, hit him, kill him. She had never felt so wretched in her life.

Finally he stopped, but continued staring at her. "Now you know what I want, Sara. Any questions?" His voice was hard. She'd never heard him sound this way before.

"No questions," she whispered.

The waiter approached and asked in accented English if everything was all right. Sara pushed her plate away and shook her head, brushing away the tears she hadn't known were there. She stood up on shaky legs. Bernie threw some bills on the table and took her arm, leading her out of the restaurant. Her tears didn't seem to bother him. Maybe he liked them.

"It's all right," he soothed. "You'll get used to it."

Never, she thought. She remembered Eileen. How could she stand it? She got carefully into his car, aware more than ever of the body mic. She prayed it had caught every ugly word.

Bernie dropped her off in front of the building with a parting, "I'll expect your answer tomorrow, Sara." She walked on wobbly legs into the foyer and took the elevator to JoAnne's floor, too shell-shocked to even have her usual qualms about getting inside the moving box.

JoAnne sat eating a tuna sandwich at her desk, and threw it down when she saw Sara. She started to smile, but when she noticed Sara's expression, she asked, "What's wrong?"

Sara closed the door and slumped into the visitor's chair and moaned. "You're not going to believe this." Carefully, she removed the tape from the microphone and the receiver and placed them on JoAnne's desk. She pushed rewind, then play.

When the tape wound down, JoAnne's mouth hung open. She closed her lips tightly, then said weakly, "I don't believe it. That's so vile." She pushed rewind, and Sara thought she was going to listen again. She wouldn't be able to stand it, she thought. Instead, JoAnne grabbed the recorder and said, "Let's take this upstairs to Jerry in Personnel."

"Wait," Sara said. "We need to make a copy. Can you do that?"

"You're smart," JoAnne exclaimed. "I'll be right back." She returned a few minutes later with another, bigger recorder and some cable. Hooking the machines together, she played the tape once more, but they couldn't hear it as it was copied to the blank tape. When it stopped, JoAnne clicked open the recorder with the copy and handed it to Sara. Sara put it in her purse, surrounded with tissue. After rewinding the tape once more, JoAnne placed the smaller recorder back in its manila envelope and handed it to Sara. "Let's go," JoAnne said. "I asked around discreetly, but no one else would say they ever went out with Bernie. It might have been just you and Eileen, or it might be that no one else would admit to going out with the creep."

Sara nodded, not surprised. At her insistence, they walked up the two flights to the top floor and entered the office of the Vice President of Personnel.

Jerry's secretary greeted them. "What can I do for you ladies?" she asked.

"Addy, we need to see Jerry," JoAnne said. "It's rather urgent. Is he available?"

"He's got someone with him right now," Addy said. She looked down at an appointment book. "I don't know how long he'll be. Do you want to wait, or should I give you a call at your desks when he's done? He doesn't have another appointment until two-thirty."

"We'll wait a few minutes," JoAnne said and sat in a visitor's chair. Sara sat next to her, clutching the manila envelope tightly. She glanced at her watch nervously. Maurice would be furious about her being away from her desk so long.

At last Jerry's office door opened. Bernie stepped out. Sara thought she'd die. She wanted to sink down onto the floor and cover her head. Bernie said goodbye to Addy, then caught sight of JoAnne and Sara.

"Hello," he said, smirking.

"Hi, Bernie," JoAnne said smoothly. She looked at him with a blank expression.

"Hi," Sara said, her voice weak.

He gave them a puzzled look but left the outer office, whistling. Sara shuddered. He wouldn't suspect, would he? It didn't matter, she realized. He'd know soon enough what she'd done. She shivered again, remembering him telling her what he wanted to do to her. It had sounded more violent than sexual. Fear fizzed in her stomach.

Addy spoke into the intercom, telling Jerry they were here to see him. A moment later, Jerry appeared in the doorway and told them to come on in.

"What can I do for you?" he asked as they settled into chairs. Jerry had a foxy look--long, thin nose, deep-set blue eyes, reddish hair. Except for the interview when she had been hired, Sara had not talked to him much. He seemed friendly enough, but she had no idea what his reaction would be to their news.

"May I?" JoAnne asked, holding out her hand. Sara gave her the package, and JoAnne hooked up the recorder.

Sara was happy to let JoAnne take charge.

"I'm afraid we have a situation here, Jerry, that is unpleasant," JoAnne told him. "It concerns Bernie Puntz."

Jerry's eyes became wary. No one in the room could forget Bernie was married to the owner's granddaughter. "What about him?" he asked.

"It seems he likes to sexually harass the women employees," JoAnne said bluntly.

"Oh no," Jerry said, his voice faint. He looked ill as he wiped his hand across his brow.

JoAnne nodded and pushed the start button. Jerry leaned forward. Sara had forgotten how long it took to get to the important part. First they listened to all that talk in the beginning that didn't mean anything. Then Bernie's voice began in that low, menacing tone, saying exactly what he wanted to do to her. Sara winced, and couldn't look at Jerry. Instead, she watched JoAnne whose face seemed carved in marble. She had no compunctions about watching Jerry's reaction.

When Bernie finished, JoAnne pushed the stop button. Silence hung in the air for what seemed like a long time. Sara took at peek at Jerry now. He'd gone pale, and she could see freckles she'd never noticed before. He wouldn't look at either of them, staring instead at his desk.

Slowly, he shook his head. "You've got him dead to rights."

"He's harassing another employee, also," JoAnne told him. "We'd rather leave her out of it, if we can. She's pretty traumatized by the whole thing. This should be enough to get him fired, shouldn't it?"

Jerry nodded, looking sick. He glanced at Sara. "Is that what you want? Just to get him fired?"

"Yes," she croaked. She cleared her throat. "Just get him out of our lives."

Sara could feel Jerry's unasked question in the air--Don't you want to sue? But he couldn't ask, couldn't suggest it. She had enough problems right now. She just wanted Bernie Puntz out of her and Eileen's life. Eileen might feel different. If she wanted to sue, Sara would stand behind her. But it wasn't the company's fault. And she wanted to keep her job. That was the important thing to her.

"I'll need to keep this," Jerry said, pointing to the tape recorder. "Do you have a copy?"

JoAnne looked at him and smiled. "Of course. When do you think we'll hear about Mr. Puntz's resignation?"

Jerry stood up and took the recorder. "By close of business today, I would expect," he said. He looked at Sara. "I appreciate what you went through. And your quick actions. You may have saved the company a lot of trouble."

Sara stood up. She was glad he'd be gone, but she wondered where he'd go and if he'd have the opportunity to do it again. She felt badly about that. Maybe Eileen would settle down, though.

Sara would never know what happened between the higher-ups behind closed doors that day. At four-thirty she received a memo about Mr. Puntz's resignation for personal reasons. She couldn't help wonder about the repercussions for her as the whistle blower. She'd worry about that later, she guessed.

At four-forty-five the phone rang, and she heard Belinda's voice.

"Belinda! How are you? Have they found out what it is?"

"I'm okay. Tired. They think they know. I'm allowed visitors now. Can you come tonight? I'd love to see you."

"Of course. Wonderful."

"I got a room on the top floor now and feel very pampered. You should see it, but I guess you will. What time can you get here?"

"If Eileen gets off on time, let's see, around seven? Is that okay?"

"That's great."

"So, what is it? Is it because of the implants?"

"No, no, they're pretty sure it's something else. They did a kidney biopsy this afternoon. I'll tell you all about it tonight." She sounded exhausted.

"Are you sure you're up to a visit? You sound so tired."

"I can't sleep, anyway. You'll distract me. We'll figure out who murdered your father, talk about old times, and then I'll be able to sleep."

Sara laughed. "Right. I'll bring pictures."

"No video?" Belinda asked. "Oh, you mean the ones from the funeral. Can't wait to see them. I'm sure that between us, we'll figure it out."

Sara laughed again. "That would be nice. We have so much else to catch up on. Oh, Belinda, I'm glad I can come see you. Are you sure you're all right?"

"I will be, I guess." Belinda sighed. "Get here as soon as you can, okay?"

"Okay! Don't start without me!"

"See you later," Belinda murmured and hung up.

Sara grabbed her purse and went to find Eileen, wondering if she'd seen the memo about Bernie.

CHAPTER 22

"Did you see the memo?" Sara asked.

Eileen jumped up from her desk and gave Sara a big hug. "How did you do it? What did you do? I can't believe it. I feel as if a weight has been taken off my chest."

Sara couldn't stop grinning. "I'll tell you all about it on the way home. I just heard from Belinda. I can go see her tonight, so we need to hurry. Are you done here?"

"You bet," Eileen said, grabbing her purse and taking out her car keys.

* * * * *

Sara pushed open the heavy hospital door right at seven. She went to the information desk to find out how to get to Belinda's new room. On the twenty-fifth floor, it involved an elevator, of course. Sighing, she got in, trying not to stare at the old woman on a stretcher accompanied by a male nurse. One woman, dressed in a powder blue suit, wore such a strong perfume that Sara could feel her eyes starting to tear.

Finally, after many stops and many deep, calming breaths, the elevator reached the top floor. Sara stepped out onto plush gray carpet and walked down mauve halls towards room 1001.

She knocked on the walnut paneled door, then stuck her head in.

"Sara!" Belinda said, her voice barely above a whisper. "Come in here."

Sara entered and approached the bed. "Can I hug you?" she asked.

"You bet," Belinda said.

196

Sara leaned down and took her friend gently into her arms. After they hugged, she held onto Belinda's shoulders and looked closely at her face. Belinda had lost weight--her cheekbones appeared chiseled, her eyes a bit sunken. But she was smiling, and Sara let go of her to sit down. She felt unexpectedly tired.

"No I.V." Sara exclaimed, suddenly noticing. She looked around the room. It looked nicer than her own bedroom in Montclair with pale green walls, dark green carpet and damask drapes patterned with leaves and vines. A wardrobe stood in one corner, a chest of drawers in another. Every spare surface held flowers and cards.

"Where's Blinky?" Sara asked.

"Making rounds, doing a few things he needs to do. I told him you were coming, and he took the opportunity."

Sara felt a bit relieved. She couldn't help remembering that Blinky was a suspect in her father's murder, and she'd just as soon not see too much of him until it was all cleared up.

"So, what did the doctors decide you have? Why don't you have an I.V. any more?"

"I have Wegener's Granulomatosis."

"What?"

Belinda smiled. "Don't ask me to spell it. It's a rare arthritic disease. Treated with steroids and chemotherapy. Just pills, no I.V. Especially not antibiotics. It's one of those diseases where the body starts attacking itself-- it's called an autoimmune disease. It can affect the sinuses, lungs and kidneys. I have some sinus involvement, and it was beginning to get to my lungs, but once I start the therapy, everything should get better."

"Wow," Sara said, letting out a long sigh. "Can they cure it?"

Belinda shook her head. "No one's ever been cured."

"Belinda! Oh, no." Sara stood up. "What does that mean?"

"They say I can still live a long life. I just have to manage the disease. It comes and goes into remission and out again. Sometimes remissions last for years, but it always comes back. I have to be followed carefully and hope my lungs or kidneys don't become involved."

Sara plunked herself back into the chair. "Jeez, Belinda. I thought once they had a diagnosis, everything would be all right."

Belinda gave a shaky laugh. "Me, too. The other thing is that the drugs have side effects. I'll take a huge dose of Prednisone to start, and that puts

197

on weight real fast plus, Blinky tells me, it will make me cranky. The other drug--Cytoxin--can cause wonderful things such as bladder cancer."

Sara shook her head. "I don't know what to say. When do you get out of here?"

"About a week or ten days. The drugs take effect rapidly, and all the symptoms will disappear as if by magic, they tell me. I'll walk out of here on my own."

"Well, that's good, anyway," Sara said. "Why couldn't they find out quicker? How many people have this, anyway? I've never heard of it."

"Only about five hundred people worldwide have ever been diagnosed with it. It's extremely rare. That's why it took so long to diagnose. Plus, I had some symptoms that are rare for the disease, too--a nodule on my elbow, even the purple spots are present only in some patients. The disease is usually seen in old men. Do I look like an old man?" She gave a shaky laugh. "It took a kidney doctor who had seen two cases to determine what I had."

Sara shook her head again. "This is all so unbelievable." She got up, walked to the bed and took Belinda's hand. "I'm glad they know what it is. I do wish they found something they could cure with a ten-day course of drugs, though." Sara fought back tears.

Belinda smiled through her own tears. "Me, too. Me, too. It sure has been interesting, now that I look back on it. You should have seen the parade of doctors through my room downstairs. It was like a Halloween party--I should have asked the nurses to throw a few fake spiderwebs into the corners and set up a table where they could bob for apples. They came, they saw, they shook their heads and left. Two of them wouldn't even come into the room. They stood in the doorway, gawking as if I were in a freak show, saying it was interesting, then leaving in a hurry. But Dr. Bravo, the kidney specialist, he's nice. He just looked me over, declared it to be Wegener's, said he'd do a kidney biopsy right away to confirm it and ordered the I.V. gone. Sara, this is so rare that Blinky had never even heard of it, and neither have any of the nurses."

"Wow!" Sara exclaimed.

"But anyway," Belinda continued, "in a few days I'll be almost back to normal. So, tell me what's gong on in your life."

Sara laughed. "You wouldn't believe it. You remember Bernie Puntz?"

Belinda looked puzzled and shook her head.

"The guy who married Margaret," Sara reminded her. "You know, the owner's granddaughter."

"That rabbit!" Belinda exclaimed. "How could I have forgotten? He worked a few offices down from mine."

"Right. In Accounting. They decided to make him a V.P."

"Well, that's not so surprising."

"No, but what he did to Eileen and me is." Sara sat down and told her what had happened during the last three days.

When she finished, Belinda said, "Wow. Makes me glad to be out of there. Aren't you worried that they'll give you a hard time now?"

"A little bit. No one likes a tattletale. But what else could I do?"

"Nothing. You did a great job. I wouldn't have thought that fast."

"Yes, you would have. I was desperate."

"So, I guess that means you haven't had much time to work on your father's murder."

"Well, I saw Kevin last night. We had a nice chat."

"Really?" Belinda quirked her eyebrows. "What about, exactly?"

"About his mother and our father, really. He's not too fond of either one."

Sara told her about their conversation.

"He calls his mother The Bank?" Belinda chuckled. "From what you've said, he doesn't sound too interested in the money."

"What else can he say? If he admits interest, he has a perfect motive. If he doesn't admit it, everyone thinks he's lying to throw off suspicion. He can't win."

"You almost sound sorry for him." Belinda gave her a sharp look.

Sara shook her head. "Not really. I just wish I could like him more."

"Well, maybe when this is all over, and if he's not guilty, you can."

"'If he's not guilty' are the operative words. I think he's right at the top of the list of suspects."

"Speaking of which," Belinda said as she got a pad of paper from her bed tray. "I made a list and some notes. See what you think." She held it out to Sara.

Belinda had listed only three suspects--Kevin, his mother, and Ira. She didn't know about Lucille and Blinky, Sara realized. She couldn't tell her about Blinky. Sara had a sudden thought which made her eyes widen. She stared at her friend. If Blinky had some unknown motive, perhaps Belinda did, too. And she would have had access to the murder weapon. Sara shook off the thought. Don't be ridiculous, she told herself, but the uneasiness wouldn't go away. Howard had shown up at the Smithfield's party, after all.

Sara read the notes. Belinda had written down the sequence of events since the party and listed all the guests names. She'd underlined, Unknown Clown. Sara read over the names, only recognizing the ones from work, JoAnne's date, Arthur, and the lawyer, Henry.

"You've left off Lucille as a suspect," she said and looked up at Belinda.

"What? Your mother? Why would she . . . I mean what motive would she have?"

"She's my aunt--my mother's sister! She hated Howard for what he did to Gloria." Sara's voice lowered to almost a whisper. "Gloria was my mother, Belinda. I can find out all kinds of things about her now."

"That's wonderful!" Belinda said. Then she frowned. "I think. Why do you say Lucille hated Howard enough that she might have killed him?"

"I guess I really don't believe that. How would she have gotten hold of the murder weapon?"

"What was it? Here, give me my notes so I can write this down."

Sara hesitated as she handed Belinda her pad. "Howard invented it. A . . . a knife."

"What kind of knife?" Belinda demanded, pencil poised over her notepad.

A knock sounded on the door, and it swung open. Blinky came in, holding a thick patient's chart.

He stopped when he saw Sara. "Hello." He smiled at her. "Good to see you. Belinda's been begging me to let you come visit her."

"Hi, Blinky," Sara said, her face flushing. She looked at his handsome face newly crisscrossed with fine lines around his eyes and mouth. Surely not the face of a murderer. She saw Belinda looking at her husband with adoration. Sara swallowed hard, suddenly sick to her stomach.

Blinky walked over to Belinda and took her hand gently in his. "Feeling any better, Babe?" he asked.

She nodded.

"I arranged airline tickets for your folks. They'll be here around noon, tomorrow."

"Thanks, Blinky," Belinda said.

"They know?" Sara asked, happy to change the subject.

Blinky turned to her. "Yes. We phoned them earlier. They insisted on coming up to see her."

Belinda gave a shaky laugh. "They'll smother me."

"With love," Sara said, smiling. "Exactly what you need."

Belinda withdrew her hand from Blinky's. "Sit down. Sara and I were talking about her father's murder, trying to figure some stuff out."

Blinky smiled indulgently and sat down in the lounge chair next to Sara. He pushed the handle to raise his feet and gave a big sigh. "That feels good," he said. He looked at Sara. "I've seen Belinda's notes. Not much to go on."

"We were just talking about the weapon," Belinda said excitedly. "Sara found out what it was."

They looked at her, waiting. Sara swallowed. "It was a knife that Howard invented."

Blinky frowned. "Not the scalpel?" he asked.

Sara nodded as she watched Belinda's reaction. "What scalpel? What are you talking about?"

"Mr. Lyndquist," Blinky began, "invented a scalpel for cosmetic surgery. It's wonderful. Fits in the hand as if made to be there, a ridge at the top of the blade so that it can only cut so deep. I've been using it ever since his partner, Ira Levine, first gave me a prototype to test."

"Why didn't you mention this before?" Belinda demanded.

"It took me awhile to put the pieces together, for one thing. When you became so ill, I sort of forgot about it. In comparison, it wasn't important, Babe." He put down the footrest on the lounge chair, stood up and took her hand.

"It was important to Sara," Belinda protested.

Blinky looked at Sara and said, "I'm sorry. Really, I am. I wasn't thinking."

Sara shrugged. "That's okay. I already knew." She didn't know what to believe. She still couldn't imagine a motive for Blinky, unless he wanted to claim the invention of the scalpel as his own. In that case, though, he'd have to murder Ira and all the other people who knew about the invention. Too many. He certainly didn't need the money.

"Want to see the pictures?" Sara asked. She fished them out of her purse and stood up. Blinky pulled the bed tray over Belinda's lap, and Sara placed the photos onto it.

"Wow," Belinda said as she took one of Howard in his casket and held it up. "This is pretty macabre." She studied it for a moment, looking first at the photo, then at Sara. "There is a slight resemblance in the shape of the face. Can't see the eyes, of course."

"Look, Belinda," Sara said, "I know I'm tired, but I'm not dead yet."

Belinda and Blinky laughed. Belinda looked at the picture again. "Yeah, I have to admit, your color is better." She put it down with an expression of distaste.

Blinky picked up another one. "I know this woman. Intimately. Breast implants and liposuction."

Belinda tried to grab the photo, but he held it away from her.

"Still looks pretty good, doesn't she?" He handed it to Sara.

"Let me see!" Belinda demanded.

Sara grinned as she studied the picture. "Good job, Blinky. Even better than you did with Belinda. The woman must have a forty-six or forty-eight inch bust and about a twenty-two inch waist. I'd demand my money back, Lin."

"Let me see!" Belinda insisted again.

Sara handed her the photograph.

It showed a tiny woman of about sixty, with hardly any breasts. She might have had a twenty-two inch waist, but only because she was so skinny.

Belinda laughed when she saw the photo. "You two!"

"No, I really did a face-lift for the woman," Blinky said. "Looks as if she needs another."

"What else is in here?" Belinda asked.

Sara pushed a few around to look. "They seem to be all out of order. That's funny, because the last time I went through them, they started with the funeral and ended with the reception."

"Here, what's this?" Belinda asked, pulling a long, red hair out of the pile and handing it to Sara.

Sara looked at it blankly for a moment. "Oh," she said. "That must be Eileen's hair. I guess she must have looked at the pictures."

Belinda and Blinky nodded and continued looking through the photos. Sara stared at the hair and suddenly remembered the perfume Eileen wore this morning. Sara had remarked on it because it smelled familiar. It smelled familiar because Miriam had been wearing the same scent at the funeral.

Sara dropped the hair onto the floor. She felt the blood drain from her face, making her dizzy. She clutched the bed.

"Blinky?" she said.

He looked up from the photo he was holding. "Sara!" He took her arm and helped her to the chair. "What's wrong?"

She collapsed into it gratefully, her thoughts swirling. "I have a new boyfriend," she heard Eileen say. "Won't be home tonight." "He has a new girlfriend," she heard Ira say. "Don't remember her name." Eileen sleeping through the burglary. Eileen sleepwalking, dieting. This morning Sara had thought it was all because of Bernie.

"What's wrong?" Belinda asked, her voice sounding far away. "Sara?"

"I . . . " Sara began, hardly recognizing herself. "I think Eileen knows Kevin, is maybe going out with him."

"What?" Belinda said. "Eileen? You think she had something to do with all this? But why?"

"I don't know," Sara said. "Maybe I'm imagining things."

"Wait," Belinda said. "Ohmygod. You remember a couple of Halloween's ago when Eileen dressed up as a clown?"

Sara looked at her blankly. "No. Was that the year I got so sick with the flu? Before she and I became roommates?"

"Yes! I'm trying to remember the clown at the party. I think the makeup was different. It must have been. She wouldn't take the chance that I'd remember. It could have been the same costume, though. I really didn't pay that much attention." Belinda's eyes had grown huge. "Sara, it couldn't be Eileen. It couldn't be."

"No," Sara said. "But maybe I should call Ira. See if he remembers Kevin's girlfriend's name. Get a description."

Blinky brought the phone over to her. She was glad the cord reached. She felt weak as a kitten and didn't want to stand up again.

With shaking hands, she got Ira's card out of her purse and dialed the warehouse number. Would he be there?

He answered on the third ring.

"Ira, this is Sara."

"Well, hello. How are you?" He sounded as if he really wanted to know. His voice warmed her inside.

"I'm okay. You all right?"

"Just fine."

"I wanted to ask you about Kevin's new girlfriend. You don't happen to remember her name, do you?"

"Um, no. Wait, maybe Ellen? Elaine? I'm not sure."

"Eileen?" Sara asked, her voice trembling.

"That's it! Eileen. Irish. Long red hair, green, green eyes. Lovely girl."

Sara remembered Eileen staying in her room the whole time Ira visited. Why had she hid? What was she hiding now?

"Sara?" Ira's voice came faintly over the line. She realized he must have said her name several times.

"My roommate's name is Eileen, she has long red hair and green eyes." But how had they met? No, they couldn't know each other.

"What a coincidence," Ira said.

"She wears the same perfume Miriam likes. Maybe Kevin gave her a bottle of it. You say his girlfriend had access to the scalpel. She has money problems. She sleepwalks."

"Sara!" Ira almost shouted. "You're jumping to conclusions."

Sara looked across the room at Belinda and Blinky who were watching her with wide eyes, Belinda shaking her head in denial.

"I have to go, Ira. I'll talk to you later."

"Sara! What are you going to do?"

She hung up without answering, staring back at Belinda and Blinky.

She got up on shaky legs and hugged Belinda. "I'm glad you're on the mend. I'll talk to you as soon as I get a chance. I have to go home now."

"Sara, don't!" Belinda begged. When Sara walked towards the door, Belinda said, "Blinky, go with her."

"No," Sara said. She turned around and looked at them. "He needs to stay here with you. I'll call you. I promise."

She thought the elevator would never come. If I get stuck in it, she thought, I'll never ride in one again, for as long as I live. But it took her down without a problem. She dashed outside to get a taxi to the Port Authority building. Then the bus home. She wondered if Eileen would be there. Or maybe she was out with Kevin, her brother.

CHAPTER 23

As she opened the door to her apartment, Sara could hear the television. She let out a breath she hadn't known she was holding.

Eileen lounged on the couch, barefoot, filing her nails and watching a horror movie.

"Eileen?" Sara yelled over the soundtrack. The TV showed the African bush, some young woman dressed in a skimpy costume being manhandled by bushmen. She screamed and screamed. A drop-dead handsome man stood nearby, tied up with vines.

"Hey, Sara," Eileen said. "How's Belinda?" She didn't turn down the sound.

"Better," Sara said. She studied her friend, unable to believe, now that she was here, that Eileen could have murdered Howard Lyndquist in cold blood. Maybe I'm wrong, she thought. She could feel her heart pounding, and she shook slightly all over. She put her purse on an end table and stood in front of the TV.

"Hey, this is the good part," Eileen said.

"I need to talk to you. Can't you turn it down?"

"Later. This will be over in a few minutes."

"Eileen," Sara shouted. "It's important."

Eileen gave her a disgusted look and turned the sound down, but not off.

Sara moved away from the TV. Eileen looked from Sara to the television, but then her attention settled on the show.

"Eileen, please."

Eileen looked at her. "What is it?"

Sara didn't know how to begin. She should have thought about it on the way home, but her mind had been spinning out of control. She clasped her hands together in front of her to stop their trembling, and sat down. "It's about my father's murder," she finally managed to say.

Eileen's eyes became wary. "What about it? You have another theory?"

"Yes, yes, I do. How did you meet my brother, Kevin?"

Eileen looked shocked. "What are you talking about?"

"You know Kevin. Ira said he was going with a girl named Eileen who has long red hair and green eyes. How did you meet him?"

Eileen looked wildly around the room, as if searching for something. "I don't know what you're talking about. There's got to be more than one girl out there named Eileen with red hair and green eyes."

"That wears the same perfume his mother wears."

"What?"

"That dresses up as a clown. Who had access to the murder weapon. Why? Why did you do it, Eileen? Please, tell me. I have to know. I almost met my father, almost knew him, but you snatched him away from me." She began to cry.

The woman on the TV screamed, startling both Sara and Eileen. Sara stopped crying and stared at Eileen.

Eileen swallowed visibly. "I . . . I don't know what you're talking about, Sara. Honestly. How would I meet Kevin? Why would I kill your father?"

"I don't know!" Sara wailed. "That's what I need you to tell me."

"Sara, you've been under a lot of strain lately. First the murder, then Belinda being ill, and that awful Bernie Puntz. I don't blame you for your imagination running away from you. But you must know I didn't murder your father! Why would I do it? What reason would I have?"

She sounded so sensible, so sure, Sara thought. Maybe I'm wrong. She wanted to be wrong. It should be some stranger who killed him. A random act of violence. But no, it had to have been someone he knew. The weapon was his own invention. The weapon missing from the warehouse after Kevin and his girlfriend had been there.

"How did you meet Kevin, Eileen?"

"I don't know Kevin, Sara. Really."

"When I talked about meeting him, you wanted to know what I thought of him."

What little color Eileen had drained from her face.

"You're in love with him. Howard was going to take away his

inheritance. You couldn't stand the thought of being poor. You wanted Kevin *and* the money. You needed the money to get away from Bernie Puntz and to help your family. Did Howard talk about disinheriting Kevin when you were there, in the warehouse with the scalpels? Did you slip two of them into your purse without really thinking, just in case? Then, did you think it out, plan it?"

"No, no," Eileen moaned, shaking her head.

Sara stood up and went to her, leaned over her. "Tell me. Please, I have to know."

The woman on the TV screamed, startling them both again. Drums began pounding, and the men surrounding the woman roared.

Sara and Eileen watched as one of the masked men started to get taller, and the mask blended into his face somehow so that he became the monster from the mask. He waved a knife high in the air and yelled. The drums beat, but softer now.

"Is the clown costume in your room, or did you get rid of it?" Sara asked. She started towards Eileen's bedroom.

"Wait!" Eileen said. Sara kept going, her roommate following. Sara flung open Eileen's closet and began rummaging around. The blow to her back didn't hurt that much. She heard something shatter and wondered vaguely if she'd been cut. Sara turned around in time to see Eileen reach into her bureau drawer and pull out a scalpel. It gleamed in Eileen's hand. Sara gasped.

"You've spoiled it all," Eileen said. Her eyes shimmered like the knife.

Sara backed away from the closet, her feet crunching on what she realized were pieces of the black ceramic panther. "Put it down, Eileen. We're friends. You can't hurt me. Please."

Eileen matched her step for step.

Sara's heart had moved towards her throat, and she was having trouble breathing. Her shoulder throbbed vaguely. But her eyes never left the scalpel as she backed away from Eileen without thinking. She didn't know why she headed for her own bedroom. As they passed through the living room, she heard the yells and screams coming faintly from the show. Her ears buzzed, and she felt faint. You can't pass out, she told herself. The phone. She needed to get to the phone and call the police. Eileen had probably turned them off. She always did when she watched one of her awful horror shows.

As she entered her bedroom, she thought wildly about how she could close and lock the door on Eileen. But her roommate stood too close. When Sara swung the door at her, Eileen simply put her foot in the way. Sara felt so small and vulnerable. Eileen seemed to loom over her, and she felt sure that any moment the scalpel would come swinging down and cut her on the face. Or the neck, like her father. Her trembling became worse. She backed slowly, watching Eileen's eyes, feeling her way with her hands behind her.

At last she reached the bedside table and the telephone. If she reached for it, she knew Eileen would attack. Now she was cornered. She should have headed for the front door and fled down the stairs. She broke eye contact with Eileen long enough to look longingly at the telephone.

"Don't try it," Eileen said.

"What are you going to do?" Sara asked, hating the high pitch of her quivering voice.

"I'm not sure, yet. Just don't touch that phone. I need to think."

They were both silent for a minute. Sara could hear each of them breathing, and the faint sound of drums on the television. A car drove by outside. A plane droned overhead. Her nerves on edge, she wanted to scream. Maybe she should scream. Suddenly, her throat felt so dry she didn't think she could make a sound.

Stall her, Sara's mind commanded her. Do anything, but stall her.

"How did you meet Kevin, Eileen?" Her voice croaked. She wiped away the sweat that had popped out on her forehead.

"Shut up. I need to think."

Sara looked at the phone again. She began to remember all that happened in the last two weeks. How she had found her father, at last. How she'd met Ira. She almost smiled when she thought about Ira. How sick Belinda was, but what a relief it hadn't been from the implants. How she'd learned more about her family. That Lucille was her aunt. Her prickly half brother, Kevin. She wanted to find out more. But now, maybe she never would. She had to do something, anything, to get out of this.

"You can't kill me here," she said softly to Eileen. "They'd know it was you for sure."

"Quiet!" Eileen's face flushed. Sara could tell she was thinking furiously but couldn't come up with a plan.

"If you take me downstairs, we might run into Mrs. Abbot or Eugene.

"Just shut up!" Eileen waved the scalpel threateningly.

"Of course, you could do it here, then drag me downstairs. But again, you might meet our nosy landlady or Eugene."

"I said, shut up!" Eileen's face flushed redder.

"The police always know when a body has been moved. They can tell somehow. I read about it in a mystery one time."

Eileen took a menacing step forward, waving the scalpel again. "Not another word, or I swear, I'll do it right now!"

Sara swallowed hard. She tore her eyes away from the knife and looked wildly around the room. Her eye fell to the drawer in the nightstand. The drawer that held the plastic gun. Had she told Eileen about it? For a moment, she couldn't remember. Then it came back to her. She'd felt silly for taking it and hadn't told her roommate.

She watched Eileen carefully, waiting for her to glance away for just a moment. Another, louder scream sounded from the TV. Eileen had been so intent on watching Sara that she jumped, startled, and looked back over her shoulder towards the sound. When she did, Sara tugged the drawer open and grabbed the gun. It felt so light and flimsy in her hand. She grasped it firmly and pointed it at Eileen's chest.

"Put the scalpel down on the bed," she said. She wanted to sound firm, but her voice came out in a rasp.

Eileen looked at her in disbelief. "Where'd you get that?"

"Never mind. Just put the damned knife down. Now!"

Instead, Eileen's grip tightened on the instrument. Her eyes wary, she began to back out of the room. Didn't we just do this in reverse? Sara asked herself. She matched her roommate pace for pace as they left the bedroom.

"Eileen, you don't want me to shoot you. Put the knife down."

Eileen stopped in the middle of the living room. "You wouldn't shoot me, Sara," she said softly.

Right, Sara thought. You don't know how right you are. "Don't test me," she said.

"I love your brother, you know. We're going to get married. He came here to find you, to see what you looked like. We bumped into each other outside and started talking. He wanted to know all about you. So, I told him. I told him what a great roommate and friend you are. I told him how you like Belinda better than me."

"Eileen!"

Eileen gave her a stubborn look. "It's true, and you know it. Just like my mother loves my brothers and sisters better than she does me. Oh, she likes the money I give her every month well enough. But it's never enough."

A commercial, louder than the show, blasted on the TV. Sara wondered vaguely how it had ended. How was this going to end? "Turn off the TV, Eileen. Please."

Eileen reached down and pushed the off button on the remote. Blessed relief. But now Sara could hear their raspy breathing. She felt the blood pounding in her forehead.

"How did you get the scalpels?" Sara asked.

"Kevin and I visited his father at the warehouse." Eileen's voice was a monotone. "I'd only met his dad once, and he didn't know that you and I were roommates. Anyway, I was looking around at all the stuff, and Kevin and his dad went into the office. I heard them shouting. I went to the door and listened. They never saw me."

"What were they arguing about?" Sara asked.

"Howard wanted Kevin to start working for him. Kevin wanted to go to college to be a journalist. Howard said it was Kevin's last chance. If he didn't come work for him, he'd disinherit him as soon as he found you. He didn't know Kevin already had. Howard's way of searching was just to write to you at Lucille's. Kevin investigated much harder than that and found this address."

"What did you do then?" Sara asked, fascinated. She had to remind herself to keep a firm grip on the gun and to watch the scalpel still glimmering in Eileen's hand.

"I went back to the room with all the inventions, worried about Kevin's inheritance."

I'll bet, Sara thought. "And you saw the scalpels and just decided to take a couple."

Eileen nodded. "I knew I had to get rid of Howard before he changed the will."

"How did you find him at the Smithfield's?"

"Kevin called me and told me Howard had finally found out more about you and planned to crash the party that night in order to meet you. Belinda neglected to invite me, so I just dressed up as a clown--"

"Wait a minute, she invited you. She invited all her old friends from Nort. I told you that."

Eileen shook her head. "It wasn't like a real invitation. It was an afterthought. She didn't bother to call me herself, just had you deliver a half-hearted invitation. I was probably too poor to be her friend any more."

"Eileen! That's not true. Belinda doesn't think that. No one thinks that."

A stubborn look crossed Eileen's face. "I know what I know," she said.

"Well, so you went as a clown."

"Yeah. I had the costume, just wore a different shirt and different makeup from what Belinda saw on Halloween. I kept out of the way of all our co-workers. When Howard left, I followed him and asked him to talk to me on the landing. He was so drunk, he did just as I wanted."

Sara shuddered. "So drunk, it was easy for you to kill him. Oh, Eileen!" She felt her grip loosening on the gun as her whole body seemed to melt with despair. "Does Kevin know you did this?"

Eileen shook her head, her face slack

"You're sure? Why did he have his friends burglar me and watch the house?"

"I don't think he did that. I think it was his mother. She probably gave them money to do it." Her voice was listless. Maybe she realized now that once Kevin found out, it would be all over between them.

Sara wondered why Kevin hadn't denied using his friends when she confronted him in the restaurant. She shrugged. It didn't matter now. Now she had to figure a way to get Eileen to drop the damned scalpel.

A loud knock sounded on the door, making them both flinch.

"Police," a voice shouted. "Open up."

Eileen looked around the room wildly, seeking escape.

"Go answer it," Sara told her, relief rushing through her. She gripped the fake gun more firmly and kept it pointed at Eileen, wondering how they knew to come.

Her roommate moved slowly towards the door. When she got there, she looked at the scalpel in her right hand as if unsure what to do with it. Suddenly, she pulled open the door with her left and stayed behind it.

A big, burly uniformed officer stood in the doorway, his gun pointed directly at Sara.

"Drop it!" he shouted.

Sara dropped the gun and stood staring at him wide-eyed as he came slowly into the room.

"Watch out!" she screamed. Eileen emerged from behind the door, scalpel poised to strike.

The officer didn't turn around. Instead he kept his eyes on Sara, his gun still pointed at her chest.

The gleaming knife came down on the back of the officer's neck. His gun went off, the shot wide of Sara. He groaned, reached around with his hand to touch the wound, then went down on his knees. As he collapsed, Sara saw the second police officer behind him, his gun also out.

"Drop it!" he yelled at Eileen.

She looked at him, the mad light in her eyes dimming as she slowly dropped the bloody knife onto the floor. She sank down after it, disintegrating into a tearful heap.

Sara found a chair and sat down with a thud. As the second officer came into the room shouting into a walkie-talkie, "Officer down! Officer down!" Sara could see Mrs. Abbot and Eugene in the hallway behind him, looking on wide-eyed.

After kicking away the scalpel, the second officer deftly handcuffed an unresisting Eileen and turned to Sara. "Are you Sara Putnam?" he asked.

She nodded.

The officer knelt down next to his partner, took out his handkerchief and pressed it against the wound. "It's not deep, Joe. You'll be all right."

"Thanks, Tony." Joe managed to turn himself around from his crouched position and sit down on the floor next to Eileen. He looked at her with disgust.

Tony used a pencil to pick up the gun. "It's plastic," he exclaimed, looking at it in amazement.

There was a commotion out in the hall, and Ira burst into the room. "Are you all right?" he asked Sara, ignoring the others.

"Yes. I'm fine. Now. How did you know to come?"

"Belinda. My number was on the packet of photos. She called me, and I told her to call Detective Beecham. He must have notified the Jersey police." Ira stopped talking to look around. "What happened?" He saw Eileen. "Eileen? What did you do?"

Eileen looked at him blankly. The second officer said, "You really must leave. This is a crime scene, and we can't have you here messing it up."

"Please. Let him stay," Sara said, "since he's already here. He can just sit on the couch."

Loud footsteps sounded on the stairs, and two men with a stretcher

212

entered the room. Joe waved them away. "I can walk," he said gruffly and stood up, swaying slightly.

The two men looked relieved. "You sure?" one asked.

Joe nodded, and winced, pushing harder against the handkerchief at his neck. He followed them out the door, not looking back.

They heard more voices on the stairs, and two more officers came rushing into the room. Ira had sat down on the couch, and Tony didn't say anything as he kept a close eye on Eileen.

"What happened?" one of the new officers asked, surveying the scene.

"This female attacked Joe. Read her her rights, will you, and take her to the station?" He turned to Sara. "Why didn't you call us before confronting her?"

"I wasn't sure. I didn't want to believe . . . "

The officer shook his head in disgust. "Tell me what happened." He sat on the arm of the couch, and flipped open a notebook.

"Let me through," a familiar voice demanded.

Sara looked out the open door to see her mother elbowing her way between Mrs. Abbot and Eugene to enter the room.

"Mom!" she exclaimed and stood up to hug her.

The two other officers maneuvered around the landlady and her son to take Eileen away. She didn't look back, and Sara watched her leave over Lucille's shoulder with a pang.

"Sara, Belinda called me a few minutes ago," Lucille said, breaking their embrace. "Said she couldn't reach you on the phone. What is going on here?" Her eyes swept the room, taking in the gun and bloody scalpel on the floor, and Ira on the couch dressed as usual in his black pants, jacket, and shoes, white tee and socks. "You must be Ira."

"Mrs. Putnam." Ira stood up and held out his hand.

As they shook, she said, "Call me Lucille."

"Lucille," he said.

The policeman cleared his throat. "Could you please tell me what happened when you arrived home this evening, Miss Putnam."

As Sara told him, she looked around the apartment as if with new eyes. Her stomach became queasy when she saw the bullet hole in the wall. Her glance fell on the statue of the woman balancing the globe on her toes. She'd have to redecorate, she thought, and almost laughed out loud, but then tears caught in her throat. I've lost so much, she thought. Then she looked at Lucille and Ira. She would get to know them better, she vowed. She'd always regret she never met her father, but she could stop searching now, admittedly with some regrets, and get on with her life.